Also by Louise Jensen

The Stolen Sisters
The Family
The Gift
The Sister
The Surrogate
The Date

Writing as Amelia Henley

The Art of Loving You
The Life We Almost Had

Louise Jensen is a global No.1 bestselling author of psychological thrillers. Louise has sold over a million copies of her books and her novels have been sold for translation in twenty-five countries, as well as being featured on the *USA Today* and *Wall Street Journal* bestsellers' lists. Louise was nominated for the Goodreads Debut Author of 2016 Award and the *Guardian*'s Not the Booker 2018. Louise's thrillers have been optioned for TV and film.

When Louise isn't writing thrillers, she turns her hand to penning love stories under the name Amelia Henley. Her novels *The Life We Almost Had* and *The Art of Loving You* are out now.

Louise lives with her husband, children, madcap dog and a rather naughty cat in Northamptonshire. She loves to hear from readers and writers and can be found at www. louisejensen.co.uk, where she regularly blogs flash fiction and writing tips.

All for You

LOUISE JENSEN

ONE PLACE. MANY STORIES

HQ
An imprint of HarperCollins*Publishers* Ltd
1 London Bridge Street
London SE1 9GF

www.harpercollins.co.uk

HarperCollins*Publishers*
1st Floor, Watermarque Building, Ringsend Road
Dublin 4, Ireland

This edition 2022

1
First published in Great Britain by
HQ, an imprint of HarperCollins*Publishers* Ltd 2022

Copyright © Louise Jensen 2021

Louise Jensen asserts the moral right to be
identified as the author of this work.
A catalogue record for this book is
available from the British Library.

ISBN: 978-0-00-853552-0

MIX
Paper from
responsible sources
FSC™ C007454

This book is produced from independently certified FSC™ paper
to ensure responsible forest management.

For more information visit: www.harpercollins.co.uk/green

This book is set in Sabon by Type-it AS, Norway

Printed and Bound in the UK using 100% Renewable Electricity at
CPI Group (UK) Ltd, Croydon, CR0 4YY

For Pete Simmons.
An integral part of our family.

PROLOGUE

Something is wrong.

I've a deep, primal instinct screaming that I need to get home to Connor. It isn't just because of the row we'd had. The horrible, hurtful things he had said, it's something else.

A knowing that, despite being seventeen, I should never have left my son alone.

Hurry.

The flash of neon orange cones blur through the window as I gather speed until the roadworks force me to a stop. The candle-shaped air freshener swings from the rear-view mirror – its strawberry scent cloying.

My fingertips drum the steering as I will the temporary traffic lights to change to green. The rain hammers against the roof of the car, windscreen wipers lurching from side to side. It isn't the crack of lightning that causes my stomach to painfully clench, or the rumble of thunder, even though storms always take me back to a time I'd rather forget, but a mother's instinct.

I've felt it before. That bowling ball of dread hurtling towards me.

Drawing in a juddering breath, I tell myself everything is

fine. It's only natural that worry gnaws at me with sharpened teeth. Every mother in our town is on high alert right now after the disappearance of two teenage boys. I have more reason to be on edge than most.

It's not as though I'm thinking Connor has been taken, but it's one thing for him to ignore my calls, he'd never ignore Kieron's.

Never.

Particularly when he had asked Kieron to call him after his hospital appointment.

Why didn't he pick up?

In my mind's eye I see him, bounding down the stairs two at a time, balancing on a chair to reach the snacks he doesn't realize I know he hides on the top of his wardrobe.

An accident, or something else?

Something worse?

My stomach churns with a sense of foreboding.

Calm down.

I've been under so much pressure lately that I'm bound to be anxious. Edgy. But… I jab at my mobile and try Connor once more. My favourite picture of him lights the screen. We took it five years ago during an unseasonably hot Easter. Before Kieron was diagnosed, before everything changed. We're on the beach, the wind whipping his dark curls around his face. His grin is wide, traces of chocolate ice cream smudged around his mouth.

We were all so happy once. I don't know how, but I have to believe that we can be again. The alternative is too painful to bear.

The phone rings and rings. Fear brushes the back of my neck.

Frantically, I try calling again, from Kieron's phone this time. He still doesn't answer.

The lights are taking an age.

Next to me, Kieron sleeps. His head lolling against the window, breath misting the glass. The dark sweep of his lashes spider across his pale skin. The hospital visit has exhausted him. The red tartan blanket I always keep in the car has slipped from his knees and I reach across and pull it over his legs. The passenger seat is swallowing his thin body. At thirteen he should be growing, but his illness is shrinking him. It's shrinking me. Sometimes I feel as though my entire family is disappearing. Aidan barely talks to me, never touches me. In bed there's an ever-increasing space between us. Both of us teetering on our respective edges of the mattress, a strip of cold sheet an invisible barrier between us. My head no longer resting on his chest, his leg never slung over mine, his fingers not stroking my hair anymore.

Connor is monosyllabic and moody in the way that seventeen-year-olds often are but he never was, before...

But it isn't just that, it's also this sickness that isn't just Kieron's. It's everybody's.

The lights turn green.

Hurry.

Before I can pull away there's a streak of yellow. Through the rain a digger trundles towards me, blocking my path.

Kieron sighs in his sleep the way his brother sighs when he's awake. Sometimes it seems the boys only communicate through a series of noises and shrugs. But that's unfair. It's hardly surprising Connor's mouth is a permanent thin line as though he's forgotten how to smile. It's not only his concern

3

about his brother on top of everything he went through before the summer that has turned my sweet-natured son into a mass of guilt and unhappiness, but the sharp truth that out of his friendship group of three, two of them have disappeared.

'The Taken', the local paper calls them, reporting that out of those who were there that tragic day, Connor is the only one left.

But Connor knows this as he hides in his room, too scared to go to school.

We *all* know this.

Tyler and Ryan have vanished without a trace and the police have no idea why.

It's up to me to keep Connor safe.

I glance at Kieron.

I'll do anything to keep both of my boys safe.

The driver of the digger raises his hand in appreciation as he passes by me. Before I can pull away, the lights revert to red once more. Frustrated, I slam my palms against the steering wheel.

Calm down.

Rationally, I know Connor hasn't been taken.

He's at home.

The door is locked.

He's okay.

But still…

He never ignores Kieron.

Never.

Hurry.

Despite the lights being red, I pull away. There's no approaching traffic. I snap on the radio again. The newsreader relays in cool, clipped tones that the missing boys haven't been found but police are following several lines of inquiry. Nobody else is missing. The unsaid 'yet' lingers in the air, and although I know Connor is safe, my foot squeezes the accelerator. Home is the only place my anxiety abates. When we're all under one roof and I can almost pretend everything is exactly how it was.

Before.

Visibility is poor. Frustrated, I slow, peering out through the teeming rain. If I have an accident I'm no use to Kieron, to anyone. My heart is racing as there's another crack of lightning. I count the seconds the way I used to with the boys when they were small.

One.

Two.

Three.

A grumble of thunder. The storm is closing in. Everything is closing in, crashing down. My stomach is a hard ball, my pulse skyrocketing as a sense of danger gallops towards me.

Hurry.

The urgency to be at home overrides the voice of caution urging me to slow down. I race past the old hospital, which has fallen into disrepair, the white and blue NHS sign crawling with ivy, and then the secondary school. I barely register the figure cloaked in black stepping onto the zebra crossing but on some level I must have noticed him as I blast the horn until he jumps back onto the path. He shakes his fist but I keep moving.

Hurry.

My chest is tight as I pull into my street, my drive-way. A whimper of fear slithers from my lips as I see the front door swinging open.

Without waking Kieron I half fall, half step out of the car, my shoes slipping on wet tarmac as I rush towards my house.

'Connor?'

The table in the hallway is lying on its side. My favourite green vase lies in shattered pieces over the oak floor. The lilies that had been left anonymously on the doorstep are strewn down the hallway.

Funeral flowers.

'Hello?' My voice is thin and shaky.

Blood smears the cream wall by the front door. Lying in a puddle of water from the vase is Connor's phone, the screen smashed. My feet race up the stairs towards his bedroom. A man's voice drifts towards me. I push open Connor's door just as shots are fired.

Instinctively, I cover my head before I realize the sound is coming from the war game blaring out of Connor's TV. His Xbox controller is tangled on the floor along with his headphones.

His bedroom is empty.

The Taken.

It's impossible.

'Connor?'

He was here.

He was safe.

The front door was locked.

Quickly, I check every room in the house until I'm back in the hallway, staring in horror at the blood on the wall, trying to make sense of it.

Connor has gone.

PART ONE

CHAPTER ONE

Lucy

Thirteen days before Connor is taken

It's there again. The car. Small and white and out of place. Parked under one of the beech trees that guard our street, lending us a sense of safety.

Who are they?

This is a family area. Most of our neighbours have four-by-fours, double garages with space on their neat blocked paved driveways for visitors' vehicles. Nobody parks on the street.

'Why are they just sitting there?' I ask Aidan as he pulls out onto the road. 'It's the third time this week.' Again, the car is parked far enough away that I can't identify the shadowy figure inside, but near enough for the driver to be able to see our house and I do have a sense that it is my home they are interested in.

My family.

I shield my eyes against the bright rays of sunlight that slant through the windscreen.

'Don't you think it's odd?'

'Don't we have more important things to worry about?' Aidan asks wearily. I bite back my retort as I take in his grey face, the way his fingers are clutching the steering wheel. He's right to be worried. We both are. There's a lot riding on today.

'Are you okay?' I twist around in my seat.

'Yeah.' Kieron flashes me a tired smile. He's so used to hospital visits they don't faze him in the slightest, although I've made him aware this one is different. I've explained to him what I'm going to ask for during our appointment and he nodded. He's been expecting it.

We all have.

Aidan drives too fast.

Our journey across town is peppered with awkward silences that I try to fill with conversation, choosing my words carefully. I'm conscious that I don't want to glare a spotlight on the things Kieron is missing out on. He'd only been discharged from hospital a few days ago after a particularly nasty infection and he'll be absent for the start of the academic year tomorrow.

'Do you think my new form teacher will send me homework too?' School is on his mind as well.

'I expect so; they don't want you falling behind.' It's not only his education that concerns me, he's missed periods before because of the frequent bacterial infections that accompany his disease, but the social aspect he is sometimes excluded from saddens me. He can't always play out with his friends. He hasn't always the energy for his swimming club. Aidan and I try not to treat him any different to Connor, but the truth is, he is different to his brother. Set apart from other thirteen-year-olds.

Since being diagnosed with PSC – Primary Sclerosing Cholangitis, a chronic liver disease – five years previously he's stopped growing at the rate of the other kids. Stopped living almost, although I'm overdramatizing again. If you asked him, Kieron would say he is happy and he is. He lives day-to-day like most kids do. Often he feels okay and thankfully he has very little pain. His side effects are manageable, mostly. But his bouts of infection and jaundice are terrifying.

It's a relief when we pull up outside the nearest entrance to the paediatric unit. Aidan drops us off before he begins the game of chance where he'll circle round the too-small area with the too-few spaces, eyes peeled for someone with keys in their hand, heading back to their vehicle.

There was a time I'd have waited, when we'd have stuck together.

Instead, we go ahead without him.

Hospitals have a smell. A taste that stings the back of the throat. So many people say they hate them but I suppose I'm more used to medical units than most. I'm comfortable amid the hustle and bustle. Inside this red-bricked building lives are changed. Lives are saved.

'Here we are!' I push through the swing doors and log our arrival on the touch-screen check-in system. We perch on hard orange plastic chairs in the cramped waiting room. It's so hot in here, my skin is sticky.

My knee jiggles with nerves. Every few seconds I glance at the door, willing Aidan to arrive before we are called through.

'I've got PSC,' I hear Kieron saying to the little girl sat next to him, curly haired doll on her lap.

'What does that mean?' she asks.

'My skin used to itch all the time but it doesn't anymore,' Kieron says simply, but it's so much more than that.

PSC – three letters with mountainous implications. Possible cancer of the bile duct being the one that lurks frequently in my mind. There's no known cause – that's the frustrating part. It can be triggered after an infection, it can be genetically predisposed or it could be an autoimmune disorder. It could be caused by something else entirely. Nobody really knows.

It isn't curable.

'Kieron?' The nurse that has come to fetch us addresses him directly. Kieron stands and follows her; I throw one last glance over my shoulder, before I step inside Mr Peters' consultation room.

'How are you today, young man?' the doctor asks.

'Fine.' Kieron raises his hand and Mr Peters high-fives him.

'He isn't,' I cut in, my tone sharper than I intended. 'Fine, I mean. He's lost weight. He barely has an appetite and he's constantly exhausted. He was on the ward last week again—'

'Let's have a look at you, shall we?' Mr Peters examines Kieron's eyes, his skin. 'We've got the results of the bloods and the latest scan.' Kieron is monitored every three to six months. 'There is some change but overall…' He trails off as a breathless, red-cheeked Aidan rockets through the door, fringe damp above apologetic eyes.

'I think it's time,' I say quietly. Mr Peters scrawls on Kieron's notes. The wait for him to speak is unbearable. My heart hammers against my ribcage. Suggesting my youngest son undergo a liver transplant is not a decision I've taken lightly. We all knew it was a probability, but prayed it wouldn't come to this. PSC is typically a slow-progressing disease. Statistically, Kieron shouldn't be at this stage after five years, but we find ourselves here anyway. It seems Mr Peters doesn't agree.

'I'm going to tweak Kieron's medication.'

'He's been in hospital three times in the past two months. He's getting weaker.'

'It's not ideal but I'm not unduly alarmed, Lucy. You know that thirty per cent of kids with PSC need a transplant around ten years after diagnosis. Kieron's not ill enough to be added to the transplant waiting list. I know it's frightening but he shouldn't suddenly deteriorate to the extent that—'

'But…' I swallow back my anger. 'Mr Peters – Rob – Kieron shouldn't have this disease full stop. It's uncommon in kids of his age and you can't predict… you can't guarantee—'

'Lucy, no one can promise—'

But it's promises I want. The promise of a future.

'Look,' I say, 'if we wait too long then Kieron could be too ill for major surgery. It's becoming clear his liver has a limited mileage and no, PSC shouldn't have progressed this quickly but it's not unheard of and it has. If Kieron's liver is at the beginning of ongoing deterioration, it's better to catch it now than wait.' I try to sound measured and calm, not come across as a hysterical mother but a hysterical mother is how I feel. Tears burn behind my eyes. I blink them away.

'It's a fine line, Lucy. Of course we don't want to wait until Kieron isn't strong enough to undergo an op but I don't see this is necessarily the beginning of liver failure—'

'But I know what—'

A hint of agitation creeps into Mr Peters' voice. 'We'll know when the time comes and—'

'There was this case where a young girl, without warning,

deteriorated so rapidly…' I'm aware that Kieron is in the room so I don't finish but I don't need to.

'That's extremely rare, Lucy.'

'I know it's rare. The disease is rare but it's happening.' I'm talking too fast. 'It's happening to us. And I just want… I just want Kieron to feel well and—'

'I'm okay, Mum.' Kieron slips his hand into mine and gives it a squeeze. He is so brave, my boy.

'Let's keep a closer eye on him.' Rob taps on his computer. 'We'll keep on the antibiotics. I'll see you in two weeks. Is the nineteenth okay?'

'But—'

'Lucy, if Kieron doesn't need surgery that's a good thing.' Aidan pulls out his mobile and opens his calendar app. 'I'm booked onto a conference on the nineteenth but Lucy can—'

'But he *will* need surgery at some stage. We can't pretend that he won't.' For a moment I stare at Rob, challenging him to meet my gaze. To talk to me as an equal rather than a parent. I'm incredulous that Aidan accepts everything he's told. I can't just put my blind faith in anyone with a white coat and a name badge, but, from the set of Rob's jaw, I know it's fruitless arguing. I can see that he has never felt the terror of a parent with a sick child. I don't want to distress Kieron so I gather my bag and my doubts and my fears and we leave.

On the way home Kieron dozes. I don't speak to Aidan. I can't say what I want to say because I have left all of my words at the hospital, all of my hope.

I stifle another yawn as we pull into our street in silence.

The spot under the beech tree is empty. The white car has gone but that doesn't ease the sense that the house is being watched.

That I am being watched.

'I'll unlock the door before we wake Kieron,' I tell Aidan as I climb out of the car.

I reach the front door but before I can slip my key into the lock I see it.

The dead bird on our doorstep.

Its black feathers are glistening, guts spilling over the concrete. My stomach drops, rollercoaster fast as I stare at it with repulsion.

'I'll get rid of it before the boys see it,' Aidan says from behind me.

'But…' I swallow hard. 'How do you think it got there?' I want to ask who put it there but I'm desperate for a rational explanation I can hold tightly against my chest.

Someone has been watching me.

'A gift from a cat, most likely,' Aidan says.

But we don't have a cat.

And neither do any of our neighbours.

It's not only the weight of the unknown future pressing down on my shoulders, but the past.

It's catching up with me.

'Guilt is a rope that wears thin' the old saying goes.

I can almost feel it tightening around my neck.

CHAPTER TWO

Lucy

Aidan snaps on a pair of blue latex gloves from his work truck and scoops up the lifeless bird – as a vet, he's used to dealing with animals. It's out of sight but I can still see its glassy eyes staring up at me.

I can't quell my feeling of panic.

Had a cat left it? There aren't any on our street and besides, I thought cats only brought dead animals to their owners.

'Mum?' Kieron calls from the car, rubbing sleep from his eyes.

'Let's get you inside.' As I usher him into the hallway, my eyes linger on the dark droplets of blood spotting the step. A chill snakes down my spine. I throw a glance over my shoulder as I close the front door.

The street is empty.

Once inside, I hang up my coat and hold my hand out to take Kieron's anorak. 'Do you want to snuggle on the sofa while I cook dinner?'

He shakes his head.

'I'll go upstairs.' He's wiped out. His footfall slow and leaden. I wish I could hoist him onto my hip and carry him the way I had before he grew too big, too heavy. It's not only a desire to hold him that floods me but a desire to be held. I miss the closeness I shared with Aidan. A sick child hasn't brought us closer together, it's pushed us apart.

Music blares from the bathroom. The Arctic Monkeys singing 'Do I Wanna Know' over the sound of running water. I knock on the door.

'Connor, we're back.'

He doesn't hear me, or pretends he doesn't.

For years, he waged his own personal war on cleanliness, fighting against washing his hair, cleaning his teeth. All that changed when he got his first girlfriend and when I recall the way that turned out, how broken he was – is – my heart contracts.

It's all my fault.

'If you stop blaming yourself, Connor might stop blaming you too,' Aidan keeps saying, but how can I?

'Do you want a game of cards or something?' I ask Kieron when we reach his room.

'No. I'm going to read.'

'Let me guess.' I place my index finger on my chin as though I'm thinking. 'The Hunger Games?' Kieron is obsessed with the trilogy, his walls are plastered with posters from the film, the pale blue paint underneath barely visible.

'Yep.'

'You'll get bored of them one day.'

'Never.'

His solar system duvet cover is patterned with planets and I turn it back so he can slip into bed. The mattress dips as I kneel across him to switch on the star-shaped fairy lights which twist around his bedstead. Before I tuck him in, I pull off his shoes and socks. A lump rises in my throat at the sight of his feet, now almost as big as Aidan's. Memories of tweaking his toes, this little piggy went to market, rise as though it were only yesterday when his only concern was the little piggy who didn't get any roast beef.

Now he might die.

Covering my mouth with a curled fist, I turn my sob into a cough. I can't think like that.

I won't.

It's a slow-progressing disease.

Not always.

Shut up, I tell the voice in my head.

'Can I fetch you a drink? A snack?' I ask once he's settled.

'No thanks, Mum.' His face relaxes as though he's safe once more in his own private space where Xbox games about war contrast with the Star Wars Lego models gathering dust on his shelves. Edward, his imaginatively named teddy bear, lies sprawled on top of his chest of drawers next to a pot of L'Oréal hair wax Connor gave him along with a half-empty bottle of Nivea aftershave. My boy is inching across the tightrope between boy and man. Will he ever reach the end of the wire and step off into his new life or will he fall? Without a liver transplant Kieron's life expectancy since diagnosis is between nine and eighteen years. He has already had five of those years. The thought that without surgical intervention he might only have four more years left steals my breath. Kieron might not make the age that Connor is right now.

I blink away tears and offer him a bright smile. 'Shepherd's pie or roast chicken?'

'A Sunday dinner on a Monday?'

'Why not.' I don't know how many Sundays he has left. God, I must stop. He's fine. Right now he is fine. Should be fine for years. 'With extra stuffing and Yorkshire puddings.'

'Thanks, Mum. Can you ask Connor to come and see me?'

'Yes, as soon as he's out of the shower.'

Connor's room is a mass of balled-up socks, crumpled T-shirts, empty crisp packets and cans littering the floor around the overflowing bin. Scuff marks cover the dove-grey walls. We must decorate.

While I wait for him to come out of the shower, I lift his uniform from his wardrobe. Today was a teacher training day but school starts again tomorrow. We should have checked his blazer still fits, he hasn't worn it since he finished school at Easter, weeks earlier than study leave actually started, because he was too upset to face everyone. Too ashamed. He isn't the only one. What happened has changed the earth beneath my feet and I still stumble against it. I'm trying to regain my footing.

I hang his blazer on the back of his door. The rules on sixth-formers wearing uniform might change now anyway. The head teacher – Mr Marshall – had insisted on it. He was big on appearances and results, but he won't be there tomorrow – one of the mums posted on the Facebook parents' group that he'd been sacked after what happened. I'm sure it's the right thing for Connor to go back, to be with his mates, Ryan and Tyler, and have a semblance of normality again.

Perhaps I'll ask Melissa and Fergus, Ryan's parents and

our oldest friends, if they want to come to Center Parcs with us in October half term. That will give us all something to look forward to. I grew up in the same street as Melissa. Ryan was born several months after Connor and the boys have always been close. We had such a great time last year. Mel whisking me off to the spa to relax while Fergus took Kieron for pancakes so Aidan could try the adrenaline sports with Connor and Ryan. They've both been so supportive.

With a change of scene, we might see a return of the old Connor. The one who joked and smiled.

I miss him.

'Lucy?' Aidan calls up the stairs.

'I'll be down in a minute.'

It smells in here of teenage boy – Lynx and feet and a whiff of something rotten.

I cross to the window to crack it open. I can't help sweeping my gaze up and down the road looking for the white car and, as I do, I remember the mutilated bird. The world is full of cars and cats. It could just be a coincidence but still goose bumps spring on my arms.

Just because I feel I deserve to be punished doesn't mean I am being punished, does it?

There's nobody around. Outside of the house on the corner where the new family moved in over the weekend is a mountain of packing boxes waiting to be recycled. I must take them over a bottle of wine and welcome them to the area.

From across the street, a movement behind the curtains. Is somebody watching me?

I'm being ridiculous. It's only old Mrs Simpkin's house. I do her weekly shopping and Aidan keeps her drive clear of snow every winter, but still, quickly I move out of sight, catching Connor's desk with my hip. His laptop screen illuminates. My eyes are drawn towards it and when I see the open tab my heart accelerates. Fleetingly, I wonder whether Ryan and Tyler are still haunted by what happened in the way that Connor seems to be.

The way that I am.

It was an accident. A horrible, terrible accident but clearly he still blames himself in the way that I still blame myself.

We have both failed the people we loved.

If only, if only, if only.

My stomach twists as I stare at the screen. How can he ever move on if he's torturing himself daily?

But then not a day goes past when I don't think of it too.

How can any of us move on?

From outside comes the tormented screech of a bird and I'm reminded of the crow on the step, the blood, the fear it must have felt in its final moments.

The fear I feel right now.

CHAPTER THREE

Connor

Connor digs his fingertips into his scalp wishing the shampoo could wash away the angry thoughts that ricochet around his mind. He presses down harder and harder until his knuckles ache and his bones feel as though they might snap. Releasing the pressure on his head, he twists the temperature dial, forcing himself to stand still while thousands of red-hot droplets of water slice at his skin like razor blades. His muscles tense, his jaw clamps shut suppressing the scream of pain that builds and builds deep in his gut. Pain is the only thing that stops his thoughts. Soon, he begins to sway, black flecks dancing in front of his eyes. Just before he passes out he yanks the dial the opposite way. The icy water is a punch to the stomach, snatching his breath. Rather than cooling his skin it hurts and he takes pleasure in that. It's no less than he deserves.

He sets the water again to warm. Spotify has been streaming 'AM' through his phone on repeat and he doesn't know how long he's been in the cubicle. It's like his own personal time machine. He daydreams he can travel back to Easter and change everything. Sometimes it's the thump on the door from his mum or dad that drags him into the present and he realizes he's been standing under the jets of water for over half an hour, minty shower gel frothing around his feet.

'Do you know how much the water bills are?' Dad would complain.

'Leave him alone, he's making up for all the years he'd sit on the edge of the bath pretending to wash.' Mum would smile at him.

Dad used to be the funny one, now they're both as stressed as each other but Mum's better at hiding it. She thinks Connor doesn't notice the black crescents that hang under her eyes like bruises. She thinks Connor's fooled by her fake smiles that don't crinkle her skin, her mouth curved, the rest of her face static and stiff, like the Mr Potato Head he and Kieron used to play with. Sometimes when she fakes a grin he longs to reach out and touch her lips, moulding them back to the thin straight line they naturally fall in nowadays. Christ, no wonder he finds it impossible to talk about his emotions. Nobody in this family discusses anything that matters. It's Ryan's dad, Fergus, who sporadically checks that Connor is okay, asks whether he wants to talk but then he was there that day too, supervising, so perhaps he feels in some way responsible even though he wasn't. His own parents pretend it never happened but it did and, because of him, things are a million times worse than they were.

Unimaginable.

Unfixable.

Reluctantly, he switches off the water, releasing a cloud of steam as he pushes open the cubicle door. He roughly dries himself before padding into his room, feeling a snap of rage as he sees Mum bent over his computer, scrolling down his screen.

'What the actual…' He marches over to his desk and slams his laptop shut, almost trapping her fingers.

'Connor, I…' A flush stains her cheeks. 'I wasn't… I didn't mean to invade your privacy. I knocked your desk when I opened the window and your laptop just came on.'

'Right.'

'Are you ready for tomorrow?' Briefly, she flashes her Mr Potato Head smile before it slips away. 'School?' she adds as though he's forgotten.

As if.

'I don't want to go.'

'But it's your last year. Your A levels.'

'I've missed too much.'

'But—'

'Will you LISTEN!' The thought of facing the other kids, the teachers, conjures a hot panic that flies out of his mouth disguised as anger.

Mum gives a barely distinguishable nod of her head. Her hands nervously wringing together.

Connor lowers his voice, not wanting his fury to drift down the landing to Kieron's room. 'I want to leave. Get an apprenticeship.'

'In what? You have a dream, Connor. You can't abandon it now.'

A sadness expands inside him as he remembers what he'd been working towards. It's gone, the passion he once felt for medicine. He'd longed to be a medical scientist, not the person who would treat symptoms like Kieron's but someone who might discover a cure for PSC and other diseases.

It seems wrong now to admit he wants to reach his goals, as if he has no claim to a full and happy life.

Mum speaks again. 'You want to go to uni—'

'I don't.' He's no longer shouting.

'Kieron would give anything to go back to school tomorrow.' She covers her mouth with her hand as soon as the words fire from her lips. Connor glares at her, hating her, but he softens when he sees that she hates herself enough for the both of them.

He despises her and he loves her. He wants her to suffer and yet he doesn't. He wants to push her away but he so badly needs a hug.

Over these past few months she's been slowly unravelling and as often as she tells Connor that it wasn't his fault, he can't look her in the eye and tell her the same although he knows she longs to hear it from him. Needs to hear it from him. Still he stabs the sharp pin of blame into her again and again with more force than necessary, the way he had once tried to fix the tail onto the paper donkey she had carefully drawn for his birthday party.

She looks so small. So tired.

'How did it go at the hospital?' His words are a white flag.

Her body droops – a balloon released of air. This time her brief smile is genuine. Grateful Connor isn't picking a fight.

'It was…' She looks at him helplessly.

'Mum, I'm not a child any more. Tell me what happened.'

'Dr Peters says that Kieron isn't at the stage of needing a transplant.'

'And you?' Connor asks. 'What do you think?' He sees the surprise on her face and notes her hesitation before she replies as though she's saying what she should, rather than what she actually feels.

'Maybe I'm overreacting and it is a little soon.'

'But… four more years, Mum.' It hangs over them.

'Potentially. It won't come to that. Mr Peters is certain and we have to trust him. He's the expert.'

'But you're—'

'About to start dinner. Kieron wants you to go and see him, okay?' She glances out of the window, chewing her lip nervously, before she leaves.

'Hey.' Connor pokes his head around Kieron's door.

'Connor!' The joy in Kieron's voice is palpable. Connor knows that in his younger brother's eyes he is Santa Claus, Luke Skywalker and James Bond all rolled into one. Connor plucks the paperback from this brother's hands. 'I'll read to you.' He settles himself on the bed, swinging his legs up, and clears his throat in readiness for the voices he'll do for each of the characters, but before he begins he double-checks.

'Are you positive you want this one? We both know the story off by heart now.'

'But I love it.'

'Are you sure it's not just Jennifer Lawrence you love?' Connor raises his eyebrows as he tilts his head towards the poster of Katniss Everdeen, crossbow in her hands.

'A bit.' Kieron blushes. 'What's it like?'

'What's what like?'

'You know…' Kieron's eyes flicker to the open door, reassuring himself Mum isn't hovering on the landing, the way she sometimes does. 'Kissing and stuff.' He lowers his voice to a whisper. 'Sex.'

'Whoa!' Connor holds out his hands. 'Easy there.'

'Tell me.'

'What makes you think I know about… sex.'

'You know everything.' Again that unwavering, misplaced trust in him.

'You'll find out for yourself soon enough, Kieron.'

'I might not.' Kieron's optimism slips along with the duvet as he sits up. 'I might not live that long.'

'Don't be so dramatic, idiot,' Connor says, hoping his voice doesn't betray his own fear. He starts to repeat the words that he has endlessly read on Google. 'Your prognosis is—'

'Connor. Don't. Just don't.'

Connor reaches for his brother's hand, their fingers linking together. Kieron is always hopeful, never self-pitying. Connor wonders whether that's his default setting or whether he's also wearing a mask. Putting on a brave face. He shouldn't have to pretend.

Connor feels sad and angry and helpless.

He feels all of those things again. He can't help pulling away, standing up.

'Please don't go. Tell me what it was like… with Hailey.'

At the mention of her name, Connor pinches the skin on his arm, digging his nails in, welcoming the pain.

The punishment.

'Connor?' Kieron prompts.

'I… Another time?'

Images strobe. Hailey's face pale, worried. Ryan and Tyler urging her on. The pleading look in her eyes as she turned to him. His indecision – his girlfriend or his friends – the nod of his head. It'll be okay.

But it wasn't okay.

It isn't.

'I… I've got to go.' He turns his back on his brother and stalks out onto the landing but the memories, the memories come with him.

Back in his room, he opens his laptop once more and studies her Facebook page. The photos of them together, his arm awkward around her shoulders. Inexperience and hope shining from their eyes. He clicks on Messenger and sends two words:

I'm sorry

Just like all his other messages, they remain unread.

CHAPTER FOUR

Lucy

In the kitchen, Aidan is peeling potatoes. The smell of herby roast chicken already drifting from the oven.

'How did you know that's what I was going to cook?'

'Because I know you.' He scrapes peelings into the bin. 'And because I was on call yesterday so we missed our roast.'

I sit at the breakfast bar. Classical music – soothing strings and a tinkling piano – drifts out of the Alexa.

Aidan pushes a coffee towards me. My favourite mug is printed with a tiny green handprint on one side and a footprint on the other. Aidan had it made for me on the first Mother's Day after I had given birth and I had cried when I'd seen it. For a long time, I wouldn't use it, it felt too precious and I was scared it would break, but as the years passed I needed that physical reminder that these impossibly small hands and feet once belonged to my child. Ever practical, Aidan reassured me that he had a spare so if it did accidentally smash I could have another.

Some things are so easily replaceable, but not everything.

'So.' I take a sip of my now lukewarm drink.

'Lucy…' There is such weariness in that one word. 'Can we just… not. Not today.'

'But we need to talk.'

'All we do is talk about Kieron and we go around in circles. Words can't heal him no matter how much we want them to.'

I know that's true but I believe that words can heal us. The right words anyway, but I fumble to find them, to pluck them out of my mind and form them on my tongue in the correct order. Lately, almost everything I say sounds accusatory or argumentative. I wish I could say what's in my heart which is, 'I need you. I love you. I want us to feel like a family again.'

'Aidan,' I whisper, hurt pulsing inside of my chest.

His sorrowful hazel eyes meet mine, the eyes I'd looked into when he'd slid the thin gold band onto my finger and promised me forever. Does he regret marrying me? Is forever too long? Too hard? Too much of everything?

Marriage takes work.

My nana had told me this when I'd splayed my fingers and glittered my engagement ring at her. I'd told her not to worry. Aidan and I were so in love I couldn't envisage a time we wouldn't be happy. Now I can't quite remember what happiness feels like. It visits us fleetingly: sharing a Saturday lunchtime pizza with Fergus and Melissa, the four of us playing rummy while we lingered over coffee; me and Aidan curled onto the sofa sharing a bottle of wine. The other night something funny came on the TV and we laughed aloud before we'd both snapped our mouths shut as though we had no right to experience any joy.

I miss him.

I miss us.

'Can I help?' Once I wouldn't have asked, we'd have stood side by side, both knowing instinctively what the other needed.

'I've got everything covered.' He's crushing garlic for the potatoes, rosemary sprigs from the garden already washed.

'What do you think about going back to Center Parcs in October half term? With Mel, Fergus and Ryan?'

'Is that fair on Kieron? He can do less this year than last.'

'He loves the pool. And the wildlife. He was so happy watching the deer and squirrels eat the food he'd put outside our lodge every day. Mel's addicted to the spa there and Fergus loves all that adrenaline stuff. It's partly why he volunteered to go along on the school residential to supervise. Or are you just worried he'll want a turn at the activities this year and you might have to—'

'Fergus offered to sit out with Kieron—'

'I know. I was only teasing.'

Aidan slices into a carrot with more force than necessary.

Wanting to change the subject, I search for something to say, topics that we might have talked about before tragedy reached out with its dirty fingers, staining our hearts with its blackness, a common ground that doesn't involve the boys but nothing comes to mind. Our conversations usually centre around Kieron and now there's Connor to worry about. Everything circles back to the kids in one way or another.

It's the ringing of my phone that breaks the silence, the screen alight with the face of my best friend.

'Hi, Melissa.' I assume she's ringing to find out how Kieron's appointment went today but instead all I can hear is the sound of her crying.

'Mel? What's wrong?'

'Have you seen Fergus?'

'We haven't seen Fergus?' I raise my questioning eyebrows

towards Aidan and he gives a shake of his head. 'Is something wrong? I can come—'

'No,' she says sharply.

'Mel… What's happened?'

'It's… He's… Fergus,' she speaks falteringly, releasing one syllable at a time. 'Fergus has left me.'

Fergus adores Mel and Ryan. Working as a pilot he's often away and when they're together they are always touching, holding hands.

'Left you?' I'm parroting her but I can't process what she's telling me.

Aidan's expression flitters between confusion and alarm. 'What's going on?' he mouths.

'Mel… Why has Fergus gone? Where has he gone?'

She ignores my question. 'He hasn't been in touch with you? Or Aidan?'

'Neither of us have heard from him, Mel… You'll be able to sort things out, won't you?'

There's a beat before she says, 'Some things can't be repaired, Lucy.'

I glance at my mug. Those tiny hands and feet.

'If Fergus gets in touch with either of you can you let me know?'

'Of course but I'll come over. Give me half an hour and—'

'No! Please don't.' There's an urgency in her voice combined with something I can't quite identify. 'Just don't. And if Fergus turns up on your doorstep, don't let him in.'

'But—'

'I'll be in touch.'

The dial tone whirrs against my ear.

'What's going on?' Aidan asks.

'He's left her.' It's hard to believe. Fergus and Melissa seemed like one of those bulletproof couples, built to stand the test of time. We haven't seen much of either of them since the residential and I recall the first time I saw Fergus afterwards.

'I'm so ashamed,' he had whispered. 'I just didn't—'

'Shhh.' I had swept him into a hug. 'Nobody is to blame.' But had he blamed himself? Is his running away a result of his festering guilt?

'Did Mel say why he's left?' Aidan's phone beeps with a message. When he reads it he tightens his grip on his handset, his skin stretched tightly over tensed muscles.

'Is that Fergus?'

'No. The Thompsons' horse isn't right. It's probably colic again. I've got to go.'

He heads towards the door, his limp more pronounced than usual, which is a sign he's tired or stressed. I wish he didn't have to leave. I'm used to him being called out at odd hours, missing meals, weekends, but tonight I've such a sense of impending doom.

I follow him as he opens the front door. The security light shines a perfect circle on the porch.

'Lucy, go back inside.' There's an edge to his voice.

'What's wrong?'

'Don't look.'

But I can't help peering over his shoulder to see what he has seen.

My stomach roils. I clamp my hands over my mouth as I stare at the macabre sight on the step.

Two dead birds. Beaks hanging open.

'Aidan?' I'm trembling. One might be a coincidence, two feels like a warning.

'Go inside, I'll take care of it.'

'Do you think…' I can hardly bear to voice my fears. 'Who do you think put them there?'

'Nobody,' he says sharply. 'Nobody left them here deliberately, Lucy, why would they? It'll be a fox or a cat or something.'

But he doesn't look at me as he speaks and I wonder whether he's trying to convince me or himself.

'But—'

'Mum?' Connor hollers down the stairs.

'Go. Everything is fine. I'll see you later.' Aidan pulls the door closed and, shaken, I press my palms against it, wanting him to remember he hasn't kissed me goodbye.

It remains closed.

'Mum! Ryan has messaged to say Fergus has moved out.'

'I'm coming.'

I head towards my son, knowing I don't have an explanation to give him. I run through the conversation with Mel in my head. Over the years, I've heard her happy and sad. Excited and exhausted. But I've never heard her… I recall her voice and try to label the emotion I heard.

'Don't come here. Just don't.'

And then it comes to me.

Fear.

She's scared.

She's not the only one.

Her son, Ryan, was there that day, with Connor. Is it all

connected? Has something happened today that could have caused a row with Fergus?

In my mind I can still see those two savaged birds on the step.

I'm frightened too.

CHAPTER FIVE

Aidan

Aidan hesitates for a moment before dropping the dead birds into the bin. Lucy has such a soft spot for animals. The birds are wild but she'd probably want to bury them in the garden under the apple tree, along with Connor's hamster and Kieron's goldfish which they'd laid to rest in shoeboxes the boys had decorated with brightly coloured felt-tip pens.

He pats his pockets. Stupidly, he forgot to pick up the keys for his work truck but he still has the keys for the Audi he'd driven to the hospital earlier. It's not as if Lucy will need to go out.

It's best she stays at home.

His hip throbs the way it does when he's stressed or exhausted or the weather is cold.

It isn't cold.

He feels terrible that he has turned away from his wife tonight when she was sad and scared, his children who need so much from him. Is this how Fergus felt when he left Melissa? Was he sorrowful as he packed his bags? Angry? What was going through his head? They'd never talked properly about what happened at the residential but Fergus seemed fine afterwards, hadn't he? Not straight away of course, he'd been apologetic, guilty but... he was okay, wasn't he?

Aidan can't believe Fergus has split from Mel without talking it through with him. He had no idea his friend was so unhappy. Last time he saw him they'd played darts in the pub and chatted about the latest updates from NASA. He seemed okay. Normal.

Can anyone ever really know what's going on in someone else's head?

As he drives, his mind switches to thoughts of his wife, not the Lucy of now, guilt-ridden and frightened, but the Lucy he'd fallen in love with.

He misses her.

He catches glimpses of her sometimes. The way she confronted Mr Peters earlier, insisting she knows what's best for Kieron and perhaps she does. Late at night sometimes he catches her poring over her computer, staying up to date with the latest research, the glow of the screen softening the lines on her face that have deepened through stress. His breath catches as he is reminded once more how much he loved his wife.

Still loves his wife.

She doesn't give up.

Early in his career as an equine vet, during those heady first years of romance, they had been lying in bed, limbs entwined, her head on his chest, his hand stroking her hair, when he'd been called to an emergency.

'Sorry.' He had trailed a finger over her collarbone before reluctantly dragging his jeans on.

'Can I come?' she had asked.

'It's freezing.'

37

'You can warm me up afterwards.' She was already dressing, knowing that he didn't want to be apart from her any more than she did from him.

The horse was one he'd visited before; its health had been deteriorating for months.

'It's time,' the owner had said, tears in her eyes.

Aidan had told Lucy to wait in the truck – he didn't want her to see him euthanize an animal – but she'd come into the stables, kneeled beside the terrified horse and stroked his nose over and over, soothing him with kind words until his nostrils stopped flaring and his eyes no longer bulged with fear. Slowly, tentatively, the horse rose onto shaky legs.

'That's impossible,' Aidan had said.

'Nothing is impossible, trust me.' Lucy had kissed him and he'd told the owner they should wait twenty-four hours before making a final decision. The following day the horse was walking, trotting, cantering.

Recovered.

A week later, Lucy was by his side while he tended to a mare in distress, her labour interminable. Nothing was going the way it should.

'The foal will be stillborn,' he told Lucy. 'If you want to leave.'

She had shaken her head, tears in her eyes. 'Come on.' She softly petted the horse. 'You'll be okay. Trust me.' She whispered words of encouragement over and over until the foal slipped into the world, perfectly healthy.

So Aidan believes in miracles. He has seen them.

And that's what he wishes for Kieron.

Trust me. He hears Lucy's whispered words. It seems foolish

to think she knows better than Mr Peters, the man with thirty years' experience in this field, but what if she's right?

She's always been the strong one. The glue that sticks their little family together, but they're becoming unstuck and he doesn't know how to hold them in place.

Kieron sick. Lucy falling apart. Connor sullen and uncommunicative.

He's tried to get his eldest son to open up to him. Several weeks ago, he had perched on the edge of Connor's bed, remembering the nights he used to tuck him in, read *The Tiger Who Came To Tea*. It all seemed so long ago. He had passed Connor a bottle of Becks and although Connor had raised his eyebrows questioningly – this was not a normal occurrence – he'd taken the bottle and raised it to his mouth. They'd sat in awkward silence for a few moments sipping their beers, Connor's eyes flicking back to his TV screen, his Xbox game still playing. Soldiers shooting each other. Bombs exploding. Aidan had glanced around the room, recalling the times he used to pace backwards and forwards, a newborn Connor cradled to his chest, hushing him in soothing tones, softly singing Bob Dylan songs. When colic had gripped his son, Aidan had taken him out in the car, driving him around in the still of the night, the engine lulling him to sleep. As the years passed, the sight of Connor in the rear-view mirror has changed. From giggling toddler to schoolboy, growing taller, but still eager to come out with his dad to visit the horses. Taking an interest in what was wrong with each animal. How Aidan could fix them. Once Aidan thought Connor would follow in his footsteps and become a vet. Now, although Aidan knows what Connor wants to do for a profession, he doesn't know the essence of who he is anymore. They have lost their connection. That night in Connor's room, Aidan had taken another sip of his beer and oh so casually asked his son if he wanted to talk about Hailey. He had watched the repugnance spread over Connor's face.

'No. I'm good,' he had said and Aidan knew it was a lie.

'When you were four and had finished preschool I heard you crying at night and you started wetting the bed again. We asked you over and over what was wrong and it was only a couple of days before you were due to start primary school that you told me. Do you remember what it was?'

Connor shrugged. 'Something stupid.' He began to peel the Becks label from his bottle, scratching at it with his nail.

'You'd heard Mum and I talking about a case of MRSA at the hospital and how somebody had died and you were terrified you'd catch it from the toilets at big school. You were funny about using the toilets at preschool anyway, always waiting until you were home, but you knew you wouldn't be able to last a whole day. You thought—'

'Yeah, Dad, that's not the same,' Connor had cut in and Aidan felt a flush of shame stain his cheeks.

'Sorry. I didn't meant to imply… I meant… it was the most worried I ever remember you being, but after you opened up to me you began to feel better.' Aidan began to pick at his own label to prevent his hand from smacking against his forehead. What had he been thinking? Of course it wasn't the same. Reassuring Connor that he could use a public toilet without the risk of dying seemed mountainous at the time but Aidan knew it had faded into nothing. It was inconsequential.

Something Connor can barely remember when he looks back. Hailey is... Hailey was...

'I've got some homework I need to get on with.' Connor had glanced pointedly at the door. Aidan wanted to scoop his son into his arms. Hold him until Connor felt able to release the emotion that was coiled tightly inside of him. Instead, he had risen to his feet. Walked out of the room, carrying the empty beer bottles and his inadequacies downstairs.

Aidan flicks his windscreen wipers on as the rain bounces of the windscreen. He could be warm and snug in front of the TV, calling out the answers to *The Chase*. Eating crunchy roast potatoes, and minted garden peas. He should be anywhere but in this car, driving, not to the Thompsons' farm as he had told Lucy, but towards trouble.

Meet me in 30 minutes, she had messaged, counting on the fact he'd be able to get away because he usually can. He is frequently on call.

It takes twenty minutes to reach the outskirts of town where they have a good chance of remaining anonymous.

He should be at home.

He is here now. Their usual meeting spot, the back of the White Swan pub, even with his windows shut he can smell hops. He pictures Lucy rattling a tray up to Kieron if he's too tired to come downstairs, her and Connor perching on the edge of his bed, dinners on laps. A family meal, not always around the table, but a family all the same.

He should be at home.

The click of the car door. A blast of damp, icy air.

'Aidan.' Her voice is thick as though she's been crying.

He can't bring himself to look at her. His fingers grip the steering wheel tightly.

He wants to stop this.

He has to stop this, it's madness. There is so much at stake. Too much. He'd tried a few days ago, told her it was over, but she'd been angry, upset, unwilling to accept it. He stares straight ahead as the windscreen wipers sweep across the glass.

Danger. Danger. Danger.

'Aidan?' Her hand lightly touches his shoulder and he shrugs it off but he can still feel the heat of her.

'This has to be the last… Lucy doesn't deserve…' His mouth dries. He hates to mention his wife's name in her presence as though the sordidness of what he's doing might somehow taint his home life.

'But I need you.' She speaks softly but Aidan knows that scratch the surface of her words and there's a sharp edge. She's scared of losing him and he's scared of losing everything and he dreads to think of how she might react if he ignores her calls and texts. Didn't turn up to meet her.

What would she say? What would she do? Fear makes people act out of character, do terrible, unforgivable things. He knows this undoubtedly to be true.

'Look,' he begins firmly, but then a shadow catches his eye.

A figure cutting through the car park. Aidan shrinks in his seat as he recognizes Connor's mate, Tyler. But it is too late. Tyler raises his hand in a wave.

He's seen him.

Seen her.

Bile stings his throat. Will Tyler tell Lucy? Tell Connor?

Aidan is supposed to be at the Thompson farm, not here. Not with her.

He watches Tyler through narrowed eyes. He could ruin everything.

But Aidan knows the only thing ruining everything is his own weakness.

Connor.

Kieron.

Lucy.

His throat swells with emotion. He turns to her.

'This has to stop. Please. I love my family and if Lucy finds out, she'll—'

'Shh.' She places a finger over his lips. 'Don't say that. You know what I want.'

Aidan knows what she wants. He knows he'll give it to her. He knows he will tell himself it will never happen again.

He knows he's a liar.

CHAPTER SIX

Lucy

Twelve days until Connor is taken

The light pushing through the window prods at the headache that's already forming behind my temples, I turn away from the brightness, one hand reaching out towards Aidan, but his side of the bed is empty, sheets cool.

It's early. The sky outside streaked with apricot. I find Aidan in the kitchen, at the breakfast bar staring at his phone, a mug of steaming coffee and a slice of half-eaten toast dripping with sticky golden honey in front of him. From Alexa, The Mamas and the Papas invite me to dream of California.

My eyes sting with tiredness. Throughout the night I had frequently checked on Kieron, the way I did with both of the boys when they were babies. Hand on chest, feeling the rise and fall. Fingers against the forehead, checking for signs of a temperature. Then, Aidan had never once called me obsessive, although obsessive is what I was.

It's what I am again.

'How did it go last night?' I yawn as I slide onto a stool.

'Last night?' He wipes crumbs from his mouth. 'Oh, the horse. Fine. So, first day of term.'

My stomach rolls with nerves.

'We're doing the right thing… for Connor?' I ask again.

Usually Aidan responds with a firm yes but this time he says, 'I hope so.' My fingers find his but he pulls his hand from under mine. 'I've got to get to work.'

As he says this we both inadvertently straighten our spines. His eyes momentarily narrow in regret because he's referenced that he still has a career before they widen into a question.

Are you sure you're doing the right thing?

My gaze is steadfast.

Yes, I'm certain.

He gives a barely imperceptible nod. After so many years of marriage we've honed the ability to have a conversation without words.

But should I have resigned? During the stretch of summer, with both boys at home, there was always something to do. Now Connor will be at school, Kieron will sleep for most of the day until he's recovered and then he too will rejoin his class. How will I fill my time? How will I define myself?

Already, I can feel myself slipping away.

I've woken Connor, checked on Kieron and now I'm dressed in faded black leggings and an old jumper of Aidan's. My heart beats faster as I open the front door; I've steeled myself to find another bird on the step, but there's nothing there. I glance up and down the street. No white car. My relief is tempered with caution and, once in the car, I keep checking my rear-view mirror until Connor throws himself onto the passenger seat in a cloud of too much deodorant and general mardy-ness. The heater is already throwing out warm air and the breakfast show I like is playing Fleetwood Mac's 'The Chain'.

Again, I yawn.

'I could drive myself?' Connor says hopefully.

'Nice try.' I throw him a smile he doesn't return. He passed his test shortly after he'd turned seventeen just before Easter, and although we'd allowed him to borrow the car once, he'd dented the wing parking and we hadn't let him take it since.

Connor turns his attention to his phone, thumbs flying over the keypad. The traffic is back-to-school terrible. Each time it clears, my foot does the lift and drop of impatience against the accelerator, but when the speedo creeps towards 35 mph I force myself to slow down.

We don't want an accident.

Another one.

I pull into Deene Street. I used to drop Connor right at the school gates but that was before he found me embarrassing.

'We're here,' I say gently.

He raises his pale face from his screen. The muscles of his jaw tight. For a second I want to take him home. Really, he's old enough to make up his own mind, but legally, he has to do something until he is eighteen and he was so set on a career in medical research. If he does leave school, I don't want his decision to be based on fear and gossip and guilt.

I know what it's like to run away from a situation. From accusing stares and pointing fingers. It didn't change the way I felt about myself inside. There are some things we can never escape.

Ryan and Tyler are waiting by the bus shelter. Tall and gangly. Wearing the Kings Park Secondary uniform but all of them scruffy somehow in the way that teenagers often are. Ties skewwhiff, laces untied. Hair sticking up at all angles. Clever enough to sit A levels but unable to grasp the concept of a brush or comb. It's reassuring they can all support each other through today.

Connor climbs out of the passenger seat, dragging his rucksack behind him. He slams the door without saying goodbye.

I open the window. 'Do you need any money for lunch?'

'Nah,' Connor says. I flash him a hard stare and he adds a begrudging, 'Thanks.'

'How's your mum?' I can't help asking Ryan, studying his face. He doesn't look like he got much sleep.

'She's…' He shrugs. 'She's not going in to work today.'

The boys begin to walk away. 'See you later,' I call after them.

Connor turns. 'Have a good day!' I say brightly. He raises his hand. I can't tell whether he is waving goodbye or dismissing me.

I drum my fingers on the steering wheel. I don't like leaving Kieron for too long but stopping by Mel's to check on her won't take too much time. As awful as the situation with her and Fergus is, there's still something in her voice last night bothering me. I can't imagine why she didn't want me to go round. We've always been so close.

She was scared.

Of what?

A chill slowly creeps across me as I recall the dead birds on my doorstep, their insides spilling out. Was it a cat or was it someone blaming Connor for what's happened and if so, are they blaming Ryan too? Had something happened at Mel and Fergus's house? The stress on us all over the past few months has been immense; I'd thought more for us being Connor's parents but perhaps just as much for Fergus because he'd been there. In charge.

I need to see her.

I rummage around in my bag for my phone so I can drop Kieron a message to tell him that I won't be long. My handset slips from my fingers, falling onto the floor, under my seat. Irritated, I undo my seatbelt and get out of the car. Crouch down and stick my arm under my seat, spidering my fingers until they brush against... not hard plastic but soft material. I pull it out.

Pink.

Pink, very sexy, very lacy, very not mine knickers.

Stunned, I lose my balance, smacking my knees against the pavement.

Whose are they? I hold them up.

No one drives the car except me and Aidan and these aren't anything to do with him, are they?

Of course not. Things are tense between us right now but that's natural with everything we're dealing with.

But, whispers doubt, he's on his phone more and more. Frequently called out at night.

I can't think the worst. With our lives in turmoil the last thing he'd have the time or energy for is an affair. I'd know if he was seeing someone. I'd just know.

Wouldn't I?

I stare at the knickers again – not practical mum pants like mine. Somebody young might wear these.

'Somebody's had a good night,' an old man cackles, nodding at the knickers I am still holding up as he walks past.

And kneeling there in the dirty kerb, littered with cigarette butts and a scrunched-up lager can, I nod that yes, somebody has had a good night.

But it wasn't me.

CHAPTER SEVEN

Connor

Tyler dribbles a scrunched-up Pepsi can across the playground. The metal sound reverberates around Connor's head along with the one single thought that spins its never-ending loop.

You shouldn't have come back.

They are not wanted here. And that's without everyone knowing the full story. After it happened, the boys had been separated but had recited statements full of half-truths and omissions. Connor sick with shock. With shame. Sick at the way they had all cobbled together a matching account so they couldn't be blamed.

They were to blame.

The other kids know it.

All future trips had been cancelled as well as the end-of-year ball.

His little group of three, once so popular, hadn't received any invitations over the summer. No swimming in the local lake. No barbecue at the country park. No parties in houses with out-of-town parents, kids left behind to study for their A levels.

The teachers know it.

He'd missed the last few weeks of school. Shell-shocked, Connor had sat his mock exams at a nearby college rather than here, in the familiar sports hall which always smelled of rubber and feet. His body was present but his mind was somewhere else entirely. On autopilot he'd picked up his pen, his hand working independently from his brain. He'd scrawled his answers to the questions but his head was only full of one thing.

Hailey.

Frequently, he'd had to bite down hard on his lip to stop himself from crying.

Afterwards, there was no cursory call from his school to see how he'd got on. There was no prep for next year sent home. No reading lists. No visit from his form tutor to see if he needed anything.

The head teacher knows it.

They'd always taken the piss out of him – Mardy Marshall – his fixation on league tables, and results. Behaviour both in and out of school – I don't care if it's Saturday, boy. You're still representing Kings Park Academy. Your behaviour is a direct reflection on the school and also a direct reflection on me. His standards were impossibly high. He was ex-military and sometimes the school felt like an army camp.

Or a prison.

'Our last year then.' Ryan breaks the silence as they climb the grey stone steps.

'Thank fuck for that.' For Tyler there is no staring at his shoes, no rounding of his shoulders, trying to make himself disappear the way that Connor and Ryan were. He put on a front half of the time. Mouthy and opinionated at school, he cowed in the shadow of his mum's boyfriend, Liam, at home. It wasn't unusual for Tyler to have a split lip, a black eye. It's how they first became friends. He and Ryan feeling sorry for Tyler, always sitting on his own at lunch, the way he often didn't seem to have any food. Ryan had offered him a crisp and they'd discovered that this boy, who was taller, louder, brasher than most of the class, was actually really funny and surprisingly ambitious. Connor assumed Tyler would end up in a dead-end job, or out of work, but Tyler had dreams.

'Gonna be a teacher,' he said after they'd hung out for a few weeks.

Connor and Ryan waited for the punchline.

'Nah. Seriously. I am.' Tyler shrugged. 'Education... it gives you opportunities, doesn't it? Gives kids who might not otherwise make something of themselves a chance.'

'What do you want to teach?' Ryan asked.

'Not sure, either History or Sociology. It's important, the way things were. The way they've changed. The changes we've yet to make. Anyway, ' he straightened his collar. 'You can call me Mr Palin.'

They all brought out the best in each other. Tyler made Connor and Ryan braver and Connor and Ryan calmed down Tyler, recognizing that his sudden flashes of anger came from a desire to be taken seriously, the way that he wasn't at home.

'Got into a scrap at the park.' He'd shrug as they'd probed about his bruises. 'You should have seen the other kid.'

Ryan and Connor would exchange a glance, their years of shared friendship meaning they could often communicate wordlessly. They didn't believe him. They'd seen the way Liam treated him. They'd stood outside his front door, hand fisted, knuckles poised to rap on the reinforced glass, hesitating when angry shouts came from inside. Tyler would run out of the door. 'Tosser,' he'd shout. Liam would chase them as they'd leg it down the six flights of stairs. Tyler's mum standing silent, watching.

'That's it. Run away with your loser mates like the cowards you are.'

Cowards. That word strikes a chord with Connor now. He wants to run away. He stops walking, drags his sleeve across his forehead to wipe away the sweat that's formed.

He can't go inside and face everyone. He just... can't.

'You okay, mate?' Tyler says. 'You look like someone has—' He shakes his head. 'Shit. Sorry.'

'I can't do this.' The air is damp, the sky grey, but perspiration still gathers in Connor's armpits. Trickles down his back.

'Me neither. Everyone's staring at us.' Ryan's breathing is laboured as he leans against the wall. 'We should have changed schools.'

'I couldn't have done. My mum couldn't afford the bus to send me to Parkfleet,' Tyler says. 'People will soon forget. Today's gossip is yesterday's chip papers.'

'Tomorrow's chip paper,' Ryan corrects.

'Whatever.' Tyler shrugs.

'And when have you ever seen chips wrapped in newspaper?'

'When have you ever not acted like a tosser?' Tyler nudges Ryan. 'Come on. We got this. Safety in numbers. Year Thirteen is our ticket to freedom.' Tyler more than any of them talked frequently of life after this. School. Parents. He was desperate to go to university far, far away and never return.

Connor flexes his fingers, the memory of Hailey's warm hand in his when they thought nobody was watching. She will never be full of last day euphoria, the ritualistic burning of school ties in the park, never shyly offer her wrist to his to fasten a corsage on the night of the school prom. She will never do any of those things.

'I can't…' He loosens his tie.

'Come on.' Ryan claps him on the back. 'We've got this.'

Ryan encourages Connor with his eyes, the way he had on their first day at primary, their first evening at Cub Scouts, the football tryouts after Ryan had spent hours coaching Connor, Ryan not joining the team until Connor was good enough.

His mum's words float back to him: 'Kieron would give anything to start back at school today,' and he knows that he can do this, not only for Ryan but for his brother.

He ascends the steps flanked by Ryan and Tyler. It isn't the same as having Hailey next to him. Their fingers brushing against each other. He misses her.

Still misses her.

'Right, losers,' Tyler says before they go to their separate lessons. 'Shall we head into town at lunchtime? Chippy? Something to look forward to?'

'Nah.' Connor shakes his head. 'Don't have any cash.'

'I've got you covered. Both of you.' From his pocket Tyler pulls out a roll of notes.

'What the…' Ryan leans forward for a closer look. 'All twenties? Where did you get them?' Tyler is always skint.

'That's for me to know.' Tyler taps the side of his nose. 'But there's more where this came from.'

The sound of the bell – shrill and piercing – makes them walk a little quicker. They pass Amber, Hailey's best friend. Connor doesn't know what to say, so he doesn't say anything at all. Instead, he slopes down the corridor, head hanging low, until he reaches his locker. Stuck to his locker door on an A4 sheet of paper is a printed-out image of Jennifer Love Hewitt in a low-cut vest top, pouting, from the movie poster for *I Know What You Did Last Summer*. Scrawled in a thick red marker, the colour of blood, across her cleavage, 'I know'.

Fucking hilarious. Connor mutters as he screws it into a ball and stuffs it deep into his pocket.

I know what you did last summer.

He clenches his jaw to stop his teeth from chattering. It's impossible for someone to know, isn't it? Not all of it? If they do, he's fucked. He glances at Ryan and Tyler.

They're all fucked.

CHAPTER EIGHT

Lucy

My eyes are trained on the rear-view mirror as I drive away from the pink knickers I'd discarded in the gutter until they're no longer visible.

I keep searching for an explanation but there isn't one. Only Aidan and I drive this car and before the pressure of Kieron's illness, the tragedy that had befallen Connor a few months ago, I'd have dismissed the very notion that Aidan might be unfaithful, but the strain we've been under is immeasurable and we've all acted out of character. Knowing this doesn't make it any easier, the thought that Aidan might have touched another woman steals my breath. He's not the sort to have a casual fling, but the idea he might have fallen in love with someone else is worse.

For thirty-four years he and I have been an 'us' and I can't picture us again as two separate entities. We met in a bar, both having leaving drinks with our friends before we headed off to uni. The heat was unbearable and we were crammed near the open door, the smell of cigarettes curling towards us from the smokers outside. He'd knocked my elbow as I lifted my glass to my mouth and was mortified he'd saturated me in Bacardi and Coke.

'There are worse things to be soaked with,' I had shouted

over Dire Straights promising 'Money for Nothing' before realising there were many ways to interpret that. 'I don't mean… oh God.' I was horribly embarrassed.

'Hmm, well I won't ask you to name one.' He lifted his eyebrows and did a weird half-wink. 'Sorry.' It was his turn to apologize. 'I was trying to master the art of the mysterious one-eyebrow raise but I can see by the horrified expression on your face I didn't quite nail it.'

'I thought you might be having some sort of medical emergency.'

'Ha! Not quite, although I am going to be a vet so I'm sure I could have sorted myself out.' This time, his face flushed red. 'I didn't mean "sort myself out" like… Another drink?'

'Yes. Alcohol is the only answer to forgetting everything up until this point. Lots of alcohol. I'm Lucy.' I stuck out my hand.

'Aidan.' He took my hand in his and a frisson of energy passed between us.

We spent the next few hours perched on a hard wooden bench in the beer garden where we could talk without yelling. Him draping his denim jacket around my shoulders when the night sucked away the remaining warmth from the day.

Neither of us wanted to go home, knowing that in each other we had found our soul mate.

'This is crazy,' he murmured when we'd finally been kicked out.

'Totally,' I agreed, but as he pressed his lips against mine under the star-speckled sky I was lost and found and his completely. Frustratingly we were heading to universities at the opposite ends of the country and tears filled my eyes as I thought about giving up my dream. Giving up him.

'If it's meant to be, we'll still be together next month, next year, next decade.' He concocted a plan that we'd meet on the first evening of each of the holidays at the same bar if we still felt this way. It felt incredibly romantic, almost something lifted out of a Hugh Grant film.

Every holiday, every year, we were there. Sometimes him first, anxiously looking at his watch, sometimes me, worried he wouldn't turn up, but always, always there. The bar is now a Specsavers but I still smile when I pass it.

Again, I glance in the rear-view mirror. This time I catch sight of a white car. My heart jumps.

Is it *the* car?

My hand shakes as I manoeuvre the gear stick into fourth. The car flies over a speed bump and lands with a jolt, jarring my spine. I slow down. The white car also slows.

Panic stamps down upon my chest.

The glaring sun prevents me from seeing who is driving. I pull into a bus stop and the car overtakes me, disappearing around the corner. Momentarily, I rest my head on the steering wheel in relief before I carry on through the housing estate we still call new although it was built in the Eighties, until I pull up outside Mel's house. I dash down the path towards the mock Tudor semi with its smooth cream render and black wooden beams. Rap the brass knocker onto the glossy black door.

Mel takes an age to answer and when she does she looks terrible. Her eyes bloodshot, hair unbrushed.

'I told you not to come.' Her voice cracks.

For a moment I'm thrown but then she dissolves into tears and I step into the hallway, into the stale fug of wine that clouds her, and envelop her into a hug. She's limp against me, crying as though her heart is broken.

And it probably is.

Melissa and Fergus.

Fergus and Melissa.

It's impossible to imagine one without the other.

I don't ask her any questions. Instead, I let her sob it out, my arms aching as I hold her up. When she eventually steps away from me, we head into the honeycomb yellow kitchen where I click on the kettle and prise the lid off the tea caddy. When I open the fridge door, the stench of strong blue cheese rushes towards me. Fergus is the only one of us that can bear it, teasing us for preferring a mild Brie or Cheddar, and I wonder whether Mel will throw it away now or leave it to fester. Milk in my hand, I close the fridge. It's covered with photos of Melissa, Fergus and Ryan and I try not to linger on them. There's one of the four of us, with Connor and Ryan when they were small. The boys holding hands as they toddled into the sea.

When I've slid her mug across to her and she's wrapped her hands around its warmth I ask, 'What happened?'

'I... I can't...'

Can't tell me?

Can't bear to think about it?

'Can't?' I gently probe but she doesn't reply. Instead, she leans back in her chair, increasing the distance between us, crossing her arms over her chest as though she's either trying to keep her feelings in or my questions out. Perhaps both.

'You said Fergus left? Have you seen him since you called me?'

She shakes her head. 'I don't think he's coming back.'

I feel a swell of sadness as she says this. As much as I love Melissa, I adore Fergus too. He's devoted to his family. I can't imagine what caused him to leave. I'm at a loss with how to comfort her, how to even begin to piece her back together when I don't know what's broken her apart.

Broken them.

'Mel. What's going on? Please tell me.' I don't promise everything will be okay because I don't know if it will. All I can do is listen the way I have so many times over the years, in the same way she always lets me offload. It always helps. I can't understand her reluctance to talk.

She's staring at the table, her eyes shiny with fresh tears that she's fighting to contain and I'm reminded of the glassy eyes of those dead crows. I'm probably on the wrong track but I ask, 'Is this connected to the boys, to Hailey?' Connor going back to school has been a source of tension in our house; I know Melissa and Fergus have struggled with what happened, Fergus's part in it, what's best for Ryan.

'No. It's not that.' She picks up her mug and takes a sip but her hands are shaking so hard tea sloshes over her fingers. I notice she's bitten her nails again, a habit she'd quit many moons ago.

I give her a chance to collect her thoughts, to speak, but she doesn't. Her lips are pursed together. Out of the two of us she's always been the talker, the oversharer. It's unsettling, her silence, and I rush to fill it, not wanting to voice the unimaginable but I ask it anyway.

'Has Fergus… has he hurt you?' He's so gentle I can't imagine it but last night she sounded scared, today she looks it.

'No.' Her voice is thin and my heart breaks for her. 'He's a good man. He… he hasn't done anything wrong.' Her breath is shallow, her chest heaving, she's trying not to cry and although part of me wants to sweep her into my arms and let her sob it out again, there's an invisible barrier between us. Her stiff spine and closed expression keeping me at bay.

The clock ticks. The fridge hums.

'Mel, if there's anything—'

'I really don't want to talk about it right now.' She shakes her head vehemently.

I'm hurt, frustrated that I'm not helping her, but I don't let it show. This isn't about me.

'Okay. But whenever you're ready, I'm here for you.'

'Same.' She changes the subject. 'How are you anyway?'

'Okay.' But she knows me too well. Detects the lie because she follows it up with, 'You don't sound okay. What is it, Lucy?'

'Nothing.'

'I've known you for nearly fifty years. Don't tell me nothing.' Now she leans forward, squeezes my fingers, back to being the warm Mel I know and love.

'Another time.' I drain my drink. I wish I could tell her about finding the knickers but it isn't fair to burden her with my problems when she has enough of her own.

'Lucy, I… I'm not shutting you out, I just… I don't…' She takes a breath. 'Please don't feel you can't talk to me if you need to because… you mean the world to me. You know that and I'd never purposefully…' Her tears begin to fall again.

'Mel, it's fine. Honestly, I'm fine. It's just…' I'm reluctant to say it aloud because there has to be a rational explanation.

There has to be.

'I found some knickers under the car seat, that's all. Knickers that aren't mine, pink and lacy.' There isn't anything else I can add.

'How did they get there?' Mel's forehead creases.

'I don't know. They wouldn't fit Aidan.' I try a weak joke knowing it isn't funny.

'Perhaps they're Hailey's?'

'Hailey's?' Surely not.

'Connor borrowed the car that time to take her out, didn't he?'

'Yes but that was ages ago. We've cleaned it since then, had it valeted anyway, when it was at the garage for its MOT.' As I say this a thought occurs to me, flooding me with relief. One of the young mechanics at the garage must have taken the Audi out when they had it, racing around town, pretending it was theirs. Impressing a pretty blonde who might wear knickers like these.

Before I can share this with Mel her phone begins to ring, Aidan's name and number flashing on her screen.

She glances at me before accepting the call.

'Hello. Lucy is here, are you looking for her?' There's a pause. 'No. I don't know. No. Bye.' She places her phone back down. 'He was calling to see if Fergus is back. Apparently he's not answering his phone and Aidan wants to know he's okay. Are any of us okay?' She gazes at me despairingly.

And I don't answer because I know that no, we're not okay. Not even close. How can we be?

We've covered up for our children. Lied. There's a constant pressure on my chest as I live in fear of being found out.

I should never have sent Connor back today.

What if...

My phone rings.

It's the school.

CHAPTER NINE

Aidan

Aidan thinks of Fergus, his oldest friend hurting and in pain. Heading off to work as a pilot, flying his lonely travels around the world with no home to come back to. He wishes Fergus would pick up his calls, reply to his text messages at least. It's not as though Fergus is the type to do anything rash but he can't help worrying.

Aidan thinks of Mel – her future now rocky and uncertain. He thinks of Tyler who had later come back to the pub car park when Aidan was finally alone, head on his steering wheel, trying to process his thoughts, his lies, and asked him if everything was okay.

He thinks of Ryan and Connor. Friends forever, their bond unbreakable and yet spider-web fragile, the past stretching the gossamer fine strands; there are things to come that could snap them altogether. The boys had always been so close. Saturday night sleepovers. Padding downstairs, in matching Spider-Man pyjamas. Would Aidan read them another story, play Uno, hide so they could find him? And then they'd grown. Aidan would stand on the landing in front of Connor's door, closed to him now, and smell pizza, cider, hear deep laughter, not the high-pitched giggles that used to make him smile, his heart aching, knowing if he stepped inside the room his son would fall silent, not craving the company of his dad anymore but irritated by it. As much as Aidan missed those times with Connor, he had consoled himself that at least his son was happy.

Then.

Aidan can't remember the last time he heard Connor laugh, that Ryan slept over.

It was before the trip.

Everything good was before that bloody trip.

He thinks of Hailey. The way she once gazed adoringly at his son before her bright flame was extinguished.

Aidan thinks of Kieron, his boy sick and suffering.

He thinks of his wife. For better, for worse. The gold wedding band that circles his finger sometimes comforting but often, nowadays, a noose around his neck.

He thinks of himself trying to hold everything together, knowing it's slipping from his grasp.

He is charged with emotion.

Sometimes he wants to lie down in the middle of the road and force the traffic to slow, stop.

He just wants everything to slow.

Stop.

CHAPTER TEN

Lucy

'It's the school,' I tell Mel, palpitations in my chest as I fumble to answer the phone, my handset almost slipping through my nervous palm.

'Is Connor okay?' I ask the instant I'm connected.

'Connor? Mrs Walsh? This is Caro— Ms Baker... I'm the new receptionist.' The voice at the end of the phone sounds young. Awkward. 'So, Kieron has been marked as absent but, basically, you haven't left a message on the absence line?'

'Sorry. It slipped my mind. He's not long out of hospital. I'm not sure when he'll be back.'

'Right, but... basically procedure is that you must ring in every day, Mrs Walsh.'

'But I can tell you now that he definitely won't be in this week.'

'Mr Marshall has actually told me—'

'Mr Marshall?' I say his name too loudly. 'He's still the head teacher?' Instinctively, my hand reaches for Mel's and she encloses my fingers inside hers.

'Yes?' There's an inflection in Ms Baker's voice, a question not a statement. She doesn't know.

She doesn't know what happened.

'Kieron won't be in for the rest of the week,' I garble before cutting the call.

'Shit,' Mel says. 'That bloody Facebook post in the mums' group said he'd been sacked.'

'I know. I guess if the board fired him if would be harsh, considering...'

'Perhaps they haven't made a final decision yet? It's only been a few weeks. How long do these things take to be decided?'

'I don't know.' I fiddle with a stray thread dangling from my sleeve.

'The boys will be okay though?' she says. 'He can't blame them, surely? He has to be impartial.'

'Of course.' I try to reassure her. Reassure myself. 'They'll be fine.'

They won't-they won't-they won't.

The hands of the clock tick out their warning as they march from the present into the future. More than anything I wish I could wind them back and step into the past. Rewrite history.

Keep us safe.

At home, I check on Kieron who's watching *The Incredibles* and then I settle myself at the kitchen table and ring Aidan. While I wait for him to answer, I run my fingertips lightly over the indents of forks stabbed against the soft pine, dents of cups banged for more juice. The marks of a family.

'Hello,' he says.

'Can you talk?'

'Yes. I'm on my way to Brampton Stables. Hands-free so don't worry. Is everything okay?'

'Mr Marshall is still the head teacher.'

'That's not ideal but it's not like Connor will see much of him, if anything.'

'I know but it's jarred me.'

'I called Mel earlier.' Aidan changes the subject.

'Yes, she said. I was there. She was… strange. She didn't tell me what's happened.'

'She doesn't have to tell you everything.'

'I'm her best friend.'

'But it's impossible to know everything about a person. Do you tell her everything?'

Crying. My heart breaking. It's all my fault, Mel. I can't bear it.

'Pretty much.' I always have.

'Well, don't push her. Look, I'm almost there, is there anything else?'

I scratch at some dried ketchup with my thumbnail, unsure whether to tell him about my discovery over the phone when I can't see his face, gauge his reaction.

'Lucy? What's wrong?'

'I found a pair of knickers under the seat in the car.'

'They're probably Hailey's,' he says without hesitation.

'That's what Mel thought.'

'I'm pulling up outside the stables now. I've got to go,' he says before I can ask whether a mechanic at the garage is the more likely option. 'Lucy, I… I do love you.'

He rings off before I can tell him that I love him too.

*

I've had a coffee and hung out the washing by the time Kieron's film is finished.

He's been in bed for thirteen hours but he still looks exhausted. Although I hope that Mr Peters is right – this is the lingering effects of Kieron's last infection – I can't help worrying this is the beginning of ongoing deterioration of his liver. It's so incredibly difficult as a mother to put your trust entirely in somebody else. To put the life of your child in another person's hands. As a mum, we're programmed to protect our young. It shouldn't feel like a failing on my part that my son has developed a chronic disease, but somehow it does.

'What do you fancy for lunch?' I ask, mentally scanning the contents of the fridge. 'We have ham, eggs, cheese. I could whip up a fluffy omelette.'

'I'm not hungry.'

'You have to eat.' I don't like giving him his medication on an empty stomach, the bile acid sequestrates his daily vitamin supplements – his body can't absorb all the nutrients he needs despite the healthy meals I cook for him. Lack of vitamin D and calcium can weaken his bones.

'Tomato soup then,' he decides.

The one thing we haven't got.

'I'll have to pop to the shops.'

'I'll have something else then. Don't go out just for me.'

'It's okay. Anything else while I'm there?' I used to shake my head when the boys begged for junk food every time I was going out, chocolate bars, biscuits, popcorn. Now I wish that Kieron was hungry for something.

'An Xbox magazine?' Kieron isn't as obsessed as Connor

is with gaming but he wants to share the same interests as his brother. Connor learns as he plays, Kieron prefers to read about new games first. How to level up. Find the Easter eggs. Build a world.

'I won't be long, don't answer the door to anyone.' I plant a kiss on the top of his head, his hair smells faintly of apples.

It isn't until I'm drawing closer to the supermarket that I notice the car behind me.

The white car.

My hands tighten on the steering wheel.

Paranoid, Aidan called me.

Obsessive.

But still, I keep seeing it.

I signal left, the car follows me. This time I slow down and try to memorize the number plate but the car speeds past me, turning right into Tesco car park. Now I am the one following them.

It must be a coincidence, there's no way anyone could have known I was coming here. No reason for anyone to follow me. The only thing trailing after me is my own guilty conscience.

But I am slow getting out of the car. Glancing around me as I zap my door locked. Walking faster than I normally would towards the store.

I scan the car park; I can see at least nine white cars. Throwing a glance over my shoulder, I spot three more.

I grab a basket rather than a trolley and stalk up and down the aisles, soup, fresh bread, magazine, grapes, toilet rolls – we seem to be forever running out. I self-scan, which takes me twice as long, before I hurry back to my car, conscious that Kieron will be waiting for his lunch.

Down the side of the driver's door runs a jagged groove. I throw the shopping in the boot and then crouch by the scratch and run my finger across it. It's deep. Too low and too uneven to have been caused by a trolley.

Someone has keyed my car deliberately, but who? Why?

Yes, again I have that cold, squirming feeling deep in the pit of my stomach. Hurriedly, I lock myself inside my vehicle. Start the engine.

There's a screech. A car speeding towards the exit.

Everything else fades away as it falls into sharp focus.

It's white.

CHAPTER ELEVEN

Connor

It's lunchtime. Connor has survived half a day but his stomach is still tight with nerves. The *I Know What You Did Last Summer* poster on his locker has set him on edge. He had sat at his desk trying to quell his mounting panic by pinching and twisting the skin on his forearm viciously between his fingers until his pain was all-consuming. He can't wait for the end of the day. He can't stick out the rest of the year in this dump. He doesn't belong here anymore. He watches as the other kids muck about, laughing, and he can't remember a time when he didn't have a cloud of guilt shadowing him. Even before Hailey, he felt horrible that he was healthy and Kieron wasn't. On some level there was the feeling he'd let his brother down. There has always been that sense he'd let his parents down.

But he can't think of it all right now. His head hurts and he wants to go for a walk to clear it.

Connor doesn't care that he hasn't any food or any cash to buy any, but when Tyler claps him on the shoulders and says, 'Chippy?' he can almost taste the salt and vinegar.

'Yeah, why not?' It isn't as though he has anywhere else to go. Anyone else to go with.

Ryan falls into step to his left. To his right, Tyler finds another can to dribble, Fanta this time. It isn't quite empty and splashes of orange stain his grubby white trainers. They're falling apart. The sole hanging down each time Tyler raises his foot. Mr Marshall will go mental if he notices Tyler isn't wearing plain black shoes.

'So where did you get this cash from?' Ryan tackles him, kicking the can into the gutter.

Tyler taps the side of his nose. 'That's for me to know. There's more to come though.'

'You gonna blow it on some Nikes?' Ryan asks.

'Nah. Saving most of it for uni. Gotta plan ahead if I want to be a teacher. Right, you losers save the bench.'

Connor and Ryan head towards the bus shelter. They sit, Ryan stifling another yawn. Dark circles under his eyes.

'How are you?' Connor asks Ryan once Tyler has gone. The three of them are close but there are some things he knows Ryan won't feel comfortable talking about in front of Tyler.

'It'll take some getting used to, being back, but—'

'I'm not talking about school.'

'I know,' Ryan says. 'It's… I dunno. I can't believe Dad would leave me.' His voice wobbles.

'He hasn't left you.'

'Whatever. Me. Mum. It's the same. He's not at home.'

'Has he called you?'

'Nah. I… I rang and texted him this morning but…' Ryan shrugs. 'You don't think it's… you know. He feels he let everyone down. He'd volunteered to supervise and… he didn't let us down. We let him down. Do you think he hates us?'

'No, I don't,' Connor says firmly. 'Your dad was cool. He told me if I ever needed to talk about it, he'd listen.'

'Perhaps you should call him then,' Ryan says with a hollow laugh. 'He might pick up.'

'Fuck it. Worth a try.' Connor finds Fergus in his address book and presses dial. Ryan watches him, his face even paler than it had been a few seconds ago. The phone rings and rings before it goes to voicemail.

'Not just me he's ignoring then.' Ryan's voice is layered with both disappointment and relief. 'Anyway, don't say anything in front of Ty. Not yet.'

Tyler is heading towards them carrying bags of chips, grease already seeping through the white paper. Steam rising.

'You legend.' Ryan masks his vulnerability with a loud voice and a bright smile as he takes his lunch.

Connor plucks a chip from the bag, it burns his fingertips, his tongue.

Hailey would never have eaten chips, she was always on a diet, but she didn't need to be. She was beautiful. Perfect in his eyes, but she'd scroll through Instagram, her hand fluttering self-consciously to cover her size fourteen tummy. It bothered her, he knew, that her best friend, Amber, was a lot smaller than her, but he honestly never noticed. He falls back into the memory of the first time he ever saw her.

It had been a year and a half ago. He had been slouched over his desk. Mrs Webb droning on about perspectives. He'd be so glad when he'd finished his GCSEs and could drop English. It wasn't that he wasn't good at it – he was – but he'd rather be focusing on his A-level choices of Biology, Chemistry, Maths and Further Maths.

Outside the classroom window, everything was grey. The playground. The wrought iron fence. The sky. There was a tap on the door. Hailey walked into the room and Connor remembers thinking that she had brought the sunshine. That she was the sunshine with a halo of blonde hair framing her pale face, her perfect skin sprinkled with freckles.

'Ah, you must be Hailey! I've been expecting you. Hailey, this is everyone. Everyone, this is Hailey. Be nice.' Mrs Webb gestured at a vacant desk in front of Connor's. As she walked towards him, her green eyes met his and Connor felt an instant attraction. Before then he'd been curious about girls. He'd been on a couple of double dates with Ryan, watched porn with Tyler, but he'd never felt…

He'd never felt *this*.

She had offered him a shy smile but although Connor's mouth wanted to break into a huge grin he didn't let it, wondering whether he'd cleaned his teeth properly, if at all. As she sat down, he raised his arm to scratch his head but he didn't have an itch. He was checking to see if his armpits smelled fresh.

They didn't.

He had kept his elbows pinned to his sides for the rest of the lesson, his eyes lost in the silky sheet of her hair and then Connor was imagining different sheets.

His bed.

Her lying next to him, kissing, touching, the curves that were so different to his last date, Sasha, who had told him he could put his hands under her T-shirt. Her body had been hard, angular, Connor's fingers had brushed against ribs and he hadn't felt turned on in the slightest. Hailey's body was different. His eyes lingered on the middle of her back where he could see the outline of her bra strap. He imagined unhooking it, sliding the straps from her shoulders. His lips kissing her neck as his hands—

'Connor!' Mrs Webb shouted and instantly he covered his lap with his hands, shame burning his cheeks.

Don't ask me to come to the front. Don't ask me to come to the front.

'I said you've got a good grasp of perspectives. Hailey's last school hasn't gone as in-depth as we have with viewpoints. Can you catch her up?'

'Suppose.' He shrugged but on the inside he was singing and dancing and turning cartwheels of joy.

The second he'd said yes was the start of something, he knew. But with hindsight, if he had known how it would turn out, the tragedy that would occur, he'd have said no. Of course he would. The year he'd spent with Hailey was the best year of his life but he'd give it all up in a heartbeat, however much it hurt, to keep her safe.

'Oi!' A shout yanks Connor back to the present. Tyler is already rising to his feet as Amber's boyfriend, Dino, jogs towards Connor. 'Sitting there like you haven't a fucking care in the world.' He places his hands under the bag and thrusts upwards so Connor is covered with chips and ketchup. Connor stands, but before he can react, Dino shoves his chest and he stumbles back against the bus shelter, the sharp corner of the bench driving into his back, his head hitting the pavement as he tumbles to the ground. He winces in pain.

'Hey!' Ryan grabs Dino. There's a scramble and Ryan's blazer tears.

'Fuck off.' Tyler is pushing Dino away. Amber is crying into a tissue. She won't look at Connor and he wants to tell her he is sorry but he knows she is not the one he really wants to tell.

'Look. I don't want any trouble.' Disorientated, Connor pulls himself to his feet.

Ryan stands shoulder to shoulder with him. He doesn't speak. Not because he is afraid, but because he knows, as Connor knows, that Dino barely knew Hailey. Likely doesn't give a shit about what happened. He's acting like a twat to impress Amber, who literally everyone in the school fancies.

Still, as Dino's eyes bore into him, they are full of hate, which slices through Connor's memory like lasers. He has seen that look before in Hailey's father's eyes at the hospital that night. The bitterness. The disdain. The vein that pulsed on the side of his neck. His jaw clenched so tightly Connor was sure he had been biting down on the words he wanted to say. In that moment, Connor knew what it was to feel so guilty that he wanted to disappear.

All he had been able to do was repeat, 'I'm sorry. I'm sorry.' Snot and tears had clogged his throat. His eyes, two swollen slits. 'I'm sorry.'

Connor's dad had led him away, throwing a glance over his shoulder at Hailey's father who stood broken and alone.

'I can't imagine…' Dad had shaken his head. He didn't say anything else. Connor had no idea whether he was angry or sad. Resentful or relieved. Whether Dad felt all of it or none of it.

He had said, 'Mum?' One word. A question. A plea. Connor had retained the childish faith that his mum could fix this. His mum could make everything better. And she had tried. It wasn't until much later that Connor understood she'd made it worse. So very, very worse.

Now he watches warily as Amber and Dino leave, their arms wrapped around each other. Connor aches with the desire to hold. To be held.

'Sorry about your blazer, Ry,' he says.

'Mum's pretty nifty with a needle and thread. She'll fix it. Are you okay?'

'Yeah. Gonna head off though. Thanks again, guys.' Before they can answer, Connor runs. He doesn't go back to school. Instead, he sprints home, faltering at the door when he sees what's on the step but, fuck it, he races upstairs, pulling off his blazer crusted in ketchup and drops it onto the floor. Sits at his computer. Opens Facebook Messenger.

'Dear Hailey', he begins. **'I have a confession to make.'**

CHAPTER TWELVE

Lucy

'Dead mouse,' is all that Connor says as he hurtles through the door and pounds up the stairs.

'Wait. What? Mouse?' I ask in hushed tones. Kieron had fallen asleep awkwardly against me as we'd watched *The Hunger Games* again. Trying not to disturb him, I peel myself from the soft sofa, every muscle aching as I stand. Cautiously I open the front door. On the step, a mouse. It's intact at least. I snap a piece of lavender from the pot under the window and poke it gently to see whether it moves.

It doesn't.

Unease worms in my belly as my eyes search the street. Everything seems as it should be, but I know that it's not.

Quickly, I nudge the mouse to one side to deal with later and then close the door on it, checking twice that I've locked it before I head up to Connor's room.

He's home earlier than he should be; he could have a free period as they often do at this age or something could have happened.

His door is closed. Hanging from a hook is a sign: Gaming in progress – eye contact/small talk unavailable. I'd thought it funny when I'd bought it as a stocking filler a few years ago. Now it just seems sad.

I knock before I step inside. Connor is hunched over his computer, his body shielding the screen.

'How was it?' I ask tentatively.

'How do you think?' His voice is thick. I don't want to push him and so I pick up the blazer that is lying on the floor, but as I slide it onto a hanger I notice it's plastered in something red.

Blood.

My heart skitters as I scan Connor for the sign of any injury but there's no staining on his shirt. I take a closer look at the blazer, draw it to my nose and sniff. Ketchup.

'Connor?' I hesitate. Not wanting to ask if everything is okay, knowing that it isn't. 'If you want to talk? About… anything,' I say.

He mutters something. I step forward but when I see what he's doing I slip away.

He's writing to Hailey again. It's incredibly sad. Endless messages to a girl who won't reply.

Who can't reply.

The doorbell rings and rings.

For a moment I don't move. I'm unsettled. Apprehension trickling down my spine.

The ringing comes again. I take a breath and open the front door. There's a lady on the step brandishing a box of chocolates.

'Hi, I wasn't sure if your bell worked. I'm Susan Golding, my family moved in at the weekend.' She gestures behind her.

'Hello. Sorry, I've been meaning to pop over and introduce myself but my son hasn't been well.'

'I hope he's on the mend now?'

For a moment I can't speak, my throat is so tight. 'He's… anyway, how are you settling in?'

'We're fine but I'm afraid Felix has been playing silly buggers. Our cat,' she adds. 'He's one for bringing us, let's call them "gifts", it sounds nicer, but he's got confused by the new area and I know of at least three houses where he's left little—' she makes speech marks with her fingers '—presents. Has he…' She screws up her face.

'We've had some dead birds on the doorstep, and a mouse,' I tell her.

Her expression is pained. 'That sounds like his handiwork. Little tyke. I'm so sorry.'

'It's okay,' I reassure her. It's more than okay. The mutilated animals I had found weren't anyone trying to scare me, Aidan was right, it was the work of a cat, nothing sinister at all. I must stop thinking the worst.

'Felix is settling in now so hopefully it won't happen again but please accept my apologies and these.' She thrusts the Thorntons towards me. I take them and my shoulders drop for the first time in days.

'I don't suppose,' I call after her as she walks away, 'that you've any visitors who have a white car?'

She shakes her head. My muscles tighten once more.

In the kitchen, I sponge off Connor's blazer and carry it out into the garden. I'll pop it on the line and fetch the washing in while I'm at it. It must be dry by now.

I notice them as soon as I step outside.

The gaps in the row of laundry blowing in the breeze.

The weather has been calm today, it seems unlikely that anything has been snatched away by the wind. But still, confused, I look around the garden, eyes seeking out clothing tangled in a bush, caught in the tree.

The only things I can see are several candy-coloured pegs dotted around the lawn, some of them are snapped as though clothes have been tugged from the line. I scoop them up, confused.

Someone has been here.

My scalp crawls.

Every instinct screams at me to go back inside but first I hurry to fetch the washing. My fingers fumbling to unpeg the clothes that are left: Aidan's work jeans; Connor's American football sweatshirt; Kieron's Captain America pyjamas. As I shove them all in the basket, it strikes me that the only items missing are mine.

Someone has been here.

How had they got in? The gate is always locked.

My pulse is skittering but I tell myself to calm down. I'd thought somebody had been leaving dead birds and mice on the doorstep to frighten me and I'd been wrong about that. Still, Felix, the new neighbourhood cat, can't be responsible for missing clothes, can he? Basket against my hip, I cross to double-check the gate is locked and then I see them.

Footprints in the border.

Someone had climbed over our fence.

The dead birds might have had a rational explanation but this...

A wave of dizziness washes over me as my scared eyes check for intruders. The garden suddenly full of places to hide. The old treehouse Aidan built when the boys were small. The dark space behind the shed. The laurel bush rustles its leaves. Gooseflesh springs up on my bare arms.

Chilled, I bustle inside. Lock the door before pulling at the handle to make sure it's secure.

Once.

Twice.

Three times.

In the lounge, I try to make casual conversation with Kieron about dinner as I hover by the window. I cross my arms over my chest, keeping my apprehension inside as I look down the street. Up the street.

It's empty.

There isn't a white car to be seen.

But still, I have the sense of being watched.

CHAPTER THIRTEEN

Connor

Connor sends his long message to Hailey and rests back in his chair, his hands tucked behind his heavy head, cradling the weight of expectation. Although he knows it's impossible he'll see the three white dots that means she'd be typing a reply, still he waits.

From downstairs, he hears the slam of the back door. It makes him jump and, turning around, he notices his mum has taken away his blazer. He guesses that she'll wash it. She didn't shout at him the way some kids' mums would. Connor's lucky to have her, but, instead of gratitude, resentment crouches in his heart ready to spring out through angry words and thoughtless gestures.

He pinches his arm hard and when he releases his fingers his skin is bright pink.

If Hailey were here she would gently tell him off. Tell him that she'd give anything to still have her mum. He remembers his shock the first time they talked about their families. He'd poured out his despair over Kieron. Not only the worry that he might die but also his frustration that the dynamics of their family had inevitably shifted. The world titling on its axis, no longer spinning around them as a four, but revolving solely around Kieron and his needs. He felt spiteful voicing it out loud. Ashamed when Hailey said, 'I wish I had a brother or a sister. Or a mum. It's just me and Dad.'

Connor was shocked. There were a ton of kids at the school from single parent families, but they all lived with their mum, not their dad. Where was Hailey's?

He threaded his fingers through hers and considered carefully what he wanted to ask. How he wanted to ask it.

'You want to know where my mum is.' Hailey quietly formed the question he was struggling to articulate.

'Yeah. I mean, only if you want to tell me.' Connor ran his index finger lightly over Hailey's wrist, feeling the pulse of her heart. Her bones. She thought she was fat but sometimes to Connor she felt so delicate he was scared she would break. That's what it felt like to really care about someone, he supposed. As well as the good – the skip of a heart when they entered a room, the shiver of expectation when they sent you a message – there was the worry. The wanting them to be okay. To never suffer. But here was Hailey telling him she had felt pain.

She had felt loss.

Hailey shifted her position until she was leaning back against his chest, his legs either side of hers. Connor lowered his head and kissed her neck.

Neither of them spoke. Connor wondered whether he should fill the silence. Whether Hailey wasn't yet ready to open up to him, however close he thought they were. But how close could they be if he hadn't even known that her mum didn't live with her? In the whirlwind three weeks they'd been together there had been much kissing. Much talk about music and movies. Nothing deep yet. Still, Connor should have picked up on the fact Hailey never mentioned her. No 'Better get home before Mum freaks,' or 'Mum wants me home by eleven.'

'She... she died.' Hailey had said eventually. Connor wrapped his arms around her chest and pulled her further back into his chest. He wondered when she died. How she died. He should have been better prepared for this conversation, with tissues at the ready and the right words to take away her pain.

'It was...' Hailey began. 'When I was really young. It's not like I properly remember her.'

'Hailey...' Whatever Connor had been expecting, it wasn't this. He didn't know what to say.

Connor shuffled around until he was kneeling in front of her. He took both of her hands in his. Her head hung low. She couldn't meet his eye and at first Connor thought that she was crying. Gently placing two fingers under her chin, he tilted her face up towards his. 'I am so, so sorry,' he said.

She shrugged. 'It was a long time ago,' but the crack in her voice told him it was still raw. Painful. 'A heart attack. She was young but it was something to do with her blood pressure. Do you want to see a photo of her?' she asked, already pulling an old Polaroid from her bag. A woman sat on the sofa, a baby in her arms. 'It's the only picture I have.'

'She looks a little like you. You must miss her?'

'I don't know any different,' she said. 'It's been just me and Dad for years. I'm glad I've got him at least but I'd... I'd give anything to have one more day with her.'

Connor recalls these words now as he pinches his arm again and again until his skin is red and stinging.

He is treating his mum terribly. How would he feel if he never saw her again? Would her absence eradicate the guilt he felt on a daily basis for ruining her life? His life. Hailey's. So many lives in tatters. How would Mum feel if she never had to see him again? The thought of being alone makes Connor panicky. Heat prickling his scalp, under his arms. But under the panic is something else.

Relief.

Sometimes he thinks Mum is so wrapped up in Kieron she wouldn't notice if he ran away.

Disappeared.

CHAPTER FOURTEEN

Aidan

Aidan soothes the frightened mare.

'Shh, Godiva.' He rhythmically strokes her nose. Godiva has Cushing's disease, a tumour in the pituitary gland. Aidan has been treating her for the past few months. Her owner, Stephanie, has both the time and the money to care for her.

The horse whimpers but she stops stamping her hooves. Instead, she muzzles into Aidan's side, accepting the comfort he is offering.

'She seems a little better?' Stephanie's question is brimming with her hope and her doubt.

'She's brighter,' Aidan confirms.

'It's such a relief.' Stephanie breaks into a smile. 'I can't imagine being without her.'

'She's a beauty. She reminds me a little of my last horse, Lancelot. Man, I miss those early morning rides.'

His Irish sports horse had fallen and broken his leg jumping a hedge, and although it was over twenty-five years ago, he still thinks about him most days. Sometimes Aidan questions whether medicine is backwards. Lancelot had been euthanized by a local vet because he was suffering and yet Aidan had months of unimaginable pain as surgeons pinned back together his pelvis. His hips still throb, a reminder in the cold weather, and when he's tired he often limps.

'Don't you ride anymore?' Stephanie asks.

'No.' He doesn't elaborate but he hasn't been on a horse since his accident. At first it wasn't possible. His bones were healing, his heart too. As soon as he was able to drive, he had visited the stable but it had been cleared, another horse lodging in Lancelot's place. He'd been handed a moth-eaten grey blanket that still smelled of Lancelot, and he had packed it carefully in a cardboard box, which he keeps in the garage. Sometimes, he still gets it out and smells it and then feels ashamed, less of a man somehow. He is supposed to be the one holding his family together, being strong.

'Aidan?'

'Sorry, I was miles away.' He gives Godiva's nose one last stroke. She is quiet now. Calm. Ready for him to check her over. He prefers to work this way. No speeding in and out. Cramming as many appointments as he can into one day. He respects the horses and they respect him.

Once he's finished his examination, he follows Stephanie to the kitchen to wash his hands. They are rough and calloused, 'worker's hands', Lucy calls them. The water is scalding, steam rising and misting the window, but his skin is so thick it doesn't burn as he rinses off the pine-scented soap, which reminds him of Christmas trees. There's a swelling in his throat as he remembers chiming bells outside the boys' bedrooms late on Christmas Eve. Taking bites out of the carrots they had laid out for Rudolph, leaving teeth marks in the vegetables. Scrawling a note using his left hand so his writing was unrecognizable: Thanks for the mince pie and glass of milk and the snacks for my reindeers. Love Santa X

'What's next for Godiva?' Stephanie asks.

Aidan explains and her face relaxes. The farmer's wife should also know better than to become over-attached to animals, but like Aidan she does anyway.

'I can't thank you enough. You're a good man.' She nods once at Aidan. 'A kind man.'

Aidan has finished up the rest of his calls and is on his way home when his mobile buzzes a text.

Her.

His insides twist painfully. He had promised himself last night that he was ending it. Tyler spotting them together really brought it home to him how easily he could be found out. The consequences if he were. He thought he had made himself clear. He loves his family, he doesn't want to lose them.

He ponders over what to say, his thumbs composing and then deleting text after text. Eventually, he says, **Half an hour**. He will tell her again, face-to-face, that it has to stop.

All of it.

It should never have started.

He pulls into the car park first. While he waits, he messages Lucy and tells her he's been called out to Godiva – she won't know he went there earlier – but he won't be long. On the end of the text he writes **I love you** but he deletes this part before he sends it. Telling each other how they felt used to come as naturally as breathing, but they've stopped lately. Their energies focused on Kieron with little left for anything else, for each other, but even if he doesn't write the words out it's ever present, the enormity of love that he's only felt a few times in his life: his parents, his wife, his children.

He wishes he could talk to his best friend. He tries to call Fergus again. Again it cuts straight to voicemail. Aidan doesn't quite know what to say so he doesn't say anything at all. He calls the airline but he's passed from department to department and nobody gives him a clear answer.

The passenger door opens. She slides into the seat.

'I wasn't sure if you'd come,' she says, but, as she meets his eye, he knows that she was confident that he would.

She's wearing a crimson tank top with yellow stars dotted over it, black ribbon sewn around the armholes. Lucy has a jumper with a similar pattern and the sight of it is like a flashing red beacon.

Look at us-look at us-look at us.

He allows her gaze to hold him.

'I can't…' He trails off. He can't carry on? He can't stop? He doesn't know what he wants.

'You're a good man. A kind man,' Stephanie had said earlier that day.

If only she knew. If only everyone knew what he was. What he was doing.

He thinks of Tyler again. His stomach had plummeted with shame when he thought he'd been caught, although out of all the secrets Aidan has, being here, with her, is probably not the worst.

What if Connor finds out?

A good man. A kind man.

Aidan is neither and he couldn't bear it if his son discovered the truth.

91

Aidan hates himself for getting into this. For not being strong enough to get out of it. He thinks of Lucy on the phone earlier, lost without her career, wanting to talk to another adult, him. Wanting reassurance.

Instead, he fed her lies.

He needs to find out the truth.

He swallows hard. Gathers his voice and asks firmly, 'Did you deliberately leave some knickers under the seat of the car last night?'

Aidan hopes he is wrong but knows she is desperate, unhappy, scared of losing him.

'Just a little warning of how quickly your life could fall apart.'

'This has to end.' He is adamant.

'Don't say that. I could make things very... difficult for you. For everyone you love. Their friends and family too. If you end this, I can promise you, someone is going to get hurt.'

Now she has been rejected, cast aside from the one she loves, she wants to destroy them all.

Aidan is close to tears, emasculated, wishing he could breathe in comfort from Lancelot's blanket, breathe in strength. Instead, he tries to pull himself together, because that's what men do, isn't it?

'I'm sorry you've been hurt,' he tells her and he is. 'But please don't hurt my wife she's—'

'Oblivious in her own little perfect world.'

'Her world is far from perfect.' Aidan's hackles rise. 'She's a good person.'

'And I'm not?'

Aidan meets her eyes and can see the pain in them. He feels that pain himself.

He's going to do the right thing.

'I'm not going to see you again. Please don't contact me anymore,' he says quietly.

'It'll be over when I say it's over.' Anger overtakes her sadness before she takes his hand. 'I need you, Aidan,' she whispers.

Everybody needs something from him. He needs... Lucy. He needs her to look at him the way she used to without her face being shadowed by worry. To hear her laughter. To hold her in his arms and whirl around the kitchen in a waltz the way they used to after watching *Strictly*.

He pulls his hand away. 'You should go.'

He can't look at her. There's a blast of air as she opens the door. He jumps as she slams it shut.

Somebody's going to get hurt.

CHAPTER FIFTEEN

Lucy

Grey clouds bunch in the darkening sky. The drizzle now a deluge, freezing rain slapping against my face. I'm frustrated as I crouch next to the footprints by the fence, trying to shield them with my open coat as the last traces of them disappear into sludge. They were the only proof I had that anyone had broken into our garden while Kieron and I were snuggled on the sofa in the lounge, unaware.

Unprepared.

'Lucy?' Aidan sticks his head out of the back door. 'What on earth are you doing?'

I head back indoors.

'And what's happened to the car?' He's spooning coffee into a mug.

I must look blank as I slip off my sodden shoes because he adds, 'The scratch down the side.'

'That was while I was parked at the supermarket. I think it might have been deliberate—'

'Deliberate? Somebody targeting you? Why? You assumed those birds were left by someone rather than an animal, didn't you?'

My resolution waivers. 'Well, yes and you were right. The

94

birds were actually left by a cat, Felix. Our new neighbour came around today and apologized.'

He doesn't say 'I told you so', instead he holds my gaze for a fraction longer than he needs to before he offers to cook dinner and this small kindness is worse than any shouting. He thinks I'm losing it in the way I had before.

I grapple to get my emotions under control, to get the situation under control. I'm fine. I am. I smile a little too brightly. 'It's okay, I made a lasagne this afternoon. It should be ready in a minute.'

'I don't smell anything?' He cracks open the oven. 'Lucy, you haven't switched it on.'

A hot scald of humiliation rushes through me. 'Sorry, I've been distracted because I thought somebody was in the garden and…'

'Lucy. Go and get changed. You're soaked through.' He sounds so weary.

Upstairs, when I open my drawer I immediately spot my blue 'Chicago Bulls' sweatshirt I like to lounge around the house in. I was convinced this was taken from the washing line earlier, and now I'm not so sure anything is missing. Had I imagined it? Is the stress of caring for a sick child, the guilt of everything that came before, causing me to lose my grip on reality? Or am I just so tired I've begun to see things that aren't there? I shed my clothes and my earlier certainty that someone is tormenting me.

It's so gloomy. I'm about to draw the curtains when I see it outside. The white car. The sight of it is a short, sharp shock bringing back into focus all of the things I had believed. I take a step backwards, my hands over my mouth.

The footprints in the mud.

The missing clothes.

The sense of being watched.

It's real. All of it.

'Aidan?' I shout.

I step forward again, back to the window. To let the person know that I know they are outside.

That I'm not scared.

Even though I am.

But the car has gone now and I doubt myself again. Had it really been there at all?

'Did you call me?' Aidan asks from the doorway, a creep of impatience in his voice.

'No. Sorry. It's okay.'

He heads back downstairs.

Full of a sense of foreboding, I put my hand across my chest and press against it, trying to slow the frantic pounding of my heart.

Is the car connected to what happened before the summer? With what happened years ago?

It's all getting mixed up in my mind but there's one common dominator in all of the tragedy that has occurred.

Me.

I am to blame and someone is coming for me.

I know it.

CHAPTER SIXTEEN

Connor

Eleven days before Connor is taken

Mum is acting weird this morning. She's in the kitchen counting the items of clothes in the laundry basket and then counting the pegs she'd thrown haphazardly on top of the washing when she fetched it in last night. She's counted everything three times now, a confused expression on her face.

Connor scatters cornflakes into a bowl – Mum stopped buying Frosties when Kieron first got sick like Tony the Tiger had something to do with it – and then he drenches them in milk, coats them in sugar.

When he's finished, he stacks his bowl in the lower part of the dishwasher knowing that Mum will move it to the upper part later. It's a small victory. But then the enormity of what happened to Hailey slams into him once more and he knows that doing his chores the wrong way won't make the slightest bit of difference.

Dad wanders into the kitchen. Looks vacantly around as though he hasn't seen the room before.

His parents are zombies.

Dad pops a slice of bread in the toaster and opens the fridge.

'Where's the butter?' He shuffles things around on each shelf.

'On the top shelf where it always is. I used it earlier,' Mum says.

'I can't—'

'For God's sake.' Mum nudges him aside. 'You men would lose your head if it wasn't... Odd.' She closes the fridge door. 'Someone has been in the house,' she says quietly.

'And stolen the butter?' Dad begins to laugh but then catches the concerned expression on her face.

'Seriously, you must have put it somewhere else.' He begins opening cupboards, the oven.

'But we always keep it—'

'Here it is!' Dad lifts it out of the microwave.

'But I didn't...' Mum looks lost.

'It's okay.' Dad rubs her arm. 'Stress makes us do weird things. No harm done.'

'Dad, can I have some cash for lunch please?'

Dad pats his pockets. Pulls out his wallet and opens it. It's empty. 'Sorry, Connor. I'm out.'

'I thought you went to the cashpoint yesterday?' Mum says.

'I didn't have time. I'll go today. I'm off now. Bye.'

'See you, Dad.' Connor bounds upstairs to fetch his rucksack.

His screen is still glowing from last night. His message to Hailey, of course, unread. He pops his heard around Kieron's door. He's still sleeping. Worry is an elastic band ball bouncing around Connor's stomach. Mum is right. Kieron isn't recovering from his bouts of jaundice and infections as quickly as he used to. He mouths a silent 'Laters.'

Mum is in the lounge. The curtains are closed and the light is on as though it's the middle of the night and not eight o'clock in the morning. Connor waits for the offer of a lift but it doesn't come. Instead, she stands in front of the window she can't see out of, laundry basket balanced on her hip, chewing her thumbnail.

Whatever.

Connor yanks open the front door. He's angry with her still. Probably always will be but...

He turns. 'You okay?' Is she too preoccupied to keep a proper eye on Kieron.

'There are twelve items of clothing and thirty-four pegs,' she says.

Connor waits for her to explain – it sounds like one of those ridiculous maths questions they got at primary school. If Harry had thirty-two biscuits and gave thirty to Hannah and two to Sarah, what does that leave Harry?

Hungry.

'Mum?'

'Have a good day.' She looks up and flashes a smile that is sadder than her saddest face.

If it wasn't for Kieron he wouldn't give her behaviour a second thought but he's tempted to ring Dad. What would he say? Mum's acting bonkers? He knows that from the butter in the microwave and yet he's still gone to work. He'll text Kieron throughout the day, make sure he's okay.

Reluctantly, Connor closes the front door behind him and fires off a message to Ryan and Tyler, arranging to meet them on the corner of Deene Street again at 8.30. He likes this time of morning. It's fresh. He winds his scarf around his neck, he doesn't mind the chill, it adds to the sensation of newness. Possibilities. The rising sun, the damp mist in the air strokes his skin. Reminds him that he is alive.

Suddenly guilty at the thought of his life stretched out in front of him, he checks his watch. It's not yet eight. He has time.

He veers a right, hurries before he changes his mind. Between the rooftops he can see the spike of the church tower, and then he's there. Slipping through the black wrought iron gates.

Connor picks his way down the winding path, careful where he treads, until he reaches the place that makes him feel lonely and sad and welcome and angry and… he supposes, comfortable. So many emotions too big for him to name.

'So…' Connor sits cross-legged in front of the headstone. He reaches out his finger and traces the butterflies that circle around her name. 'I've gone back to school. Shocking, I know.'

He pauses – a beat long enough for the answer that comes only in his mind.

'Yeah.' He shakes his head. 'It's as bad as I thought. Nobody is really talking to me except Ryan and Tyler.' Again he pauses. 'I know. I know. It's only a few more months but then what?' The silent voice reminds him of his hopes and dreams.

'Yeah, but…' His voice catches. 'If I go away to uni then you'll still be stuck here on your own and I'm sorry.' His throat is too small to release the rest of his apologies.

I'm sorry I'm alive.

I'm sorry you're not.

But he knows that he doesn't have to always speak out loud; on some level, she hears him anyway.

He presses his palm against the butterflies again, thinks of flying and freedom and he wonders what happens... after.

Is there a good place and a bad place? Where will he end up? Away from everyone he loves? What if Kieron ends up there soon? His brother is nothing but goodness just like...

He lowers his forehead onto the cold marble.

Sugar and spice and all things nice.

He wraps his arms around the headstone and wishes he were holding her. He can't bring comfort to her now. He couldn't then. He is...

Snakes and snails and puppy dog tails.

Connor stumbles to his feet. It's too much to bear.

He half runs towards the gates, past the car parking spaces that are all empty, save one, sole car.

It's white.

CHAPTER SEVENTEEN

Aidan

Melissa is on Aidan's mind as he drives towards his first appointment. Fergus too. The memories of the four of them were tightly woven together but now they're beginning to unravel. Shared holidays. Christmases. Birthdays. Barbecues on sunny summer days. Barbecues in pelting rain. The girls holding umbrellas over the grill as Aidan and Fergus turned charred sausages and pink-in-the-middle burgers.

He still hasn't managed to talk to Fergus despite his efforts to reach him. It shames him that he doesn't know where one of his closet friends is living, but does he really have the right to refer to Fergus as his best friend? To call him that? He has let him down. His loyalty is stretched. Thoughts of the future dull and jaded. For now, Lucy will take Melissa's side. Where does that leave him? Boys versus girls? He doesn't want to choose. He wants to head back home and kiss his wife goodbye. Hold her tightly. It isn't too late, they can still be a two.

He approaches the church where he uttered his wedding vows. The promises he made, and broke. The love he felt that day can be summoned in an instant along with the image of

Lucy with pink and purple confetti in her hair. Crystal tiara glinting in the sun.

Her smile.

Her hope.

Their dreams.

At their wedding reception, she had hitched up her dress, the train still trailing on the floor, and had strode confidently onto the stage. The band smiling knowingly at each other.

'Come here, husband,' she had beckoned.

'Oh no.' He had been smiling as he had shaken his head.

She'd put her hands on her hips. 'Is this our first married row?'

The guests began to chant his name, Aidan, Aidan, and he had joined Lucy, laughing as she handed him a microphone, knowing what was coming.

The room melted away as they sang a song – their song – 'Islands in the Stream'.

There's a lyric about tender love that now makes despair rise from his stomach. He is an island, lost, alone, lonely.

He never thought marriage would be so hard.

Out of the corner of his eye, he spots Connor speeding out of the graveyard. Is he just cutting through or had he lingered? Poured his heart out to the girl who couldn't offer him comfort. He should stop. Talk to his son. Tell him that he has felt everything that Connor feels but has he? Aidan is drifting apart from his family. It's stupid to risk them. Risk everything. He never should have started it but he's in too deep and he doesn't know how to clamber out unscathed.

I can promise you. Someone is going to get hurt.

Aidan turns up the radio to drown out the whispering threats in his mind.

The Sixties station is playing Elvis. He remembers the song although he can't instantly place the title, but he knows it's from that film – *The Trouble With Girls*.

He turns into Byron Street. Ryan and Tyler are messing around, kicking a can and shoving each other. Aidan wonders what they are laughing about. He clenches his jaw, it wouldn't be about him, would it? He thought he and Tyler had come to an understanding? Tyler slips off the kerb and Aidan has to swerve to avoid him. The boys laugh again and momentarily Aidan is angry the boys are so happy and carefree while Kieron is lying at home, isolated.

Tyler jumps back onto the pavement, but the boys carry on jostling each other, unaware of the dangers of doing so. Tyler hasn't notice it's Aidan driving, not like in the pub car park, where his eyes met Aidan's through his smeared windscreen.

Someone is going to get hurt.

He accelerates and again twists the volume dial, identifying the song now: 'Clean Up Your Own Backyard'.

Last night, he had arrived home and stripped off his clothes. Shoved them roughly into the washing machine. Watching them spin round and round before standing in the shower and scrubbing at his skin, but he had still felt dirty.

Still feels dirty.

He wants to clean up his own backyard but he doesn't know where to start.

Someone is going to get hurt.

CHAPTER EIGHTEEN

Connor

Connor stalks away from the graveyard, hands thrust into pockets.

'Wait!' a voice calls from behind him.

He spins around to face the woman who is jogging towards him, holding out his scarf.

'Thanks.' He takes it from her and winds it back around his neck. She looks vaguely familiar. He's probably seen her here. You get to know the regulars: the middle-aged lady in the straw hat, with the fat Jack Russell. The pensioner who, rain or shine, is always smart in a suit. The man only a few years older than Connor who wears an orange high-vis and carries a flask in one hand and a bunch of pink roses in the other.

'Cold this morning.' She yanks on her zip although it's already done up as far as it will go, the neck of her red jumper barely visible. 'I need a scarf like yours. Is it warm?'

'Yeah. Suppose.' Connor is uncomfortable with small talk. 'Anyway, gotta go.' He heads off but she falls into step beside him.

'I'll walk with you. I'm going to the cashpoint,' she says.

He tries to ignore her. He relishes these precious few moments when it's just him and his thoughts.

'I've seen you before? At the cemetery?' she asks.

He shrugs, hoping she'll go away.

She doesn't.

He makes a show out of pulling his ear buds from his pocket, lowering his head and engrossing himself in working the knots free that have formed in the cable, hoping she'll take the hint.

'You're tangling the wire even more. Want me to try?' She holds out her hand.

Connor hesitates. They're only cheap but he doesn't want to pass them over to a complete stranger.

'You into that grime or whatever the in thing is right now?' she asks.

'Nah.' He glances at his hands. She's right – he's been twisting the knots tighter. He hands them over. 'I like Oasis. The Arctic Monkeys.' Old-school vinyls that Fergus used to play whenever he was at Ryan's. He'd taught him a lot about music.

'Ooh, indie boy. I was a goth when I was young.'

'The Cure and all that Sisters of Mercy shit?'

'Nah, I was all The Smiths – depressed as fuck. I stomped around hating my mum for my crap body and my crap life and my crap everything. Until she wasn't there anymore and I couldn't blame her. That's who I was visiting today. In the cemetery.'

Connor doesn't answer. Partly because he is uncomfortable with a stranger divulging such personal information and partly because he is wondering how he'd feel if his mum wasn't around anymore. Knowing he'd miss her. Would she miss him if it were the other way around or was she so fixated on Kieron she'd be glad she had one less responsibility?

They turn onto Deene Street.

Connor raises a hand at Ryan and Tyler.

'These your mates?'

'Yeah. This is Ryan. Tyler.'

'The three wise monkeys, eh?'

'What?' Connor wasn't sure if she'd just insulted them.

'You know, hear no evil, speak no evil, see no evil. Between you, you've got it all covered.'

'Right,' Ryan monotones. 'And you are?'

'A friend of Connor's here.'

Connor kicks at the kerb, embarrassed. He's known her all of ten minutes and she's old.

'Here you go. All sorted.' She drops his ear buds back into his hand.

'Ta.' He stuffs them back into his pocket.

'You lot off to school?'

'Yeah.'

'Last year?'

'Of sixth form.' Connor pointedly checks his watch, hoping she'll take the hint. 'We've gotta—'

'And you still have to wear a uniform – unlucky!'

Ryan raises his eyebrows at Connor in a let's-get-out-of-here-way but she's still talking.

'I customized mine. Was really into sewing. I stitched those fabric badges you get with different band names on into the inside of my blazer, covered the lining. I was a rebel on the inside even if the teachers couldn't see it on the outside. I knew they were there. Don't suppose you boys sew. Learn loads of useless crap at school but not the basics.'

'Actually we do.' Connor begins to walk away but she falls

into step beside him and so he stands still again, not wanting to turn up at the gates with her in tow.

'Like what?' she asks.

'Mr Marshall – our head teacher – is ex-military and told us he had to learn to sew buttons on his uniform and stuff when he was stationed somewhere remote and one time he made us all learn. Told us real men were good with a needle and cotton.'

'Ah. So you could totally rock that uniform. Make those blazers your own!'

'Nah. Mr Marshall would have a fit,' Connor says. 'He's pretty strict. Look, we really have to—'

'One of those Ofsted league table obsessed ones, is he?'

'Yeah. He's always stressing about what people say about the school,' Ryan says. Behind him Tyler is jerking his head towards the direction of the school, mouthing, 'Let's go.' They try to sidle away but she jumps in with another question.

'I guess it's a reflection on him?'

'Suppose.' Connor knows what people are saying about the school since the trip. What they think of Mr Marshall's supervisory skills. 'He's not that bad,' Connor says, not sure where his sense of loyalty springs from. 'He just...' What. Have. You. Done. Boy? Eyes flashing hard and cruel. 'Cares.'

'You'd never get away with "the dog ate my homework" then?' She laughs.

'Has anybody got away with that, ever?' Connor asks rhetorically.

'I did! No really,' she carries on as Connor looks at her in surprise. Now this he does want to hear. 'I remember it so clearly. It was French and I hadn't bothered to do the essay I was supposed to, so I told my teacher – Mrs Mira – that the dog ate my homework. At home time she marched up to the gates to where my mum was waiting with our pet poodle. 'Is this the dog that ate an entire homework book?' she demanded.

'Busted!' Tyler says.

'You'd think, right? But no, Mum didn't break eye contact as she said, "Yes, Tootsie did and I must say the notepaper you send the kids home with isn't very good quality. It's clogged up her bowels something awful."'

The boys laughed. Their eagerness to ditch her momentarily forgotten.

'I can't imagine my mum lying for me, although she does for that waster she lives with,' Tyler says.

'At least he sticks around,' Ryan mutters.

'Your parents separated?' She puts a hand on Ryan's arm. He moves away from her, obviously uncomfortable, and doesn't answer but still she says, 'I'm sorry, that's rough. What about you, Connor? Are your parents together?'

Connor wants to tell her to stop being so nosy but he can't bring himself to be so rude when she's being so friendly. 'Yeah.'

'Are they happy?'

He shifts from foot to foot. He'd hardly tell a complete stranger if they weren't. 'We really gotta go.' He takes a step, hoping that this time she won't follow them. She doesn't.

'Of course. You don't want to get detention and be late home. Kieron will be waiting. Nice to meet you guys.' She flashes a bright smile as she walks away.

Connor is confused and unnerved as he watches her leave. Has he mentioned Kieron? He can't remember. He can't recall giving her his name either but then again, at the graveyard, his emotions were high, they always were. He could have told her. He sees her reach the corner. Instead of turning right towards the cashpoint she heads left, circling back the way they had come. Before she vanishes, she pulls something out of her pocket. A bunch of keys?

'Shit. I've forgotten to do that thing for Maths,' Ryan says. 'All this stuff with Mum and Dad has really…' He falters, he'd told Tyler the basics now but hadn't really said much else in front of him. 'Well, it's really fucking shit. Do you think I'll get an extension?'

'Nope. Marshall would love an excuse to kick any of us out.'

'I could get it done over lunch.'

'Nah.' Tyler shakes his head. 'I'm buying us all chips again.'

'Get you, money bags.'

'Yeah, king of the fucking world, that's me. Told you there's plenty more where it came from.'

'Where did it come from?'

'Couldn't possibly tell you. I'd have to kill you. I've done my maths, Ryan, I'll help you do yours now, it didn't take long.'

Ryan crouches and pulls out his book and pen. Tyler squats beside him, telling him what to write. Making sure he understands how to arrive at the answers. Tyler is often judged on his appearance, his behaviour, but he's the brainiest out of the three of them. He'll make a great teacher one day.

When Ryan's finished, he stuffs everything back in his rucksack.

As they turn to head towards the school, a white car crawls past the bottom of the street, slowing to watch them.

Connor doesn't feel the eyes in his back, as sharp as a knife. He doesn't hear the click of a camera.

He doesn't feel the hate.

CHAPTER NINETEEN

Lucy

The smoke alarm shrieks, a plume of black smoke escaping the toaster. My fingertips burn as I pull out the charred bread and drop it into the bin. It's hard to the keep the tidal wave of hopelessness at bay. Already this morning I've washed my hair with conditioner instead of shampoo and left the iron plugged in after I'd finished pressing Connor's school shirts. I'm heavy with the feeling I'm only seconds away from losing my mind. I throw open the back door to let in some fresh air, scanning the garden again, eyes landing on the empty washing line before I pull them away. It's a beautiful day, the sun bouncing off the windows of the shed. The memory of the footprints in the border punches at me. I shield my eyes, just for a second imagining someone peeping at me from behind the glass.

'Mum?' Kieron calls from the sofa.

'Coming,' I reply with a false note of brightness as I close the door and lock it.

'Did you burn my toast?' Kieron asks.

'Yes, sorry. I got distracted.' I pick up my mug and take a sip, my drink now lukewarm and unappealing.

'Dad says you're always distracted. Do you wish you were

at work, rather than stuck here with me?' His bottom lip trembles.

'I'm not stuck here. I want to be here. You're the most important thing—'

'And Connor?'

'Of course, Connor too.'

'He…' Kieron trails off. Hugs the duvet a little closer.

'He?' I gently prompt.

'It doesn't matter.'

'Kieron. If there's something I need to know?'

'He thinks you love me more than him.'

There's a choke in my throat as I ask, 'Did he tell you that?'

'I heard him telling Hailey once. She was saying how lucky Connor was having a mum when she didn't and they started talking about families. I didn't mean to listen. I know you love us both and I don't think Connor was upset because he had Hailey then but now he doesn't have her… Mum, he looks so sad all the time.'

I want to weep into my cold coffee. 'I love you both equally.' I've dreaded Connor feeling somehow less when Kieron often has to come first. I'm going to put it right. Everything. Starting with the bloody bread.

'Let's pop to the shops and get a loaf.'

'I'm too tired.' He snuggles further down onto the sofa and draws the blanket up to his chin.

'I don't want to leave you alone.'

'Mum. I'm not a baby. I'm thirteen. Just because I'm small for my age—'

'It isn't that.'

'Why can't I stay here then?' A lengthy sigh lets me know he thinks I'm being overprotective.

Am I?

I gather my courage, my keys and my purse.

'Don't answer the door or the phone. I'll be fifteen minutes.'

Nothing can go wrong in fifteen minutes, can it?

My edginess returns the minute I step outside of the front door. I go to a different supermarket to the Tesco my car was keyed in. Hurry into the safety of bright lights and garish Halloween pumpkins grinning their toothless grin at me, knowing that soon they'll be replaced by tubs of Quality Street. Their eyes seem to follow me as I stalk away from their orange faces but although I round the corner I still have the sense I'm being watched. I throw a glance over my shoulder and realize that I am being watched.

'Agnes?' I step towards her. She looks smaller. Frailer. A sheet of A4 paper clutched to her chest.

'Lucy, I…' She looks embarrassed. 'I've just picked up an application form.'

'You're applying for a job? Here?'

'I… I've been…' Her eyes dart left to right before settling on mine. 'Struck off.'

I don't know what to say. She's been a nurse for twenty-five years. Conscientious, she rarely took a day off until she fell pregnant in her forties after years of trying. Tragically, her little boy was stillborn and although she took months off work to grieve she was never the same again.

I envelop her in a hug, remembering with clarity those first seconds when you meet your baby who is fragile and precious and utterly dependent on you. The fierce desire to protect them. The ache in your chest as you realize, even then, that the world is sometimes too big. Too cruel for the innocent. The new and the helpless. How you wonder what they'll grow up to be. Who they'll grow up to be. And it happens in the beat of a heart, the blink of an eye. I think of my favourite mug, those tiny imprinted hands and feet. Sometimes when I see it I am back in that day, singing 'Hush little baby' while I counted tiny fingers and toes, eyes, ears, nose. I wonder whether Agnes has any visual reminder of her baby who will never grow and I wonder if it would bring her any comfort, even if she had.

'Sorry' is such a small word. Insignificant and often misused but it is all I have to offer as I step back and meet her red-rimmed eyes.

'I made a mistake, many mistakes actually, but the last mix-up with medication could have been fatal. I'm lucky nobody died. I... I just can't focus on anything. This...' She flaps her application form. 'Even this is too much. Too soon. But... we're so behind on the mortgage, the building society are threatening eviction.'

'Is there anything I can do?'

It seems so unfair that she's lost her job; I understand risks can't be taken when it comes to patients, but nurses are only human. Fallible. Although we'd hate to think it, when our health is in their hands, the health of our loved ones, sometimes doctors make mistakes too.

I should know.

I am one.

Was.

I was an orthopaedic surgeon until a few weeks ago. Not to save lives as such – that weight of responsibility is heavy to bear – but to salvage them. I was so grateful that Aidan's shattered pelvis had been pieced back together after his riding accident I decided to specialize in orthopaedics. I have rebuilt bodies. Rebuilt lives. Made the immobile, mobile. Granted people the greatest freedom of all, the freedom to walk again. It's not that I believe I'm a God, but we all do what we can, don't we?

Often it's the little things that make the biggest difference. Smiling at someone in the street. Casual conversation with a stranger in the check-out queue. Who knows what dark thoughts lurk inside someone's mind? What impact a friendly gesture can make. Kindness is contagious – be a carrier. But Agnes needs more than a smile, a kind word.

'I could lend you some money?' I offer. Although we've currently dropped to one wage our savings account is healthy, for now.

'Thanks. But I couldn't. I hear you've left the hospital?'

'Yes, I resigned to spend more time with Kieron.' It's half the truth. 'But… Agnes.'

'It's okay.' She touches my arm. 'I couldn't just take money without earning it, it wouldn't be right.' She gives a wry laugh. 'Not that anything feels right. How could… God… let a child die? How could medicine? Everything I trained for… I should have been able… I…' She dissolves into tears.

'I know.' I hug her again, ignoring the curious glance of a woman slowly pushing a trolley past us.

Agnes's eyes are full of anguish as they meet mine. 'If I could just save one more child, make it right, but now I've been struck off I can't even do that. I just…' She shakes her head. 'I'd better get home and fill this application in.'

'Wait. I can ask Aidan if he has any jobs at the practice? I know it's not exactly saving children but you could make a child very happy by saving their pet?'

She swipes at the tears on her cheeks with her sleeve. 'Would he have me… after?'

'I'm sure he will.' I'm confident he'll understand.

I punch her number into my phone and promise that I'll be in touch before I hurry away. I've been far longer than my promised fifteen minutes.

But what can go wrong in fifteen minutes?

When I get home, I know.

Everything.

CHAPTER TWENTY

Aidan

Aidan drums his fingers on the bar trying to make a decision. It isn't just because he's tired that he should avoid alcohol. He shouldn't be in a pub. He doesn't want to arrive home stinking of beer, with clouded judgement and loose lips. He has to remain clear-headed. He eyes up the bottles of Becks Blue in the fridge, the Heineken Zero, but nudged by the awkward conversation that awaits him, can't resist ordering a pint of the guest ale – Just the Job – as well as a glass of house white. He carries them over to the table and places them down, licks a splash of beer from the back of his hand.

He slides into the seat next to her and raises his glass before realizing there is nothing to celebrate, and lowers it again.

'So…' He's awkward. Unsure.

Melissa sips her drink, places it down on a crumpled Guinness mat, before immediately picking it up and taking a slug this time. 'You wanted to talk?' She meets Aidan's eyes. Hers are bloodshot, red-rimmed with sadness.

'Yeah…' He wipes his frothy moustache. The ale is going down too quickly. 'But how are you first?' Aidan should care. He *does* care, but what he really wants to discuss is Lucy. He hears Mel speaking but he isn't paying attention, his mind on his own marriage, his own family, not hers. He inhales deeply and breathes out his selfishness. Places his hand over hers and focuses on what she is saying.

'It's not looking like Fergus is going to come back. I've no idea where he's living. Ryan is… God knows. They don't talk a lot at that age, do they? He seems okay one minute but angry the next but then teenagers often are. Fergus has really distanced himself from everyone.' Aidan knows that. His messages to his friend have remained unopened. He squeezes her hand, encouraging her to go on. 'I don't know how Ryan will cope if his dad meets someone new, has kids.' She isn't crying, although she's close to tears. 'Not that I can see him with anyone else but… My mind is constantly full of what-ifs. I don't suppose he's been in touch with you?' Mel asks.

Aidan shakes his head. 'He hasn't, Sorry. Try not to worry. He'll be in touch when he's ready.'

'Do you really think so?'

'I do. Yes.' Aidan can't let on to Mel just how worried he is about his friend, she already looks like she has the weight of the world on her shoulders. 'Has he turned up for work, do you know?' he asks casually as though he hadn't rung the airline to try to find out.

'I'm pretty sure he has or they'd have rung the landline to find out where he was. It's not like he has an office I could ring and ask to speak to him or turn up at. Goodness knows where and when he's supposed to be flying.' She chews her nail. 'Everything is such a mess. Everything.' She pauses. 'Not just with Fergus either. I can't believe Mr Marshall went back this year, can you? He hasn't said anything to Ryan yet but he's worried. I'm worried.'

'Us too. Lucy persuaded Connor to finish his exams but if we'd known that Mr Marshall would still be the head we'd have let Connor transfer to another sixth form. It must be hard on the boys seeing him but also hard for him seeing them. Can you imagine the gossip he's subjected to amongst the staff? I wouldn't want to go into that environment every day.' He takes another sip of his drink. 'That's what I wanted to talk to you about today. Gossip.' He fiddles with a beer mat. 'Lucy.' However insistent his wife is that she's left her post solely because of Kieron, he doesn't believe her. 'I wish she hadn't been so hasty handing in her notice at the hospital after the school trip. Kieron is... well he's not great at the moment but Mr Peters says he'll pick up again. God knows how Lucy will occupy her time once he goes back to school. She's... well she's not behaving rationally. She's become so obsessive over Kieron and I know it's partly because of... well, you know. But also because she's let her career go.'

'I don't know what to say,' Mel says, her eyes pooled with sympathy. 'I'll give her a call later, see if I can get her to open up.'

'I'd appreciate that. She's so fixated on Kieron. She doesn't talk to me, not properly. I've no idea what she's thinking half the time. You know how she fell apart after...' He can't bring himself to say it but Mel is their oldest friend. She knows. She takes his hand. Gives it a reassuring squeeze.

'What happened then is not going to happen now. Don't take her not opening up to you personally. We all have our secrets, don't we?' Her eyes don't meet his. Instead, she drains her drink.

'Another?' she asks.

Aidan turns his phone over to check the time. He's had nine missed calls from Lucy.

There's a tightening in his stomach. Something must be wrong.

'I've got to go.' He hurriedly pecks Mel on the cheek and jogs out of the pub before she's even said goodbye, unlocking his mobile in his hand. His notifications shoved aside by a text.

Don't ignore me or you'll regret it.

Followed by another message, this time a photo.

The back of three boys.

Connor, Ryan and Tyler.

A message follows:

Remember this isn't the only interesting thing I have saved on my phone...

He waits for something else but it doesn't come. But the implications are clear.

Someone is going to get hurt.

He needs to make sure it isn't his son.

CHAPTER TWENTY-ONE

Lucy

Kieron is burning up. He's had infections before – many of them – but none hitting as hard and fast as this one. His chest lifts and drops with rapid breaths. His skin is clammy.

I call 999 before soothing him with soft words and impossible promises.

'You'll be okay.'

But will he?

My thoughts are dark and chaotic, a murder of crows fighting and scratching for dominance inside of my mind.

I'm so scared.

That's one thing Aidan can't always understand. No amount of medical training, experience can detach you from the primal emotional response a mother feels when her child is sick.

I ring Aidan again from the back of the ambulance. Still, he doesn't pick up.

The paramedics don't race towards Wheatfield General with flashing lights and a blaring siren but I urge them to drive faster, making sure they know I'm a doctor. In the young medic's eyes I see the why-are-you-freaking-out-then look. He wouldn't be quite so blasé if he were a parent. If this were his child.

Treatment starts almost as soon as Kieron is admitted. The staff here know him – know me. Paracetamol is given to lower his temperature – something other parents are always surprised about, expecting some newfangled drug with a complicated name they have never even heard of. Kieron doesn't flinch as he's hooked up to an IV to administer the antibiotics to fight his infection. Bloods are taken. He looks so small in the bed.

One of the nurses cracks a joke about not being able to keep Kieron away from the canteen's jam sponge and custard, but Kieron doesn't raise a smile. It's worrying how quiet he is. How resigned he looks to it all. This is the place Kieron is growing up, where innocence is lost. Where children are faced with their own mortality and parents confront their biggest nightmares.

Mr Peters arrives. 'Didn't think we'd see you back so soon.' He smiles at Kieron, a reassuring stretch of his mouth, flash of his teeth, but it does not calm this agitation that builds and builds until I fear I might explode with it all: the emotion, the fear, the sense of helplessness.

'Are you going to—'

'Let's give the antibiotics time to kick in.'

Waiting is a game parents of sick children know so well. I'm an expert player but I still feel there is more that can be done.

'I really—'

Mr Peters cuts me off again as though I am nothing. Nobody.

'Lucy.' He checks his watch as though he has somewhere

more pressing to be. 'I appreciate your medical training but orthopaedics—'

'But you know—'

'I'm sorry. I really have to get to a meeting. I wanted to pop in and see Kieron when I heard he'd been readmitted. I'll be back later, around six. Let's talk then.' He marches towards the doors without a backward glance and there's nothing else I can do but sit by Kieron's bed as he sleeps. The ward is busy but I feel so lonely. So utterly, hopelessly, irretrievably lonely.

It's a relief when Aidan calls me back.

'Kieron's in hospital. He's got another infection,' I blurt out as soon as we are connected.

'So soon? Has Mr Peters seen him?'

'Yes. I tried to talk to him again about Kieron's long-term prognosis but he...' My throat contracts. 'He didn't listen.'

'I'll be with you both as soon as I can. Do you need anything?'

'Can you pop into the school and let Connor know that Kieron's been readmitted? I don't want to tell him by text.'

'You want me to go to the school?' Aidan asks me to clarify. I know what he is really asking is does he have to face Mr Marshall. He doesn't want to. Neither of us do. And yet we send Connor to school every day. It isn't fair. A wave of guilt washes over me. I'm still feeling terrible from Kieron's revelation that Connor thinks I love his brother more than him. I teeter on a high wire between my two children. How do other parents make it seem so effortless?

Aidan strides through the door. I fling my arms around his neck, breathing in his comforting smell of hay and horses and something else...

'Have you been drinking?' I ask, hearing the note of irritation rising in my voice.

'Just a quick one.'

Aidan turns his attention to Kieron and they begin to chat. Shortly afterwards, the doors fly open again and Connor hurries towards us flanked by Tyler and Ryan. Five people around one bed will be frowned upon but Tyler and Ryan are fond of Kieron.

'Ten minutes,' I say sternly, but I'm pleased they are here. Kieron is too.

'Doesn't seem like five minutes since we visited you here last time, Kier,' says Ryan. 'You fancy one of the nurses or something?'

A flush spreads across Kieron's neck but he doesn't deny it.

'You do!' Connor perches on the side of the bed. 'You never said. Who?'

Kieron shakes his head. 'No one,' he mumbles.

'An older woman! Once you're home I'll come round and race you on a game of *Forza* on Xbox. Take your mind off her,' Tyler says.

'I don't have that one yet.' Kieron glances at Connor, knowing that if his brother has it, he will lend him it.

'I'll treat you to your own copy. I've come into a bit of cash.' Tyler taps his pockets.

'Yesss,' says Kieron. Tyler holds up his hand and Kieron high-fives it.

Kieron's excitement is heart-warming. I glance across at Aidan expecting him to be sharing my smile, but the muscle in the side of his cheek is twitching.

He's angry.

Tyler must feel eyes on him because he meets Aidan's glare and something passes between them, thick and private.

'Are you all right? Aidan?' I pull his attention away from Tyler.

He shrugs. Tries to smile but then a look of utter despair passes over his face.

'What's wrong?'

'I need to tell you something.' Before I can react, he is taking my hand, his palm is clammy. He leads me out into the corridor.

Whatever he has to say, he's nervous.

I'm nervous.

He is gripping my fingers too tightly, and when I wiggle mine to loosen his grip, he lets me go. I want to snatch his hand again because I am frightened – I don't know why – but he has moved away from me. He's leaning against the wall and I scan his face anxiously trying to decipher what's going on in his head but I can't read him.

I'm holding my breath as he begins to speak.

'Lucy…' Again the anguished expression. 'Please don't judge me for this…'

CHAPTER TWENTY-TWO

Aidan

'Please don't judge me for this...' Aidan stops speaking, his unfinished sentence hanging in the air.

'Judge you for what?' Lucy's voice is measured and calm, but she looks at him with wariness and confusion.

'I feel...' He begins but the words tie themselves in knots on his tongue.

'You seem...' Lucy nudges. 'In there, you seemed angry. You were glaring at poor Tyler.' She gazes at him questioningly.

'I'm just... Just...'

'Angry.' She says it simply.

'Yes.' There is so much fury coiled tightly inside of him. How can he explain to her that his lungs feel as though they're wrapped in barbed wire, which cuts deep and sharp and painful each time he takes a breath. 'Listening to Tyler laugh and joke, it's... it's... when I hear them in there like that, the three of them, okay not Connor so much but it...' He places his palm across his heart. 'I feel it here. This rage that builds and builds. The injustice. The senselessness. It seems so... unfair.'

'That they're healthy and living the life we want Kieron to. School. Friends.'

'God, it sounds so awful doesn't it, it's not like I wish anything would happen to Tyler or Ryan but…'

'It's okay to hate them a bit.'

Aidan looks at Lucy in surprise and she flashes him a quick smile. 'Sometimes I hate everyone a bit too. It's only natural. The why-me's. The why-us's. Illness is so random but sometimes it can feel so personal, like an attack.'

Aidan nods. He doesn't know why he is surprised she knows how he feels – she feels it too. All at once he wants to drop to his knees, wrap his arms around her legs and push his face into her hip. Let her stroke his hair, soothe him, like a mother would a child.

'I wish…' He swallows hard. 'I wish Kieron was hanging out with his mates right now and… and…' His eyes well. He closes them and presses his fingertips hard against his lids. This is not how a man should behave. This is not how a father should behave but nevertheless tears leak down his cheek.

'It's okay to cry.' Lucy's arms snake around his shaking shoulders. 'It's okay. Shhh.'

He allows her to hold him.

'It's okay. Shhh.'

Each syllable as soft as down.

He clings to her tightly, until his body has stopped shaking and then he releases his grip although he doesn't let her go.

She kisses his cheek, still wet with tears. 'Is there anything else you want to talk about?' she whispers.

He tries to say no but those two letters stick in his throat along with the lie and the shame and his guilt.

He gently pushes her away.

'Sorry. It just got a bit… much.' He says 'much' at the same time she says 'shit' and they both laugh. It's a release. He raises her palm to his mouth and presses his lips against it.

'Are you staying here tonight?' He already knows she will be. She always does when Kieron is admitted.

'Yes. How long are you hanging around for?'

'About another half an hour. I've still got two more appointments today. I'll drop Ryan and Tyler home on my way so you can have some quiet time with Connor and Kieron. I'll come back to say goodnight and pick Connor up when I'm done.' It's not the right time but still he asks, 'Is it odd, Lucy? Being in the hospital? Without working, I mean. Do you miss it?'

'No,' she tells him but her eyes say yes. 'A little. I have thought about coming back but...' She stares at the floor. 'I've so much on my mind I wouldn't be fully present if I was here and if I made a mistake...'

'It might be good to have something else to—'

'I saw Agnes earlier.'

For a moment Aidan is thrown and then he remembers – the nurse who lost a child. His stomach tightens with sadness.

'She's been struck off.'

'Why?'

'Because she wasn't fully present. And she made mistakes.'

They both fall silent. It is her who speaks first. 'Anyway, she'd be good at the practice. Answering the phone. It's not exactly life and death, is it? Not too much responsibility?'

Aidan is confused for a moment. 'My practice?'

'Yes. Donna doesn't come in every day now, does she?' Since Donna had become a grandmother she'd drastically reduced her hours and once her daughter returned to work following her maternity leave she'd offered to look after the baby full-time. 'You can't do everything alone, Aidan. Immunization reminders. Ordering stock. Invoicing. It's no wonder you're tired. You need somebody full-time again. Agnes can manage your diary and—'

'No,' he says bluntly. 'I mean. I'm not sure right now what we'll do to replace Donna and—'

'I know you're fond of her and she's been with you since the beginning but you will need someone.'

We all need someone.

'Let me have a think.' He pulls her to him and kisses the top of her head. A traitor's kiss. He knows he can't let Agnes near the practice. He can't let anybody into his life right now.

He can't risk anyone finding out the truth.

The less people close to him, keeping track, the better.

Somebody's going to get hurt.

CHAPTER TWENTY-THREE

Lucy

Ten days until Connor is taken

In the early hours, I watch Kieron sleep. It's impossible to stop my mind hopping from one black thought to another. The walls of the ward begin to close in on me. My breath coming in short, painful gasps. I stumble outside and sit on a hard wooden bench at the hospital entrance. The rising sun shimmers, painting the sky with streaks of salmon and orange. The world is so beautiful; I am floored by an overwhelming sadness. I so desperately want Kieron to be around to see it in ten years.

Twenty.

Thirty.

An ambulance speeds into a parking bay, blue lights flashing. The paramedics yank open the doors and lift out an unconscious man on a stretcher, before a woman weeping into a tissue steps out of the back of the van. I turn away from the rawness of her pain and scurry back inside.

Kieron is still dozing. Sandra, a nurse I know well, brings me a coffee, strong and black. The heat coming through the polystyrene cup burns my fingers. I blow away the curling steam before taking a sip, feeling the scald on my tongue.

'No point suggesting that you go home and rest, is there?' Sandra keeps her voice low.

'I'm okay. I slept.'

She raises her eyebrows; we both know I'd risen frequently to watch the nurses carrying out their observations. It wasn't that I didn't trust them but ultimately no one is as invested in Kieron's health and wellbeing as me. Not even the professionals.

By the time Aidan arrives, Kieron has woken, had a drink, pushed some Weetabix half-heartedly around a bowl and is dozing again.

'Morning.' He plants a kiss on the top of my head. He hands me one of those large supermarket bags for life. 'Emergency supplies,' he whispers. Peeking inside, I see bottles of water, Jaffa cakes, honey granola bars along with the paperback from my bedside table, Kieron's current read – a Goosebumps book along with his dog-eared copy of *The Hunger Games* – and some fresh clothes.

'Thanks.'

'How is he?' Aidan gently strokes Kieron's forehead.

'Don't wake him.'

'Rough night?'

'Yes.'

Aidan yawns. It doesn't look like he's slept much either. He has bags under his eyes, dozens of red blood vessels streaking the whites around his eyeballs.

'You look shattered.' I place my hand against his usually clean-shaven cheek, his stubble rough beneath my skin.

'I'm all right. Do you think you'll be home today?' he asks.

'I'm not sure. Did Connor get off to school okay?'

'Yes. Look, I've got to get going – can you tell Kieron I came when he wakes.'

I promise to do that and once he leaves I try to read my book – uplit it was marketed as – but it's horribly depressing. There's already been an attempted suicide and it made me cross. The thought of someone wanting to die while my boy is fighting to live.

Lonely, I rattle off a text to both Melissa and Fergus. Once they'd have visited with armfuls of unsuitable gifts – too-old-for-Kieron magazines, cans of fizzy drinks and sweets.

Neither reply.

It's late afternoon. I'm lying next to Kieron reading aloud. Katniss Everdeen is raising her bow. Kieron's pale lips mouth the words with me, his face is as white as the bed sheets.

My phone buzzes a text.

I read the message.

Oh God.

My vision narrows, the clatter of the ward swells around me before ebbing away.

Oh God, no.

I read it again. Those words, dripping with fear.

What can I do? I feel so helpless.

The desire to do something drives me to my feet. There's a rush of blood to my head as I stand and I wobble, my hip knocking Kieron's bedside cabinet, his jug of water crashing to the floor.

Someone calls my name but it sounds muffled, far away.

Oh, God.

I can't focus on anything but that text.

Despite the stifling temperature of the ward, I am suddenly icy, icy cold.

Connor.

CHAPTER TWENTY-FOUR

Connor

Something was wrong.

Connor and Ryan had waited at Deene Street for Tyler that morning, but he hadn't shown up. Unusually, he hadn't replied to their messages.

'Did he seem okay when you and Dad dropped him off last night?' Connor had asked Ryan. Tyler had seemed fine at the hospital.

'Yeah. Your dad took me home first but Tyler was... normal on the journey.'

Connor's thumbs flew over the keypad of his phone. 'I've told him we're heading in.'

They had raced up the steps, passing Amber on the way. She glowered at Connor and he lowered his head, felt the heat on his cheeks.

'Can't wait to be out of this dump.'

'You and me both.'

'Boys!' Mr Marshall's voice boomed down the corridor. 'You're late for class. Don't forget I'm watching you. Both of you.'

Connor had hurried towards his form room knowing that to be true. He felt Mr Marshall's angry eyes on him even when he wasn't at school. The way Mum felt she was always being watched by some random in a white car. Connor had thought she was batshit crazy but now he wondered whether it was true. Whether everyone is watching someone. Feeling shivers running down their spine. The hairs on the back of their neck standing on end.

Come to think of it, he'd been noticing a white car lately. Outside the graveyard. Crawling down the street as he walked with Ryan and Tyler. He tried to dismiss it. It's only because Mum kept going on that he's started to believe her. There are hundreds of white cars.

Thousands.

Nevertheless, he was on edge. Waiting for something to happen.

Something bad.

Where was Tyler?

The class had started by the time Connor took his seat. Dumped his pencil case on his desk. Into the wood was a fresh scratch, a deep groove. Words gouged out with a compass.

I KNOW.

It happened mid-afternoon, like something out of a film. Police marching into the classroom while the kids exchanged uneasy glances. A few years ago, uniformed officers would have been a source of excitement. Jokes. But there have been too many shootings at American schools. Too many terrorist attacks all over the world. His generation don't have the innocence of those before. They don't believe people are inherently good. They've grown up with Twitter, Facebook, YouTube, the worst of humanity streaked across their screens.

One of the policemen whispered to their teacher before addressing the class.

'We're going to be calling you in one by one to speak to you.' The officer caught Connor's eye. Connor's hand had crept over the '**I KNOW**' on his desk, his palm was hot as though the words burned into his skin, branding him.

When the police had left the room, Connor's eyes began to sting. He blinked furiously. He would not cry.

For a minute, he allowed himself to forget that Mum was no longer the person he trusted most in the world. To forget that the last time he had relied on her to make everything better it had all fallen apart. Connor sent her a text from underneath his desk.

Police here asking questions. Do you think it's about the residential?

He slips his phone back into his bag. He couldn't concentrate, wondering when he'd be called, expecting to be the first.

He is.

Connor has only ever been inside the head teacher's office when he's been in trouble. He thought he'd known fear before as he'd sat in the low chair opposite the big desk, Mr Marshall peering down at him over his glasses, Connor's palms damp as he waited for his punishment: detention; a letter home to his parents. But this… this is fear.

An officer sits behind Mr Marshall's desk. Mr Marshall stands by the window, the sunlight reflecting off the glass in the picture frames which hold the 'Ofsted Outstanding' certificates the school has been awarded with. Connor hears the thud-thud-thud of his own heart. Like the hem on his trousers, he's unravelling. The truth rising from his stomach through his throat, choking him. He coughs his confession back down and waits.

'Connor Walsh,' the officer says. 'I'm PC Johnston. You're close friends with Tyler Palin?'

'Umm.' He glances over to Mr Marshall. 'Yeah.'

'And when was the last time you saw Tyler?'

'Umm.' He can't seem to stop faltering as he speaks. 'Yesterday. He came to the hospital with me to visit my brother, along with Ryan… Ryan Horner. They left at about five.'

'Alone?'

'No. My dad dropped them off. Is Tyler in trouble?' Connor can't stop his knee from juddering as he speaks. He places his hand on his leg and pushes his foot down into the muddy brown carpet.

'Have you had any contact since? Phone? Text?'

'No. We messaged him this morning, me and Ryan, Tyler was late meeting us so we came in without him. What's happened?'

'Tyler didn't arrive home last night. His mum has reported him missing.'

The word hangs heavy in the air. 'Missing?' Connor repeats as though he doesn't know what it means. There has to be a mistake. His confused eyes flicker around the room as though they might find Tyler before they land back on the officer who is watching him intently. Connor tugs his collar away from his neck, suddenly hot. Heat sweeps over his cheeks as he struggles to make sense of the situation.

'You think something has happened to him?'

'Not necessarily.'

'But… you must. You're here and he's been missing less than twenty-four hours. You wouldn't be looking if—'

'You watch too much TV. There is no set time period before we investigate a report. Each missing person case is judged individually. Tyler is under eighteen and doesn't have a history for staying out at night and not turning up for school. We're just trying to establish the facts. Is there anywhere he might be? Any reason he might have run away?'

I know.

'No.'

'Nothing we should know about?'

I know.

Connor's eyes flicker to Mr Marshall. He is dragged back into a memory of the first evening of their residential trip.

'I'm knackered.' Ryan had speared a piece of sausage onto his fork. 'I thought it would be relaxing here, a holiday.'

It had been cold for Easter. When the letters had first circulated last year telling parents the school intended to run its first ever sixth-form trip, the expectation of the pupils had been lazing around in the sun, sneaking cans of dark fruits into the dorms. Ryan wasn't keen that his dad was coming along to supervise but it hadn't put Connor off at all. He couldn't wait to spend quality time with Hailey but his heart had sank when he scanned the jam-packed itinerary and realized they had activities scheduled every day.

'After dinner,' Mr Marshall had announced, 'Miss Webb thinks that as young adults you should be treated as such and be able to choose what you do in the evenings. Go out and have some fun.'

Excitement rustled through the dining hall.

'I, on the other hand.' He cast a slow glance around the room. 'Think that's a very bad idea. How you behave is a direct reflection on the school, which is?' He cupped his hand to his ear.

'A direct reflection on you, sir,' was begrudgingly muttered.

'Absolutely. But I'm not a complete killjoy. You can choose to go in the games room where you'll find a pool table, air hockey and ping-pong; upstairs there's a TV room; the room at the end of this corridor is a quiet space for those who want to read; or you can, of course, return to your dorms and get an early night because tomorrow we'll be up at 5.30 for the sunrise hike.'

Groans rippled around the room as kids stood up and began to disperse.

'One last thing!' Mr Marshall stared directly at Connor and Hailey, the only couple. 'No boys in the girls' rooms and vice versa.'

Connor nodded. Uncomfortable under his steely stare.

Fergus ambled over, hands in pockets, a smile on his face.

'Don't worry,' he said, 'I'm not going to ruin your street cred by hanging out with you.'

'Ryan doesn't have any street cred,' Tyler laughed.

'What are you going to do?' Fergus asked.

'Dunno. Probably the games room. Game of pool?' He looked at Connor.

'Then I shall go to the quiet room and have a game of scrabble with Miss Webb.'

'Scrabble?' Tyler raised his eyebrows. 'Is that what you call it now?'

Ryan elbowed him in the ribs.

'Ow. I was only kidding.'

As soon as Fergus left the room, Tyler appraised them all in turn. 'Let's make this trip interesting. Dares.'

'Dares? What are we, like twelve?' Connor shook his head and began to lead Hailey away.

'Come on, Connor. This is our last trip together. Soon we'll be out in the real world, university, jobs, we might not see much of each other. Let's have some fun while we can. Ryan?'

Ryan shrugged. 'Dunno. Risky when my dad is here supervising but... Yeah, I guess. If Connor's in?'

Connor's heart and head raged. He wanted to be alone with his girlfriend but he didn't want to let down his mates and Tyler was right, this might be the last time they were away together.

'What do you have in mind?'

'A surprise. Meet outside in an hour.'

'Outside. But we're supposed to remain on the premises.' Connor didn't want to get on the wrong side of Mr Marshall.

'They can't keep track of everybody with so many different places we can go. Besides, Marshall will never expect anyone to defy him. What do you say? I've got it all planned out. A dare a night.'

The trip was Monday to Friday. Four nights. Three friends. And Hailey. They wouldn't expect her to take part, and as Connor thought that, he realized that was what he felt: expectation. Don't let your mates down. Don't act scared. Weak. It was stupid, this need to impress Ryan and Tyler, and unnecessary. If he said no there'd be some gentle ribbing but they wouldn't really care.

He looked at Hailey, she shrugged. 'It's up to you.'

Did girls feel the same? Did they push each other to their limits? They'd probably think this was ridiculous. Immature. And it was all of those things, but something else too.

A rush.

They met an hour later.

'I've checked where everyone is. Marshall is standing to attention in the corner of the games room like the fun sponge he is,' Tyler informed them.

'He's not that bad,' said Hailey.

'And my dad?' Ryan asked.

'He's in the quiet room with Miss Webb.'

'Playing Scrabble?'

'No. They're… you know, chatting. Let's go.'

Tyler did the first dare; it was only fair. It was crazy hurtling down the zip wire without any safety equipment, in the dark, the lights from their phones casting the dimmest of glows but Tyler's euphoria was infectious. The buzz Connor got watching him must only have been a fraction of the hot adrenaline coursing through Tyler's veins. Even Hailey was on a high as they stumbled back to the centre, feet falling into potholes. They'd snuck back in through the fire exit Tyler had propped open afterwards and swaggered back to their dorms carrying their coats and a sense of achievement. They were brave. Defiant. Untouchable.

They were fucking, fucking stupid kids, but they didn't deserve what happened.

Nobody deserved that.

I know.

Now, PC Johnston clears his throat, causing Connor to free fall back into reality, grappling for the last question he was asked. 'Umm, no. There's nothing you should know about.' Connor shifts under the weight of Mr Marshall's stare on him. Waits for the blow of his words.

But they don't come.

PC Johnston leans back in his chair. 'That's all then, Connor.'

Connor stands, his knees weakening as the officer adds, 'For now.'

It's the change of lesson and the corridor is teeming with kids. Connor punches out another text to Mum: **Tyler is missing. I'm scared.**

And then he walks mindlessly towards his next class amongst the throng of pupils as though he is one of them.

As though he hasn't done anything wrong.

CHAPTER TWENTY-FIVE

Aidan

The radio announces the local news as Aidan is driving home.

Boy from Kings Park Secondary sixth form missing.

Several lines of inquiry are being followed.

As yet there are no leads.

Aidan swerves into a lay-by. He is shaking. He cracks open the window. Breathes in deeply.

His phone rings – an unknown number. He presses accept.

'Aidan Walsh? This is PC Johnston. We'd like to ask you a few questions.'

Aidan tastes the vomit in the back of his throat.

CHAPTER TWENTY-SIX

Lucy

When the boys were small they had a Stretch Armstrong action figure. They'd each tug on an arm, laughing as the limbs grew and grew, wondering if he would snap. I feel like that toy now. Wishing I could snake one arm out around Connor and keep the other one here around Kieron.

The despair in Connor's text is pressing down on me. I'm deliberating whether I should leave my youngest son alone while I go home and check on my eldest when my phone rings.

Aidan.

'Christ, Lucy, have you heard about Tyler?'

'Yes. Connor texted me. How—'

'The police have called me. God, when I heard a boy was missing from the sixth form on the radio I was worried it might be Connor. I have to go into the station.'

'The police station?' It sounds stupid as it comes out of my mouth, it would hardly be the fire station. 'But why?'

'I was the last person to see Tyler apparently, when I dropped him off.'

I let that thought settle before I ask, 'Did anything seem… off?'

'Nope. Nothing. I keep going back over it but he was fine.

We left you and Connor at the hospital and the boys seemed in good spirits. I dropped Ryan first and Tyler said he'd see him in the morning. We chatted about Kieron for the rest of the journey. Tyler thanked me for the lift as he climbed out the car. It was all… normal.'

'Did you notice anyone weird hanging around outside of his flats.'

'No. I didn't take much notice though.'

'Did you watch while he went inside?'

'No, but why would I? He's seventeen. Not seven. Look, I don't know how long I'll be at the station but I'll come to the ward afterwards.'

'Can you go home instead? Connor's understandably upset.'

'Okay. I'll come tomorrow afternoon after my rounds but ring if you need me before.'

The stretch in my shoulders gives a little. It's a solution, not ideal but at least I can stay here and know that Connor won't be alone.

Nine days until Connor is taken

The second I wake after an uncomfortable and unsettled night I call Connor. I don't know whether he's getting ready for school or angry with me. Hurt I didn't come home. My shoulders twinge, my arms aching for both of my boys. I had a choice and I chose to stay with Kieron. Not because he's my favourite but because I'd never forgive myself if I wasn't here and something happened. I must explain that to Connor again. I assumed he was old enough to understand but after Kieron telling me that Connor thinks I love his brother more than him I must make things clear. I don't want him to bury his resentment, let it fester until his relationship with me is poisoned. Toxic feelings will eventually seep out. Nothing stays hidden forever, does it?

There's a shift in my stomach. A discomfort born of the inevitability of the truth escaping.

What exactly did Connor tell the police yesterday?

Sandra is on shift again. She hands me a steaming coffee before taking Kieron's temperature. 'Much better! You might be able to go home later.'

'Hope so,' Kieron says.

We've only been away a few days but it seems longer. Usually, it's like a bubble in here. The outside world pales into insignificance, not quite real. The news about Tyler has popped that bubble. How distraught his mum must be, the thought of not knowing where your child is, is unimaginable. Oh God. I chew my fingers, the skin around my nails already broken. Where is Tyler? I'm so fond of him. How can he be here one second and gone the next? He's a hulking great teenager not a bloody rabbit in a hat. I wrench off a piece of skin with my teeth and my finger begins to bleed. I wipe it on my trousers. What if it were Connor? What would we do?

Missing.

A soft word with hard connotations.

At nine, I call Aidan and check Connor went to school and then call the school to make sure he is there. He is, but still it's impossible to relax.

What can have happened to Tyler? My knee jitters up and down.

Missing.

*

The day is endless. Minutes ticking past slowly and painfully. At 4 p.m., I phone Connor, he should be home from school but he doesn't reply. I text and ask him to ring me.

By teatime, Mr Peters still hasn't been on his rounds. Kieron is given a tray with a jacket potato heaped with grated cheese that hasn't properly melted, with slices of overripe tomatoes, soft and squidgy, and pale-green iceberg that's lost its crunch. He's still eating when Aidan arrives.

'Hey, buddy!' Aidan high-fives Kieron. 'You coming home today or what?'

'I don't know.' Kieron looks questioningly at me.

'I'm not sure.' Impatience creeps into my voice. 'Dr Peters hasn't been round yet so it will likely be the morning now. Have you seen Connor today?'

'Not since he left for school. He'll be at home now.'

I usher Aidan away from the bed, out of Kieron's ear-shot. I speak in a low voice. 'Connor hasn't answered my calls or replied to my texts.'

'That's not unusual,' Aidan says.

'I know but I can't stop thinking about Tyler.' Panic flutters in my throat. Where did he sleep last night? Where will he sleep tonight? 'People don't just... disappear?'

'He might have run away?' Aidan suggests. 'He doesn't get on with his mum's boyfriend, Liam.'

'No.' I don't believe that. 'He wouldn't miss school, he sees his exams as a way to escape. He's set on becoming a teacher. It doesn't make sense. It's so worrying. I'm going to call Connor again.'

He still doesn't reply. My chest is tight. 'We need to make sure he's okay. That he isn't... that he hasn't.' It's hard to breathe. Where is my son? Where is Tyler?

'Calm down, Lucy. I can guarantee you Connor is okay.'

'How?' There's a lack of concern in his tone that unnerves me. 'How can you guarantee me that. You don't know what's happened to Tyler.'

'I just know Connor, okay,' Aidan says. 'He'll be in his room. His phone out of battery or on silent.' His expression is unreadable. I have no idea whether he actually believes this or not, all I know is that I have a mother's instinct something is wrong.

Something has happened to Connor.

CHAPTER TWENTY-SEVEN

Connor

Connor sits on his gaming chair in his bedroom. He doesn't pick up his Xbox controller. He doesn't stream Spotify. He just... sits.

Time is irrelevant and he's not sure how much has passed before his door bursts open and his dad whizzes in.

'Connor! Your mother is worried sick about you. She's been trying to reach you!'

It passes through Connor's mind that if she were that worried she'd have come home to check on him, make sure he was safe. One of his best friends has disappeared off the face of the planet, for God's sake. At the very least she could have nipped home yesterday. Given him a hug, but no, she won't leave Kieron alone in hospital, not even for an hour. She probably wouldn't give a toss if Connor was the one who was ill. The one who was missing. Bitterness trickles down his throat as he swallows his anger down. He loves Kieron and understands she won't leave his side but he needs her too right now. Tyler has vanished into thin air.

It's scary.

'I'll give Mum a ring while I make some dinner and let

her know that you're safe, but can you get in touch with her too?' Aidan asks.

'Yeah, I'll text her but I'm not hungry.' Connor's stomach is so tightly clenched he can't face the thought of food.

Instead, he goes on to Facebook as soon as his dad leaves the room. Pinches the soft skin on the inside of his thighs hard as Hailey's profile picture loads slowly via their sluggish Wi-Fi. Her fringe, her green eyes, her bright smile. When Connor sees her, he is sad and happy at the same time. He reaches out a finger and traces her cheek.

Cold.

Hard.

She's gone. His bright and beautiful girlfriend is gone. He can't help torturing himself. Scrolling through her photo albums. There are photos of her and her dad at a zoo, standing in front of a cage, monkeys hanging from the bar behind them. Pictures of her and Connor smiling up at the camera, his arm stretched upwards as he takes a selfie. It brings him both comfort and anguish to see her but he can't stop himself. He wonders if Facebook removes profiles if they are inactive for a period of time. He's scared they might. He scrolls down the posts. The most recent one was made by Amber – a photo of the two girls with their arms looped around each other's neck, shrieking with laughter, unaware the photo was being taken.

I miss you babe!! X Amber had written. Further down there are a stream of similar posts. The 'OMGs' and the 'how tragics'. Most written by kids who hadn't ever talked to Hailey before. The same ones who make a show of ignoring Connor in class as though they care. The same ones who think it's funny to tape printouts of stills from the *I Know What You Did Last Summer* movie. Gouge words into the wood of his desk.

I know.

It isn't funny.

Tossers.

The last update Hailey posted was during the second day of the residential. She's bundled up in a yellow quilted jacket, her cheeks pink with cold, a harness around her waist and a safety helmet capping her head as she gives the thumbs-up in front of the steep hill they had just abseiled down. That was the day of Ryan's dare.

'No fucking way,' Ryan had said as Tyler pointed up at the disused railway bridge. 'I'm not abseiling down that!'

'You're mental,' Connor had said.

'Chill!' Tyler raised his hands. 'You don't have to but I've "borrowed" all the safety gear, the helmet, the harness. It will be exactly the same as what we did earlier.'

'Yeah, but without anyone having a clue about what they're doing.'

'I know!' Tyler said. 'You'll be safe. It'll be a buzz.'

'My dad will have a fit if he realizes we're missing and finds me doing… that.' Ryan said.

'Your dad didn't notice we'd snuck out last time, did he?' Tyler pointed out. 'He'll be hanging out with Miss Webb again. He won't even know we've gone.'

'What do you reckon, Connor?' Ryan asked.

Connor looked up at the arches and shrugged. 'I dunno. Shall we get up there and see how high it is.'

'Too bloody high,' said Ryan, but still they climbed onto

the bridge. The sky stretched out before them, a sheet of indigo, twinkling with stars. They weren't too far from their town but it was a different world. The air smelled fresher. The moon popped brighter.

'I'll do it!' Hailey's breath billowed from her mouth. 'I loved abseiling earlier.'

'No,' Connor said.

'Oh right, so basically I can risk my neck but not your girlfriend – cheers, mate!' Ryan said.

'And I can make up my own mind!' Hailey said indignantly.

'Yeah, but if you go abseiling who's gonna keep me warm?' Connor had wrapped his arms around her waist and pulled her close to him. 'Don't be so selfish!' He grinned as he rubbed the tip of his cold nose against hers.

She pressed her lips against his. 'You're forgiven.'

'Let's go back to the dorm,' Connor said. 'Ryan, you never took the piss when I wouldn't take part in the hot chilli challenge at Amber's Christmas party.'

'He was the only one who didn't take the piss,' Tyler said.

'Yeah.' It was only now Connor could laugh about it. 'You've nothing to prove.'

'No but...' Ryan huffed out air. 'Harness me up.'

When he completed the abseil Ryan was euphoric, they all were. Two dares. They really should have stopped there because it was Connor's turn next and that...

There's a tap on his door. Dad says, 'I've left you a bacon sandwich out here if you change your mind about eating.'

Connor replies with a gruff 'Cheers,' and wipes tears from his cheek. Boys shouldn't cry but he frequently does.

'You're forgiven,' she had said that night. Sometimes he

closes his eyes and tries to hear her voice, those words, but they evade him, lingering just out of his reach.

He doesn't go and get his food. Instead, he types another 'I'm sorry' message to Hailey that will again remain unread.

Unanswered.

CHAPTER TWENTY-EIGHT

Aidan

Aidan sits at the kitchen table, a mug of cold coffee in front of him forming a skin. He really should have cooked more of a substantial meal than bacon sandwiches but his forehead actually aches with worry. Connor, Kieron, Lucy. None of his family are doing well and he doesn't know how to make it right. He doesn't know how to not make it worse.

During his interview with the police, he had felt the guilt visibly oozing out of him; in the twitching of his fingers, in his eyes that couldn't quite look directly at the two faces sat impassively opposite him. What would happen to his family if he were sent to jail?

He deeply regrets everything.

All of it.

The screen of his phone lights, demanding attention. Her name illuminated and the sight of it tightens the knot of anxiety in his stomach.

At first he wanted to save her name under something else entirely but he had so many clients on his phone he knew that Lucy wouldn't be suspicious about another woman contacting him.

His wife trusts him.

She shouldn't.

Reluctantly he opens the message.

Shame about Tyler. How easily kids can disappear…

A tremble begins in his hands, before sweeping through his body, until every inch of him is shaking violently – his arms, his legs, his head.

His heart actually stops for a second when his phone starts to ring, jerking back into action again when he sees it's only Lucy.

He licks his lips. His throat is parched.

He answers the call.

At first, he can't hear anything but crying until she manages to splutter out, 'Aidan, it… it's Kieron. You have to come… Oh God, Aidan. Please come now.'

CHAPTER TWENTY-NINE

Connor

Five days until Connor is taken

Connor barely notices the coldness of the wall he sits on, the vibrations that run up his legs as his heels kick back against the brick. He can't shake the image of Kieron hooked up to machines and wires. When his brother had developed sepsis a few days ago, he'd heard the fear in his parents' voices, seen blind panic in their eyes. But his mum had noticed the signs quickly and her speedy reaction had meant that Kieron was okay. But still, the thought of him in ICU sends his stomach spinning.

He's okay.

Connor tilts his head back and stares up at the stars sprinkled over the deep navy sky, the moon a sliver between clouds. He wonders if Tyler is looking at the moon, thinking of home, of him and Ryan. It is comforting somehow to imagine that he is.

It's cold tonight. Connor pulls his hood over his head and crosses his arms over his chest.

Ryan is late.

Once Connor wouldn't have given this a second thought but since Tyler disappeared his heart beats faster, his eyes darting from left to right, searching for his friend, relieved when he sees Ryan jogging towards him.

'Sorry,' Ryan says. 'Had a nightmare getting away from Mum tonight. She was really upset. Crying and shit.'

'Because of your dad?'

'Yeah.' Ryan scuffs the toe of his trainer against the kerb. 'Sometimes she wants me to stay in with her and sometimes she wants to be alone.'

'Still no word from him?'

'No. I don't… I don't understand what I've done,' Ryan says softly, and then angrily, 'Fuck him. I don't need him.'

'You don't mean that.'

'I do.'

'No. You don't.' Connor jumps down from the wall and places his hand on his friend's shoulder. Ryan turns towards him. Despite the gloom, Connor can see the tears in his friend's eyes.

'No,' he says softly. 'I don't.'

When they were little and Ryan was upset, Connor always knew how to cheer him up: giving him one of his football stickers for his album; splitting a Snickers in half; letting him win on FIFA on the Xbox. How can he make up for a lost father? It's impossible.

'Anyways. How's your bro?' Ryan changes the subject.

'Much better. Hopefully coming home tomorrow.'

'Cool. Can't wait to see him.'

'He's been asking after you. And Tyler.'

'What did you tell him?'

'Nothing, Mum doesn't want him to know Tyler's missing but he's gonna find out.' It has been five days now.

'Not if we find him. Come on, let's get moving.'

They had both been getting up for school a couple of hours earlier than usual and checking under the railway bridge and the old shopping precinct where the homeless people sleep to see if Tyler was there.

He never was.

After school, when Connor wasn't at the hospital with Kieron, they visited the places they regularly hung out, along with the areas of town they didn't usually go to. Connor is beginning to lose hope.

He picks up his crowbar from the top of the wall. It's cold and heavy in his hands.

'We can break the boards off the old shopfronts tonight. Have a look inside.'

They fall into step, heading across town, speculating again about what might have happened to Tyler.

'You don't reckon it's because of what we did? You know. The residential?' Connor stares at the pavement, wishing he could drop his shame here along with the dog-ends and the empty crisp packets. Walk away from his guilt.

'Don't even.' Ryan's voice is sharp.

'You haven't noticed anyone following you? Watching you?' Connor clamps the crowbar tighter in his hand.

'What? No. Don't be soft. No one has taken Tyler. No one else has gone missing.'

Yet.

'But why hasn't he been in touch?' Again, Connor asks the impossible question. 'He wouldn't... he'd get in touch with us if he could.'

If.

Connor clenches the bar in his fingers harder until his wrists ache and his rising tears disappear.

'I still think that tosser Liam has done something to him,' Ryan says angrily. 'Fuck knows what Tyler's mum sees in him. He's a bully.'

The boys had been to Tyler's flat a couple of times to see if his mum had heard from him and on their last visit Liam had told them to piss off and chased them down the stairs. Connor had arrived home shaking with both anger and fear.

'Liam might have hurt Tyler,' he blurted out to his dad. Rather than dismissing him, Aidan rang the police and reported Connor's suspicions. 'We've already ruled him out of our inquiries,' he was told but Aidan believed Connor. 'It makes sense. Liam's a nasty piece of work who wanted Tyler out of the way. He had the motive and the opportunity.'

The precinct is derelict. The council have turned most of the streetlights off and even the gangs of kids that hang out here in the daylight don't come back at night. Just a few years ago this had been the centre of a thriving community. Mums would gather in the coffee shop, rocking prams back and forth with one hand, cappuccino in the other. There had been a selection of shops: a bookshop; a butcher's; a fancy dress shop; one that sold crystals and homeopathic remedies. Connor always liked it when they walked past that one, the smell of incense drifting out, comforting. They never went inside though. Mum didn't believe in alternative healthcare.

'This board is loose.' Ryan tugs at it with his fingers.

Connor slides the crowbar underneath the wood and lifts. He meets resistance and he pushes harder. It takes a few minutes before the board springs away from the empty windowpane. The next board is easier and soon there's a big enough gap for Connor and Ryan to squeeze through, their feet crunching on broken glass as they step into the old fancy dress shop.

It's the smell that hits them first.

'Hang on.' Ryan activates the torch on his mobile but his hand is shaking so much the light judders as he sweeps his phone around the room. From the walls, Pennywise the clown from *IT* glares down at them from a torn poster, while on another, it's the Joker from *Batman*.

'Remember that Halloween when we came here and rented out costumes for the primary school party?' Ryan whispers.

'Yeah. I was Woody and you were Buzz Lightyear.'

'This place is trashed.' The counter in the corner was black and charred. The stench of urine clogged Connor's throat.

They stick close together, edging their way around the room.

A noise. From beyond the door to the stockroom.

Ryan lowers his torch. Connor picks up on the tension radiating from him.

The fear.

He feels it too.

'Should we call the police?' Ryan whispers.

'No.' Connor is dizzy. Afraid. But also impatient, he doesn't want to wait for the police. He wants to… know. He wants to stop wondering all the time where his friend is, whether he is scared. Alone. Hurt…

Alive.

In sync, they shuffle forwards, careful not too tread to heavily on the glass that litters the floor.

Shh.

Again, the sound of something moving.

They hesitate.

Connor's heart hammering against his ribcage.

He's torn between fight or flight. Desperate to run away but what if it's Tyler back there? Hurt?

He moves slowly towards the door.

Reaches for the handle.

Raises his crowbar in his other hand.

Beside him, he can hear Ryan's short, shallow breaths.

Connor begins to count, softly.

One.

Two.

Three.

Simultaneously, he throws open the door as Ryan raises his torch.

'Fuck!' Ryan jumps as two rats scurry past them. 'Shit, man. I thought…' He sweeps the light around the room. 'Urghh, rats. Let's get out of here.'

'No wait.' Connor strides over to a small skip against the wall. 'Shine your torch over here.'

The light glints off the metal clothes rails on the top of the skip. Connor pulls them out. Underneath are some torn costumes. He can't reach any deeper.

'I'm getting in.'

Inside the skip, anxiety causes a heat that's insufferable. The air suddenly thin. He feels…

Trapped.

Is this the way Hailey…

He shakes away the thought before it can properly form

and crouches down. Rummages around the rubbish. The stench causing his stomach to roil. Something slimy, a rotting banana skin. Something hard, a row of coat hooks. And then…

Fingers.

A hand.

Connor whimpers but then he realizes the hand is hard. Plastic. One of the shop mannequins.

'Christ.' He begins to smile. 'If Tyler could see us now.' They both laugh before remembering he is the reason they are doing this.

Later, the boys have said goodbye and Connor is almost home.

An owl hoots.

A dog barks.

His road is quiet.

There's an occasional chink of light pressing through a gap in the curtains but most of the houses are in darkness.

It's late but his father's truck is missing from the driveway. Connor hurries towards his house, wanting to slip the crowbar back in the shed before Dad gets home.

He's a few feet away from his house when he notices them. The figure standing under the orangey glow of the streetlight. Connor hesitates. It's impossible to tell where the person is looking but Connor knows.

They are looking at him.

He is convinced of this from the scratch of fear at the back of his neck, the coldness in his stomach.

No one else has gone missing.

Yet.

Connor tries to tell himself he is paranoid. Edgy from Tyler's disappearance and Kieron's health scare, but he carries a constant sense that something terrible is going to happen. His mum had thought someone was watching the house but what if they weren't watching the house, but him?

He raises the crowbar and smacks it against his palm. It's reassuringly solid but Connor knows that his bravado is nothing but an empty threat. Somebody had been hurt before because of him and he couldn't bear for it to happen again.

He hurries forward. Sensing eyes burning into his back.

The keys slip through his fingers. His heart racing as he bends to retrieve them. As his fingers fumble to jab the key into the lock, he throws a glance over his shoulder.

The figure is still there.

Waiting.

For what?

For who?

Shivers snake down Connor's spine as he pushes into his hallway then locks the door behind him.

Home.

But even here he doesn't feel safe.

Since Tyler vanished nowhere feels safe.

CHAPTER THIRTY

Lucy

Four days until Connor is taken

The ward is too loud: the chatter of visitors; the clatter of trolleys. Too hot.

I hear him before I see him, polished shoes squeaking across the lino. I raise my eyes to his troubled face. See his uncertainty, his worry.

'Fergus?' I'm surprised he's here. He hasn't replied to any of my texts since he left Melissa and I can't unpick whether I'm angry he has stayed away for so long or pleased to see a friendly face. Mel's popped in when she can but her visits have been fleeting, short.

He can't quite look at me, instead turning his attention to Kieron. 'How are you, mate?' he asks.

'Bored.'

'Funny you should say that.' Fergus hands Kieron a bag of Skittles, a bottle of Tango and a book with a cover that frankly looks like erotica – a woman with sharp fangs protruding from red glossy lips, wearing a low-cut dress, draped over a smouldering man in a cape.

'Cool!' Kieron snatches up the book and immediately begins to read.

'Lucy, can we talk?' Fergus asks tentatively. Shifting his gaze from Kieron to me. Something unreadable in his expression.

'Hang on a sec.' I nip down the ward to find Sandra.

'I want to grab some food with my friend, I haven't seen him for ages,' I tell her. 'But last time I went to the canteen and left Kieron—' It's all too fresh in my mind.

'I'll stay with him,' she assures me.

'That's settled.' I rejoin Fergus. 'We can go and get some lunch. Kieron, is that okay? We won't be long?'

He nods, engrossed in his story. It's still a wrench to leave him.

The canteen is quiet except for the gurgle and hiss of the coffee machine. There's a heavy tang of oil in the air, a trough brimming with golden chips basking under a heat lamp. We both opt for a mozzarella and pesto panini – it only takes a minute to toast them.

'So…' I wait while Fergus takes a bite, pinching the melted cheese string that stretches between the bread and his mouth, licking his fingers.

He swallows. 'I came to say goodbye, really. I'm moving away.'

I don't know what to say. Thirty years of shared memories tumble together before breaking apart. 'But… Fergus… but you can't.' I'd been clinging on to the hope that he and Mel would sort things out. 'Does Mel know? Ryan? Aidan?'

'Mel knows. I'm still thinking about the best way to handle things with Ryan and no, I haven't spoken to Aidan.'

'But you're going to tell him?'

A film of tears glazes his grey eyes. 'A clean break is…

it's easier. Aidan will try to talk me out of it but my mind is made up. I thought you could tell him? I'm moving back to Scotland.'

'Back to…?' I am incredulous. 'But you haven't lived there since you were a child. What about your family?'

'It is for my family. Mum isn't well and with Dad passing last year, she needs me.'

'But you can't just… leave. Melissa needs you. Ryan needs you.'

For a second Fergus crumples into himself before he straightens his spine.

'My mum needs me more.'

'I know there's been some sort of falling out between you and Mel but surely it's nothing you can't work through? You can't just give up on twenty years of marriage.'

'I'm not just anything.'

'Sorry.' I'm saying all the wrong things. Hundreds of words swim around my mind and I sift through them trying to fish out the ones that won't make me sound critical or accusing. 'I know this won't have been a decision you've made lightly, Fergus, but… we care. Me and Aidan.' I rub his arm. 'We're here for you.'

'I'll miss you, Lucy. If you can keep an eye on Ryan for me.'

'Can't you stay? Until he's finished his exams at least? I'm not saying you shouldn't be there for your mum, of course you should help but… Fergus, you could ask Melissa and Ryan to go with you after he's finished sixth form or move your mum down here. You don't have to end your marriage.'

Fergus runs his thumbnail along the edge of the table.

'Except it's not the real reason you're leaving, is it?' I study him. 'Tell me why, Fergus. Please.'

I'm wondering if it's to do with the residential. 'I'm so ashamed,' he had whispered afterwards and I'd thought he'd meant ashamed of himself but what if it was Ryan he was ashamed of instead? Ryan he blames?

He doesn't look at me, instead poking his finger into the mound of salt and spreading it around the table like a child. Part of me wants to place my hand on top of his and tell him to stop. Talk. But I know you can't always force people to tell the truth. I think of Connor with his secrets. Aidan's furtive behaviour.

The things I try to keep hidden.

Fergus continues staring at the Formica, peeling a strip away from the edge of the table, before he lets it fall to the floor, as though he is peeling away the layers of our friendship, tossing away years of shared memories.

It hurts.

'You know,' I try a different tactic, 'Tyler is missing. Connor is so upset. Ryan must be too. We all are.'

Fergus's face closes down. If he's shocked or concerned he doesn't show it.

'Where do you think Tyler is?'

He shrugs, detached; probably consciously he's already made the break from us all but still... a boy is missing.

'The police talked to Aidan.'

This time there's a flicker of something in his eyes but he quickly lowers them, making a show of checking his watch, not a discreet glance, but raising his wrist. This is so out of character. The Fergus I know cares about everyone. He cares deeply. I try to nudge him into a memory.

'Do you remember when Connor, Aidan and Tyler—'

'Lucy, I've got to go. Take care.' In an instant, he's on his feet, stalking away without a backward glance.

It feels so final.

Kieron is napping. I have a book balanced on my lap but my tears are blurring the page, my head full of Fergus. Melissa. Aidan. Me.

Fergus and Melissa will never reconcile and it isn't just their loss, it is ours. I glance at Kieron, he's unaware that the fabric of his world has changed and his world is small, Melissa, Fergus and Ryan making up a huge part of it.

Next to me, the mother begins to sing to her little girl, 'Hush little baby', a lullaby. A promise. And the sound of it triggers a memory. Once I had sung that song myself.

I begin to cry properly, not sure who I am crying for: Mel and Fergus, me and Aidan, Connor, Kieron, Ryan. I cry for us all. I can't wind the clock back, make everything the same as it was, but oh, how I long to.

'Don't say a word,' she is crooning next to me.

The tissue pulls at my skin as I drag it across my cheeks, trying to force myself to breathe slowly, pull myself together.

It will be okay. It will be okay.

But the soft voice in my head is drowned out by a harsher one.

Are you sure?

Carefully, I take Kieron's hand. We are a four. A family of four and our unit is the most important thing, but I picture the despair on Fergus's face, his sense of loss that reached out and brushed me with its fingertips and I am haunted by all of the things that are out of my control.

Get better, my darling, please.

I clasp Kieron's hand between mine. He stirs. I'm holding him too tightly.

But I can't let go.

I won't.

The first sign I have that something is wrong is when Mr Peters wants to speak to me and Aidan away from Kieron's bed.

'I'm so sorry,' he begins. 'The results of Kieron's latest liver function test since his sepsis aren't… aren't what we'd want. I was hoping not to have to say this for a good few years but he was lucky to pull through sepsis. Patients with such compromised immune systems often don't, but there has been some damage.'

Fear crawls up my throat along with the questions I'm terrified of knowing the answer too.

'You. You believe…' I swallow hard. 'It's time to put Kieron on the transplant list.'

'I do. Yes.'

Aidan gasps. Mr Peters shifts his gaze over to him, he doesn't look at me as he continues to speak.

'I understand this is a shock.'

And it is. Although I've been expecting it, the bottom drops out of my heart. My world. I can feel the tremble of Aidan's hand in mine and I can't tell which of us is shaking, probably both of us.

'How long is the waiting list?' It is Aidan who finds his words first. Whirling around my mind are things that can go wrong while we wait.

'I can't give you a timescale, sorry.'

Hot tears are forming behind my eyes, spilling down my cheeks.

'But…' I clear my throat, but my voice is still quiet. 'You could move him up the list?'

'Lucy, no! That would be unethical. Immoral. I could lose my job.'

'I could lose my son.' This time I can't hold back my choking sobs as I cling to Aidan, he's my driftwood in a storm. He holds me tight and although I try to compose myself as quickly as I can, it takes a few moments until I can speak.

'Rob.' My tone is pleading as I begin to address the doctor, but I can't find anything else to say.

'We do everything we can for kids. We go all out. You know it's rare that a child doesn't make it. Very rare.'

'Promise me he'll be okay,' I ask unfairly.

'Lucy, you're a doctor. You know we can't promise.'

I break down again. Break apart. I can't hold myself together.

'Let's go home.' Aidan takes my arm. 'We're still okay to take Kieron home?' he asks Mr Peters.

'Of course. We'll be monitoring him closely. I've drawn you up a new prescription, you can collect this from the pharmacy on your way out.'

Aidan grips the steering wheel so tightly I can see the white bone of his knuckles protruding underneath his stretched skin.

He's terrified.

I'm terrified.

My shuddering breath won't go back to normal. I want to

curl myself into a ball, hug my knees to my chest and close my eyes tightly.

Block everything out.

The car speeds. I stare mindlessly out of the window.

Grey sky.

Grey buildings.

Grey road.

I name things the things I can see to distract myself from my tumultuous thoughts but it doesn't work. Instead, I bite my lip so hard that it hurts, crushing the soft skin between my teeth until I taste the blood on my tongue.

'We're home!' Kieron says excitedly as we turn onto our street.

And it's there.

Again.

Underneath the beech tree, the white car.

I glare at it.

Instead of my usual fear, a growing indignation pulls back my shoulders, straightens my spine.

How dare they?

How dare whoever it is that's following me, trying to scare me, be here today of all days.

Haven't I been through enough?

I glance at my family. Haven't we been through enough?

My upset morphs into anger. Rage bubbling beneath my skin.

The second Aidan stops on our driveway, I throw open my door and run back towards the road.

'Lucy! No!' I hear him call behind me, but my arms are pumping by my sides, my blood pumping in my veins.

I should be scared as I approach the car but Kieron's decline has taken all of my fear.

I'm almost at the car. Ready to confront the person who has been watching me.

Today.

Now.

CHAPTER THIRTY-ONE

Connor

The shouting rises above the sound of his Xbox game. Connor crosses to his window. Mum is running down the street, yelling, 'Get out and face me, you coward,' literally shaking her fist at the white car speeding away. Dad calling her name. Kieron sitting stiffly in the back of the car.

He pounds down the stairs.

'Come on, Kieron.' Connor grabs his brother's bag. 'Let's get you inside.'

'I don't understand what's happening?' Kieron is pale. Scared.

'Mum's just…' Connor shrugs. 'I dunno. She's okay now. She's coming back, look.'

Dad's guiding Mum back to the house, his arm around her shoulders.

'Who was she shouting at in that car?' Kieron asks.

'Probably the person who parked across our drive the other day and blocked her in,' Connor lies.

'But—'

'What's the goss from the hospital then?'

'Fergus came to visit.'

'Really?' Connor's hurt that Fergus hasn't been in contact

with him but then he reminds himself that he hasn't been in touch with Ryan either and he feels bereft on behalf of his friend along with a desire to protect him.

'Let's not tell Ryan.'

'Why?'

'Because… Just because.' He leaves it at that. 'Ryan said he might pop over later.' Unless Mel wants him to stay with her. She's not coping well.

'And Tyler?'

'Nah. He's… he's got a job now.'

'Wondered where he was getting his money from. He's going to buy me *Forza* for my Xbox.'

'I know. You're lucky.'

'And Fergus bought me a book.' As soon as they are in Kieron's bedroom he pulls it from his bag and hands it to Connor. 'Look, she's a vampire and her boobs are massive.'

They sprawl on the bed and Connor begins to read aloud to his brother.

His parents trudge slowly up the stairs, Mum rambling about the washing and there being too many pegs on the line. Dad trying to reassure her. Mum keeps mentioning the car. Connor wonders whether to tell her that since Tyler had disappeared he has seen it too and is scared the driver is after him.

'You haven't slept properly in days,' Dad says. 'And Mr Peters… You've had a huge shock. Let's get you back in your own bed, you can get some proper rest.' It's as though she suddenly is the child and this is worrying.

'I don't understand what's happening,' she keeps saying over and over, almost in tears.

Connor doesn't understand either but he reads another

chapter of the book, louder this time, but not loud enough to mask his parents.

'Are you sure Mum's okay?' Kieron whispers. He's afraid. Hell, Connor is afraid.

'She's exhausted, stressed.' He says this solely to reassure Kieron but then there's a pang of guilt in his chest as he realizes it's true. Him and Kieron aren't the only ones going through something. 'Back in a sec.' He tentatively walks into his parents' bedroom.

'Mum? Can I make you a cup of tea or something?' he offers.

'No thanks, Connor.' She doesn't even give him her Mr Potato Head smile.

'Let Mum rest, I'll go to the chippy,' Dad says.

Connor waits for mum to say all the grease is bad for them but instead she says, 'None for me,' as she slips off her shoes and lays down. Dad pulls the covers over her and Connor is wrapped in the warmth of the memory of Dad sitting on the edge of his bed, reading him *Paddington* until he fell asleep. He wonders if mum feels the same sense of safety that he used to. The overwhelming security of being loved. He wishes he could recapture those feelings, stretches for them sometimes, but they are out of his reach. He wants to tell Mum that he loves her but he can't say the words, instead he tells her goodnight. Even though it's only 4.30 he doesn't think he'll see her again today, she's already half asleep.

By eight o'clock, him, Dad and Kieron have eaten fish, chips and mushy peas and yawned through a couple of episodes of *The Simpsons*. The past few days has caught up with them all.

'I've got to go and check on a horse,' Dad says. 'Don't

disturb your mum. She needs to catch up on her rest after days of kipping on a camp bed. You two look shattered as well. Early night?'

It is stupidly early but if Connor goes to bed Kieron will too, besides he's barely slept since Tyler vanished. It's embarrassing going to bed this early but by 8.15 he is tucked up, surrendering to sleep.

Connor jolts upright from another nightmare, heart hammering, sheets drenched with sweat. He's clawing at his chest, remembering the cold, putrid water filling his lungs before his hands had grappled for Hailey.

He covers his face, not wanting to remember his dare again, but he can't help it. Tyler going missing has brought everything he was trying to forget back, with frightening clarity.

'No way.' Connor had stared at the lake. The moon reflecting a lonely circle on the far side of the black water. Something to aim for, if he was going to swim across, which he absolutely wasn't.

'Chicken.' Tyler had tucked his elbows into his waist and flapped his arm like a bird.

'I'm not scared.' But he was. Connor was a strong swimmer but the thought of taking his clothes off in front of the others, his pale flesh covered in goose bumps, the shrinkage the cold water would cause, made him shiver. It wasn't something he'd want Hailey to witness. 'I don't have a towel.'

'I do.' Tyler patted his rucksack.

Hailey slipped her hand into his. The reassuring squeeze of her fingers told him that she wouldn't judge him if he didn't do it. In return he tightened his fingers around hers thanking her for not trying to talk him out of it in front of the others.

'Fuck's sake.' Connor was angry with Tyler, angry with himself. They were seventeen. Too old for this shit really. 'I can't even see the other side.'

'We kayaked across it earlier – you know it's not as far as it looks,' Tyler said.

In a boat. With a paddle. It was stupid. Every summer his mum drummed into him never to swim unsupervised in a lake. He should walk away.

'Seriously, Con.' The whites of Ryan's eyes glowed bright. 'It's okay. Remember Pleasureland?'

A shared memory passed between them. They must have been about ten. A day trip to the seaside with their parents. Mum and Melissa sprawled on the sand, faces upturned to the sun. Fergus fetching pints of beer in plastic glasses from the beach bar. Dad pushing coins into his hand telling them to go to the fair on the pier, and have a good time. The euphoria they had felt as they scrambled up the steps to the giant inflatable slide, the sensation of climbing into the sky. His stomach plummeting as he realized how high they were. The tears that gathered as he tried to force himself down the slide but his body had been frozen in fear.

'It's okay. Whatever,' Ryan had said then, heading back down the steps the way that they had come. Ignoring the smirks of the other kids as they took in Connor's tear-stained face. At the bottom, Ryan had bought candyfloss with the rest of the money and they'd headed back to their parents, Ryan never once laughing at him.

Connor knew he wouldn't now either.

Hailey shuffled closer to him, their thighs pressing together. It was cold. It wasn't fair to keep her hanging around outside. He needed to make a decision. Briefly he thought about ushering her back to the dorm. What's the worst that could happen? Hurt pride and a bit of light piss-taking. Or should he get it over with and hold on to his dignity?

'Let's get this done,' he had said.

'We'll run around to the other side, to the wooden walkway bit where they tether the kayaks. Hailey can bring your clothes round. Meet you there soon.' Tyler said.

'Connor…' Ryan clapped him on the back. 'You'll be fine.'

Hailey stood on tiptoes and pressed her lips hard against his and then her mouth against his ear.

'This is dangerous. You should just say no.'

'I'll be okay.' He flexed his biceps and she laughed but he wasn't feeling like a man at all as he picked his way down to the shore, more like a scared boy. A stupid boy. He unlaced his boots and pulled them off, followed by his socks. The ground was damp. Freezing under his feet. Quickly he undid his belt, unzipped his jeans and tugged them down.

The pebbles were sharp as he picked his way across them. Something ripped his skin. It stung. Great, now he was probably bleeding. He glanced around for the others, but they'd been swallowed by the night. He couldn't hear their footsteps, but in the distance, Tyler's voice. If he started now they'd be there when he climbed out, Hailey holding the towel wide and open. Enveloping him in its warmth.

He dipped a toe into the water. It was freezing. He hesitated. But then he remembered all the times his mum had ripped a plaster off a scraped knee or elbow.

'Best to get it over with,' she'd say before kissing the wound better.

Connor hobbled over the uneven ground. The slime in the water covered his feet, his knees, his hips. He took a moment. His breath catching in his chest. His limbs already turning numb.

This was stupid.

He plunged forward, face wet. The lake was pungent – something rotten like eggs and he could taste it on his tongue, smell it in his nostrils. Front crawl was always his best stroke and he set off at a reasonable pace, trying not to tire himself too soon, but not wanting to hang around longer than he had to. His arms sliced through the water.

Three strokes, head turn, breath.

Three strokes, head turn, breath.

Every now and then he would glance forward, fix his eyes on the moon, knowing that Hailey was waiting the other side.

God, it was cold.

His pace was slower than usual. His body felt heavy. For a split second he worried that he wouldn't make it but his nerves drove him forward. Harder. Faster.

'Come on Connor. Almost there!'

He heard the shouts, looked up. Shadowed on the shore were the others.

Connor stopped, his body shifting from horizontal to vertical, raised his arm and waved.

It was while he was treading water he felt it. A slither of something against his toes. In a knee-jerk reaction, he kicked it off. His feet flailed furiously. Something tangled around his ankle, slippery and strong. He should have relaxed. He dived underwater and tried to free himself, but panic had a hold of him as tight as the reeds that wrapped around him. He tried to swim forwards, pull himself free, was dragged underwater. Water filled his mouth, his throat, stung his eyes. Frantically, he paddled his hands, tried to kick his legs. Broke free of the surface, coughing and spluttering.

He couldn't keep still, had to keep treading water or he'd sink, but the more he fought to be free the more tangled he became.

'Help!' The scream tore from somewhere deep in his belly but still his voice sounded small in the vastness of the lake. The blackness of the night. 'Help.'

'Very funny!' Tyler shouted back.

Connor dipped again. Water in his ears. His eyes. Everywhere. His strength was seeping away, but the desire to live was fierce. He plunged under the water and prised his fingers in between the weed and his ankle. Tugged once.

Twice.

Three times.

It didn't snap.

It didn't even give a little. His lungs were on fire. Desperate for air, he broke free of the surface, the cool breeze immediately chilling his face. He was scared, more than scared, he was terrified.

He thought of Kieron, how much he wanted to survive, and curling around his terror was a shame that he had thrown his life away for a stupid dare.

'Help.'

He couldn't stay afloat for much longer. His body as heavy as iron.

A cry.

A splash.

Someone swimming towards him.

Hailey.

'Connor!' She reached him and he wound his arms around her neck, tried to calm himself down.

Failed to calm himself down.

He was heavy. Too heavy for her and she disappeared underwater before she rose again, heaving water out of her mouth.

'Do…' She struggled for breath. 'Do you have cramp?'

'Something…' His voice was too high, like a girl's. 'Something around my ankle.'

Without a word, she threw herself under the water again. He felt her hands travel down his body, his chest, his stomach, his legs. He was falling. Without meaning to he drew his knee up abruptly to fall back into the momentum of treading water and somehow pushed Hailey away from him.

She didn't surface.

Even more panicked, his hands snaked through the water trying to find her clothes to drag her back up.

'Hailey!' he called, grasping nothing but air. 'Hailey!'

More splashes. Tyler and Ryan calling at him to hold on, that they were coming.

He couldn't feel Hailey.

Hear her.

See her.

He couldn't find her.

She was gone.

Sitting up in bed now, he pinches himself, in short, sharp

snaps all over his arms, but he can't stop his mind racing. Hailey is gone and it's all his fault. He folds his fingers into his palms, draws his knees to his chest and wraps his arms around them. Dropping his forehead onto his kneecaps with a jolt, feeling bone against bone, fighting the urge to do it again, harder, to hurt himself.

He needs to speak to someone, not about Hailey but about… anything. Crap. Take his mind off her and his guilt and his regret. Mindless chatter to slow his heart and still his mind so he can sleep again. Ryan never goes to bed until at least midnight. Connor doesn't usually either. He tries to FaceTime but Ryan doesn't pick up.

He waits a few minutes, imagining Ryan pausing his Xbox, picking up his phone and he calls him again.

And again.

He can't remember a time Ryan wasn't at the end of his phone but his calls remain unanswered.

There was that figure standing near the school.

The sense of eyes on his back.

Mum chasing away the car.

Christ, what has happened to Tyler?

He curls into a ball on his side, reassuring himself that Ryan can't have disappeared like Tyler. Any second now he'll call back.

He stares at his phone, willing it to ring so he knows Ryan is okay.

It doesn't.

CHAPTER THIRTY-TWO

Lucy

Three days until Connor is taken

It's almost simultaneous. Connor heading out of the front door for school and Mel ringing.

'Lucy, am I too late to catch Ryan? He's not answering his mobile, is he still there?' Her questions come at me in a rush.

'Ryan?' I rub the sleep from my eyes. It had been a rough night.

'He's forgotten his essay. I've just found it in his room.'

'Ryan hasn't been here this morning.'

'But he stayed with you last night?'

'No. Was he supposed to?' Connor hadn't told me.

There's an edge to her voice. An edge to mine.

'No. But he went out in the evening, said he was going to yours. I fell asleep and I've just woken up. So he isn't there? Lucy, he's been out all night.' Her voice sounds small and high against the blood pounding in my ears.

I pace the room, unsure what to say. My heart is racing. 'Mel…' I'm helpless. 'Don't worry. I'm sure he's fine.'

'But where is he?'

'Have you tried Fergus?'

'Fergus. God. No. I'll try him from the landline. Hold

on.' I hear her mutter under her breath, 'Pick up, pick up, pick up.'

'He's not answering.' Her fear crawls over my skin. 'Lucy. What should I do?'

I shake my head although she cannot see me. It's horrible to hear her pain, her anxiety, wishing I could make it better but knowing that I can't.

'What if he's had an accident? Should I call the hospitals? The police. I should call the police, shouldn't I?'

'Yes, but I'm sure wherever he is… I'm sure he isn't hurt.'

Unbidden, my hand reaches out and scoops back the curtain. There's no white car. I'm not even sure now that it's them I am frightened of – this unknown person – them that's causing the pounding feeling in my chest. It's all become mixed up in my head with the dread that squeezes me tighter and tighter every day.

We talk for a few minutes more and I try to remain calm for Mel's sake but calm is the last thing I feel.

It's all too close to home.

CHAPTER THIRTY-THREE

Connor

Ryan isn't at their usual meeting place on Deene Street. Connor has waited for fifteen minutes, his unease growing with each passing second until his whole body is coiled with tension.

Something is wrong.

At a loss to know what to do, he heads to school to see if Ryan is there, planning to leave and go to his house if he isn't, but as soon as he walks through the doors he knows something is very wrong.

Mrs Webb is waiting by the door, ushering everyone inside.

'Straight into the hall.' Her face is serious.

'Why?' Through the windows, Connor can see the flash of blue lights, the police car pulling into the car park.

Ryan.

An intense heat scorches his face and he feels he might faint. He reaches out a hand to touch the wall and steady himself but before he can make contact he is swept down the corridor in a tide of kids, all of them speculating what is going on. But Connor knows.

Ryan.

His phone buzzes, a text from Mum, but before he can

open it Mr Marshall claps his hands. 'Everyone settle down.' He waits for the noise to fall. 'Now I don't want to cause any concern but...' His eyes sweep around the hall. 'You all know that a week ago Tyler Palin disappeared.' He pauses. 'I'm sorry to say that last night Ryan Horner also went out and didn't make it home. Does anybody have any idea where he might be?' There's a silence that Connor hasn't heard in the hall before. 'You won't get in any trouble if you can tell us anything that might help find him.'

The whispering begins, the exchanging of horrified glances.

'The officers will want to speak to you all, starting with those in Ryan's classes, followed by everyone who knew him. Nobody is to leave school premises today, not even at lunchtime. If you're upset, please speak to your form tutor. Right. That's all for now.'

Connor stands.

'Not you, Connor.' Mr Marshall gestures at him to stay where he is. 'You'll be the first person the police will speak to, naturally.'

Naturally.

It is PC Amin this time asking questions. Connor's tongue is thick, his mouth dry, he is close to tears.

'Ryan will be okay, won't he? When did he go missing?' Connor asks again. He can't get his head round it. Where is he? He can't remember not having him by his side. Joint birthday parties; the boys dressed as pirates, matching eye patches and stuffed parrots on their shoulders; the junior football team, both boys refusing to play if the other was on the sub bench; getting drunk at the park for the first time, staggering home, holding each other up, collapsing into laughter every few steps. 'Something's happened to him. I know it.' Connor drops his head into his hands; it's too heavy for his neck. The room is spinning.

'Have some water,' PC Amin urges.

Connor watches his hand reach for the glass as though it's someone else's hand. Someone else in his body. He's floating high above himself. He takes a sip. The water is cold and, as it trickles down his throat, he begins to cool down.

'Take some deep breaths,' PC Amin says. He breathes with Connor.

In. Out.

In. Out.

'Better?'

'Yeah.' Connor sits back in the chair.

'If you need a break—'

'No.' Connor is closest to Ryan. He wants to help.

'Connor. PC Amin has a lot of people to talk to.' Mr Marshall has been pacing the room but now he places his palms on the desk and leans in to Connor. Traces of tobacco on his breath, clinging to his clothes. Connor thought he was always dead against smoking.

'If there's nothing helpful you can—'

'I'll ascertain what's helpful and what isn't, Mr Marshall,' PC Amin says firmly.

Connor can't look at Mr Marshall. He knows his nostrils will be flaring. He likes to be the one in control. Anger radiates from him but all he can feel is terror, not because of his head teacher but because he might never see his best friend again.

There are so many people he might never see again, who are such an important part of his life.

Fergus.

Tyler.

Ryan.

Hailey.

Where will he be without them? Who will he be? He begins to hyperventilate again. The world isn't safe. Who else is at risk? Kieron? Him?

Connor struggles to calm himself.

'Okay?' PC Amin asks gently when Connor has taken another few deep breaths. He nods.

'Talk me through yesterday,' PC Amin asks.

'It was… normal. School was school. We walked home together as far as Deene Street, that's when we go our separate ways. Ryan said he might be over later to visit Kieron and…' Connor shrugs. 'He didn't come round.'

'Did you go out last night, Connor?'

'No. I stayed in with my family.'

'And your family consists of?'

'My brother, Kieron, he's just out of hospital so I was spending some time with him. My mum, she went to bed really early, she'd been sleeping on the ward and was knackered. And my dad, although he went out after tea.'

'Where did he go?'

'Dunno. He's a vet so he's often called out at night.'

'Did it strike you as odd that Ryan didn't come to your house after he said he might?'

'No. His parents have split up and sometimes his mum wants Ryan to stay in with her. She's a mess.'

'Where is Ryan's dad?'

'Dunno. Ryan hasn't heard from him since he moved out.'

'He must be upset about that?'

'Yeah. I guess.' Connor can't keep his body still, everything moving, his toes, his knees, his fingers curling and uncurling.

'Could Ryan have gone to him?'

'He doesn't know where he is.'

'And you haven't had any contact with Ryan since you said goodbye yesterday on Deene Street. No texts?'

'No.' Connor shakes his head. 'Oh. I tried to FaceTime him last night but he didn't pick up. God, was he... was he missing then? I thought...I had a weird feeling that something was wrong, but I thought I was paranoid because of Tyler, but now they're both...' Connor's voice sticks in his throat. He covers his face with his hands for a few moments. 'Sorry. Carry on.'

'Ryan's mum has told us that he left his house around 8.30. Told her he was heading over to yours.'

There's a short, sharp jab to Connor's stomach, the knowledge that Ryan is missing because he'd left his house to see Connor, a punch to his gut. Is it his fault? Is everything his fault? He begins to shake. His legs, his body, his teeth clattering together, it seems impossible that PC Amin can't hear them rattling in his skull.

'Let's talk about the residential.' PC Amin leans back on his chair while Connor leans forward in his, dragging in a deep breath.

'Obviously the tragedy with Hailey was... tragic,' the officer says.

No shit.

Connor steals a glance at Mr Marshall. He is looking out

of the window but Connor sees the stiffness in his shoulders, the clench in his jaw.

'We were properly supervised but...'

'We're not here to investigate that, Connor, but the fact is there were three of you there that night, not counting Hailey of course, and two of you are now missing. I know tensions have been high here. I need you to be honest with me. You won't get into trouble, but if you have the slightest suspicion that Tyler and Ryan's disappearance could in someway be connected—'

'I don't.' Again Connor glances at Mr Marshall. 'The trip was really well organized. It was an accident, just an accident.' Even to him, his words don't ring true. Anxiously, he waits but when the officer doesn't speak again he can't help asking, 'You don't think it's connected, do you?'

'Do you?' PC Amin throws back.

Connor looks at Mr Marshall, standing next to the Ofsted 'Outstanding' certificate. If he wasn't in the room Connor might tell the officer everything but he doesn't know where to start. Who to blame.

'There's no connection,' Mr Marshall answers for him. 'How can there be?'

There's a pause before PC Amin nods. 'That'll be all for now, Connor.'

Connor stumbles out of the room on legs that feel too weak to support him. He staggers into the toilets, drops to his knees and vomits.

Later, he heads home, vulnerable without his friends either side of him. Jumping as traffic speeds past him, muttering 'fuck' under his breath when a white car slows before roaring off again. He's walking faster than usual.

Outside of the newsagents the A-board is out as usual, advertising the early edition of the local paper.

'THE TAKEN', screams the headlines.

Connor can't help going into the shop, picking up a copy. On the front page are grainy photos of Ryan and Tyler. He recognizes them – they're pulled from Facebook. There's also a third photo, Hailey.

The words swim in front of his eyes and it takes Connor several attempts to get his whirring mind to unravel any of the sentences.

Two out of the three boys have disappeared.

Coincidence?

Something to hide?

He leaves the shop, the unpaid-for newspaper still in his hands, his feet walking methodically towards his house.

The Taken.

Two down.

One to go.

CHAPTER THIRTY-FOUR

Lucy

Two days until Connor is taken

'Lucy?' Aidan pulls a face. 'You've made the coffee with cold water.'

'Have I?' I press my fingertips against the kettle, it's warm but, as I take his mug, I can see his drink is cold and unappealing. Undissolved granules floating on the surface. 'Sorry. I didn't get much sleep last night.'

'I don't expect any of us did. With Ryan going missing yesterday—'

'What's that about Ryan?' Connor trudges into the kitchen.

'You're awake early for a Saturday.' He looks as though he's barely slept. Skin pale, eyes circled with heavy black bags.

'Mum! Ryan?'

'Sorry. I... We... Mel hasn't been in touch yet.' I'd spoken to her yesterday, her mum was with her, along with the police, so she didn't want me to go round. She said she'd told Fergus, but I didn't know whether he was coming home although I thought he probably would. How could he not?

'Mel's promised to call the second there's news.' My voice diminishes with every disappointing word I tell my son.

Connor sits down heavily on a chair.

'I'm so sorry.' I rub his back the way I would when he was a baby after a night feed.

'Ryan will be okay. Won't he, Lucy?' Aidan says.

'I… I hope so,' I say quietly. Aidan glares at me but it's the best I can offer because in truth I just don't know and Connor is too old to want false promises.

'Where can he be?' Connor asks, his gaze flicking between me and Aidan. My heart goes out to him. He looks so confused. So scared.

'He's probably with Fergus,' Aidan says unconvincingly. Connor shakes his head, a tear spilling down his cheek. I haven't seen him cry since he was eight and he went flying over the handlebars of his bike, landing face down on the tarmac. It's unbearable. I want to tell him I feel his pain, all of it, but I can't.

'Connor…' What can I say? I take his hand and he lets me hold it in the way he had that day all those weeks ago when I had to give him terrible, terrible news.

'What if…' He squeezes my fingers. 'What if I'm taken next?'

'You won't be.' This time my voice is steady, certain.

'We're not going to let anything happen to you,' Aidan says. Both of us on the same page for once. 'You'll be safe inside this weekend and on Monday—'

'Ryan and Tyler will probably be back?' Connor asks with hopeful eyes.

'Probably,' Aidan reassures him and Connor's face relaxes a little. He isn't too old for false promises after all.

Aidan refuses the offer of breakfast before he heads out. After the cold coffee I can't say I blame him. I am making scrambled eggs for Connor. It's my second attempt. My hands shook so much the first time that I'd dropped most of the shell into the pan. I gaze out of the window into the garden at the empty washing line. The borders where the footprints had been.

The smoke alarm begins to shriek.

'Mum!'

'Shit.' I grab at the pan but my fingers land too far down the handle and pain sears through my skin. I turn on the cold tap and soothe my burned hand under running water.

The letterbox clatters.

'I'll fetch the post,' Connor says.

'Okay,' I replied, because you would, wouldn't you? You'd never expect something as innocuous as an envelope dropping onto the doormat to be so dangerous.

So damaging.

CHAPTER THIRTY-FIVE

Connor

The envelope isn't addressed to anyone. Assuming it's junk, Connor tears it open.

AN EYE FOR AN EYE.

The world begins to spin.

'Connor?' Kieron calls from the top of the stairs. 'Connor, can we play—'

'Shut. Up.' Connor shouts.

There's anger in his voice. He swallows hard. He never usually speaks to Kieron like that but he doesn't know how much more he can take.

Someone knows.

Hysteria beats furiously in his chest.

They had come for Tyler.

Ryan.

They were coming for him.

CHAPTER THIRTY-SIX

Lucy

'Why did you shout at Kieron?' I rush into the hallway. Notice that Connor is holding a piece of paper. 'What is it?'

Connor doesn't answer so I pluck the letter from his fingertips. My face freezes as I read the words.

AN EYE FOR AN EYE.

'How ridiculous.' My voice is tense. 'It must be from some religious group.'

Hold it together.

I make a show out of screwing it up, dropping it into the bin in the kitchen. I begin to load the dishwasher. My hand is trembling so much a glass slips through my fingers and shatters against the floor. I pick up a shard but it nicks my skin. I wince. Blood drips onto my T-shirt.

Hold it together.

'Connor, can you—'

'No,' He snaps. His earlier fragility has been replaced with a hard shell. I understand that he is exhausted, on edge, but I want to yell back at him that he isn't the only one with problems. Instead, I fetch the dustpan and brush and crouch down again, sweeping up the mess. It's a relief not to be standing. My scared, shaking legs no longer capable of supporting me.

But I have to act as though I believe the letter is not aimed at us.

Aimed at me.

CHAPTER THIRTY-SEVEN

Aidan

The local station is drifting from the speakers, the drive-time presenters discussing the news.

'So what are our thoughts on "The Taken", as the evening paper has dubbed them? Tweet us using #TheTaken.'

Aidan swerves off the road, tyres bumping over the grass verge. He slams his foot on the brake and sits, his foot pushing against the pedal, his fingers clenched around the steering wheel. His whole body rigid.

'It's shocking that two teenage boys from our town have gone missing, isn't it, Steve? @Dps1978_1 says "worried to let my own kids out". If I was a parent I'd feel the same.'

'I can tell you, Helen, my kids have all grown and you never stop worrying about them. Here's another tweet from @Lgray591: "2 of the 3 boys were involved in the tragedy at Penton Outwards Bounds Centre. Coincidence?"'

'Can it be connected, Steve? We can't speculate too much. The other boy involved must be terrified that two of his friends are missing.'

'Another tweet from @cb247drive: "2 down, 1 to go". That sounds ominous.'

'It does. But let's not forget that although they are seventeen, they are children so show some respect.'

Aidan snaps off the radio. He hopes Lucy isn't listening. When he arrives home, it's a relief to find her with both boys on the sofa, watching one of the *Batman* movies but if people are gossiping, how long can he shield his wife and sons from the damage idle tongues can cause?

He kisses the top of Lucy's head. Her face is grey. She looks exhausted. Her top is on inside out.

'Hey.' He gently tugs at the label on the outside. 'I hope you haven't been out like this?'

'Oh.' She looks confused. 'I was in a rush to get changed. I got blood on my other top.'

'Blood?'

'I dropped a glass putting it in the dishwasher and cut my finger.'

'Are you okay?'

'Yes,' she says, but he can see she isn't. He had hoped she'd relax once Kieron came home but then they didn't know the results of his latest liver function test.

They didn't know about Ryan.

Every time Ryan pops into his head there's a tightening of his chest. He's practically grown up in this house, in this family. Aidan recalls the time the boys were wrestling in the garden and Ryan lost a tooth. He'd come running into the kitchen to show Aidan. It was Aidan who had helped him wrap it in tissue and pop it under the pillow on the bottom bunk in Connor's room. It was Aidan who slipped into the room when the boys were fast asleep, replacing the tooth with a shiny pound coin.

However distressed he feels, it must be a million times worse for Melissa, and Fergus. Had it not been for Tyler also going missing, the obvious explanation is that Fergus has taken Ryan, but if that was the case Ryan would have been in touch with Mel, with Connor.

He'd tried to call Fergus again today, left another voicemail. It didn't seem right to mention Ryan over text but he had little choice.

I'm so sorry about Ryan, he had sent. He didn't get a reply, he wasn't really expecting one, but this time he could see that Fergus had opened the message. That had to be a good sign, didn't it?

He has to keep believing that they will all get through this. He'll be the positive one. He crouches before Lucy and takes her hands. 'Everything will be okay.' Their gazes lock. He sees that she wants to believe him and wanting something is always the start, isn't it? 'We'll be okay. All of us.' This it what he wants more than anything, and as she nods, squeezing his fingers, he is relieved that she wants this too. Wants them. He's been so distracted, so caught up in *her* and all the implications of their ill-fated relationship he's almost forgotten what's most important.

His wife.

His children.

Everything he needs is right here. He has such a lot of making up to do he doesn't quite know where to start but he says, 'I'll cook tonight. Do you want a cup of tea while you wait?'

It's a small kindness but Lucy's eyes fill with tears.

He is floored by a love that is fierce. 'Look. I don't have to go to this conference on Monday.'

'But your CPD?'

Vets have to undertake 105 hours of Continuing Professional Development over a three-year period.

'I know, but I can do it another time. You're more important. All of you. You absolutely come first.'

For a moment his words hang heavy, the frown that creases Lucy's forehead disappears and he can imagine her holding his promises to her chest. She's wavering but still she says, 'But they won't give you a refund now, and you've paid for the hotel room.'

'It's fine.'

'No… go. You're only half an hour away, you're often called out further than that. If we need you, you can come back. Look… when you come home everything will be different.' She touches his face, her palm is warm as it rests on his cheek.

'Go, Dad.' Connor chimes in. 'Staying here won't bring Ryan and Tyler back and I'm not going to school next week if they haven't been found so you know I'll be safe.'

'But Kieron's got to see Dr Peters.'

'He won't tell us anything new. Kieron's only just been discharged but I'll take him to be cautious and to book the next appointment.'

Now Aidan is the one who's unsure. 'I don't know—'

'Mum does and she wants you to go and she wants a cup of tea!' Kieron pipes up. 'And while you're making it, I'll have a hot chocolate please!'

Aidan forces a laugh for his son. 'You lot are so bossy. Want anything, Connor?'

'Is a beer out of the question?'

Aidan doesn't answer but while he waits for the kettle to boil he uncaps a bottle of Becks from the fridge.

He scoops the teabag out of Lucy's mug and stamps too firmly on the pedal for the bin. It tips open, spilling rubbish across the kitchen. He tosses back in a banana skin, an eggshell. Scoops up a screwed-up piece of paper. That should be in the recycling. As he carries it towards the back door, he can't help opening it.

AN EYE FOR AN EYE.

It stops him in his tracks.

AN EYE FOR AN EYE.

Revenge.

That one word is cold and hard and terrifying.

AN EYE FOR AN EYE.

Oh God. He wants to grab his family and run. Do they know? How will he explain? He stares at the letter wondering who found it.

Lucy?

Connor?

Kieron?

More importantly, did they guess it was for him?

CHAPTER THIRTY-EIGHT

Lucy

The day that Connor is taken

I wake at first light, disorientated and distressed. In my dreams I'd heard a baby crying and I'd stumbled through the dark trying to reach it but I couldn't.

'I'm leaving for the conference now.' Aidan bends down and gives me a minty kiss. 'I want to arrive early and get my bearings. I'll have breakfast there.'

I squint at the clock. It's 7 a.m., Kieron's hospital appointment isn't until one but I drag my leaden limbs out of bed. I have six hours and there's lots to do before we go. The flush of positivity I'd experienced last night has faded under the weight of my nightmare.

Missing baby.

Missing children.

As soon as I'm up, I ring Melissa to check if she's okay but she doesn't pick up. I call her landline but that too rings and rings without answer. I'm worried there's been a development I don't know about until she texts that she doesn't want to tie up the phone line just in case there's news.

Connor is already downstairs, in his pyjamas, shaking cereal into a bowl. He looks as exhausted as I am.

'Morning,' I yawn as I fill the kettle. 'Are you okay?'

'My mates are missing, Mum. Of course I'm not okay.'

He's been like this all weekend. His moods veering from light to dark to light again. He's scared for his friends, himself, I understand, but I've been biting my tongue and I'm so close to snapping. My eyes are stinging with tiredness and I can't unravel my tangled thoughts. The past few days have been such a lot to cope with. Too much.

'I just meant… I'm glad you're staying home from school today.'

'Yeah, but you can't keep me prisoner forever.'

'I'm not…' I lower my voice. 'I'm not keeping you prisoner but—'

'It's all right for you. I've been stuck in the house all bloody weekend. At least you've been able to go out.'

'To the supermarket. I've hardly been out having fun.'

'And the walks "to clear your head".'

'You could have come.'

'You could have asked. 'He looks at me with such contempt. I shrivel under his gaze until he is the towering adult and I am the reproached child.

'You're right.' I take a breath. We both need to calm down. 'I assumed you'd say if you wanted to get out and you were gaming with Kieron, but I should have made a point of asking you. Why don't you come with us today? To the hospital? It would help with Kieron if you're there.' It wouldn't really make any difference but I don't want Connor sitting alone, brooding, while all of his classmates are at school.

'So you want me with you when you need my help,' comes back the stinging reply. 'I don't want to come.'

I react too quickly. 'There's loads of things I don't want to do but I do them anyway. For Kieron, for—'

'Don't say for me!' Connor's fury streaks towards me. 'You never fucking do anything for me.'

'That's not true!' I don't want to fuel his anger but he's been snapping at me all weekend and now I quietly defend myself, 'I—'

'Fucked my life up!' He is screaming now. Out of control. I know it isn't me he's really furious with, not really, but it still hurts to hear him say, 'You don't know what it's been like for me and do you care? You pack me off to that... that shit-hole every day where Mr Marshall glares at me and a bunch of twats think it's funny to wind me up about what happened.'

'I can't imagine anyone would—'

'I am NOT imagining it. I've had posters taped to my locker – "I know what you did last summer" like the film. And words scratched into my desk: "I know".'

'Connor, I'm sorry but—'

'But you love Kieron more than me.'

'I really don't!'

'You do. You love Kieron more than anyone else!'

His rage is absolute. I'm unprepared. Doubting myself. Too tired, too worried, to process his assault. It's like being underwater. I'm hearing everything. Seeing everything. But it's all muffled. I don't feel well. Increasingly breaking out in a sweat, head light, limbs heavy.

I can't cope anymore.

I've gone to extraordinary lengths for both of my children, as any parent would. I love them equally. Even if at this moment I do not like the red-faced, furious teenager stood in front of me, who is still talking too loud.

'Well it bloody seems like it. You literally wouldn't care if I vanished like Ryan and Tyler. That you'd be glad.'

'Of course I wouldn't—'

'Yeah.' He crosses his arms and leans back against the wall. 'You have to say that. Perhaps I'll try it, I'll disappear and then we'll both know how you really feel, won't we? I hate you.' He runs back into his bedroom and I am left shaking. Wishing he could know what's in my head, my heart, how I try to give both children the attention they need but sometimes, like now, it's impossible.

The doorbell rings. A quick check of my watch reveals it's only eight. Probably the postman.

I open the front door and there, on the step, are a bunch of flowers. There's no card. For a second I stare at them suspiciously, unsure what to do. Who left them or how to interpret the gesture. It's ridiculous to think the worst. I thought the dead birds and mice had been left on the step as some kind of warning but they'd only been left there by a cat. These were probably left by a neighbour in support of all we're going through.

Probably.

The Taken.

Reluctantly, I pick up the flowers. It's understandable Connor is so stressed. I pop back into the kitchen and fill my favourite green vase with water before I dump the bouquet inside and leave it on the hall table but as I walk away the pungent smell of lilies fills my nostrils and I remember what they are traditionally used for.

They're funeral flowers.

I drop to my knees seeing the future flash before me. Kieron's small coffin. His body giving up before he reached the top of the transplant list. Connor hating me. Blaming me for it all. Aidan snapping under the pressure.

I'm alone.

I'm alone.

I'm alone.

A wife without a husband. A mother without any children.

Help me.

I cannot cope with this. I just... can't.

The flowers. The white car. Connor. Kieron. Aidan.

Hailey.

I'm so so sorry for the things I did, for the things I didn't do.

'I hate you,' Connor had screamed.

I hate me too.

The smell from the flowers fills my nostrils, I crawl down the hallway from them.

A spinning top of thoughts, whirring faster and faster until I'm dizzy.

Missing.

Taken.

Funerals.

Death.

Missing.

Taken.

Funerals.

Death.

I must get up. I must pull myself together, but instead, begin to hum under my breath, a song that is both soothing and painful to me.

I can't seem to stop.

CHAPTER THIRTY-NINE

Aidan

He shouldn't have come to the conference. It's the first lecture of the day and all he can think about is Lucy driving Kieron to the hospital. He wishes he were with her to support her. She's not as strong as she believes. No one is infallible. He's worried she's falling apart again, but he doesn't know whether he thinks this because he almost expects it. They have had such a lot to deal with this year. But it isn't normal, putting the butter in the microwave, being so forgetful. Seeing a white car everywhere. Making coffee with cold water. Not realizing you're wearing your top inside out. Standing in the garden in the pouring rain because she's convinced someone has stolen the washing, that someone is after her. She's a million miles away from the poised, polished Lucy he fell in love with. The stress is unravelling her and he has to be the one to hold her together. His arms ache to hold her, to stroke her hair and promise her that everything will be okay even if he doesn't know how, or when. He shouldn't be here.

His phone buzzes.

Her.

He didn't meet her yesterday as she demanded. He hasn't replied to her last few messages.

He opens this one.

Ignore me & you'll be SORRY

CHAPTER FORTY

Lucy

Our appointment with Dr Peters is over and I have not said the things I wanted to say, my carefully rehearsed questions stuck in my throat. I don't want Kieron to hear the desperation in my voice.

Dr Peters holds open the door and ruffles Kieron's hair as he walks back out into the waiting room.

'I'll be out in a minute, Kieron.' I step back inside the room and look pointedly at the door until Mr Peters closes it. He wears a look of resignation. He knows what's coming.

'Rob.' I meet his gaze, addressing him as a friend although I'm painfully aware we are not equal. He holds Kieron's life in his hands.

'Have you ever lost a patient?' I open with.

'Lucy—'

'Please. Have you?'

'Yes, but not a child. Kieron—'

'We see it as doctors, death; we comfort the relatives and send them on their way and we may go home and dwell on them, for hours, days, weeks but ultimately our pain fades, we move on. There's always another patient. But… for those families there is never another mother. Another father.' I curl my nails into my palms, I will not cry. 'There will never be another Kieron.'

'I'm doing all I can.'

'When you lose a patient you analyse everything you did, questioning if there was anything else you could have done. If you could perhaps have saved them if you'd tried something different. With Kieron, you could try something different.'

I step closer to him, smelling the stale coffee on his breath.

'Lucy. I feel for you, I really do but what you're asking is... wrong.'

'It's—'

'Wrong. Right for Kieron perhaps but if we replace the child on the top of that list with Kieron, what becomes of that other child? Of their family? It's immoral and unethical and highly unfair of you to put me in this position.'

'I know.' My voice is small. I do know. And it's not like I want anybody else's child to die, I just want mine to live. Any parent would understand that. But Rob Peters isn't a parent and he will not change his mind. 'I had to ask.' I swipe away the tears on my cheeks.

'Lucy.' He passes me a tissue from the box on his desk. 'It's easy to say don't worry but you're so... fraught and Kieron will pick up on it. You know with kids we pull out all the stops. It's not like we have to tissue match a liver the way we would with a heart or kidney. It's easier—'

'Nothing about this is easy,' I whisper. 'Nothing.' Impossible decisions. Unimaginable consequences. He has made his choice and I know he won't change his mind. I hadn't really expected him to. There's a roundness to my shoulders, a stoop to my spine as I trudge back out to the waiting room to find Kieron.

'Mum,' he says, 'Connor isn't answering his phone. He told me to ring him straight after my appointment and tell him how I got on.'

'Perhaps he's on silent.' I guide him towards the car park.

'No. He said he'd be waiting for my call and then he'd set up the Xbox so we could play as soon as I got in. I've tried him five times. He never ignores me.'

Hearing Kieron say this unsettles me, because he's right. Connor never ignores Kieron. I pull out my phone and call him myself, knowing that if he's not picking up to his brother, he won't to me.

He doesn't.

I usher Kieron towards the car again, faster this time.

Kieron falls asleep quickly in the car. I am left with my thoughts and my worry.

A knowing that something is wrong with Connor.

Why isn't he picking up to Kieron?

Despite being seventeen, I should never have left my son alone. Tyler is missing. Ryan is missing. Connor is horribly upset and I'd just… left him.

Hurry.

The flash of neon orange cones blur through the window as I gather speed until the roadworks force me to a stop. The candle-shaped air freshener swings from the rear-view mirror – its strawberry scent cloying.

My fingertips drum the steering while I wait for the temporary traffic lights to change to green, the rain hammering against the roof of the car, windscreen wipers lurching from side to side. It isn't the crack of lightning that causes my stomach to painfully clench, or the rumble of thunder even though storms always take me back to the time I'd rather forget, but a mother's instinct.

I've felt it before. That bowling ball of dread hurtling towards me.

While I wait, I try Connor's phone again, calling from mine and then from Kieron's. He doesn't pick up.

Drawing in a juddering breath, I tell myself everything is fine.

The lights turn green.

Hurry.

Before I can pull away, there's a streak of yellow and through the rain a digger trundles towards me, blocking my path.

The song finishes playing on the radio, the news begins. The presenter mentions 'The Taken' and I snap it off. Doesn't he realize he's talking about real people, real lives. Connor has never been the same since the trip, since he lost Hailey, and being discussed on air, on social media, strangers dissecting his life, is horrific. If I could shield him from it all, I would.

I'll do anything to keep both of my boys safe.

The driver of the digger raises his hand in appreciation as he passes by me. Before I can pull away the lights revert to red once more. The storm builds. My anxiety builds.

My stomach churns with a sense of foreboding.

'You never fucking do anything for me.'

I can understand him ignoring my calls, but Kieron's?

'You fucked my life up!'

Is he still angry?

'You love Kieron more than anyone.'

Is he so hurt he's ignoring us both?

'You'd be glad if I disappeared like Ryan and Tyler.'

Despite the lights still being red, I pull away. There is no approaching traffic.

Visibility is poor. My heart is racing, as there's another crack of lightning. I count the seconds the way I used to with the boys when they were small.

One.

Two.

Three.

A grumble of thunder. The storm is closing in. Everything is closing in, crashing down. My stomach is a hard ball, my pulse skyrocketing as a sense of danger gallops towards me.

Hurry.

The urgency to be at home overrides the voice of caution urging me to slow down.

My chest is tight as I pull into my street, my drive-way. A whimper of fear leaching from my lips as I see the front door swinging open.

Without waking Kieron, I half fall, half step out of the car, my shoes slipping on wet tarmac as I rush towards my house.

'Connor?' I am calling his name although there is a part of me instinctively knowing that he won't answer.

Can't answer.

'Connor?'

The table in the hallway is lying on its side. My favourite green vase lies in shattered pieces over the oak floor. The lilies that had been left anonymously on the doorstep that I thought were from a well-meaning neighbour are strewn down the hallway.

Funeral flowers.

'Hello?' My voice is thin and shaky.

The cream wall by the front door is smeared in blood. Connor's phone is on the floor, lying in a puddle of water from the vase. His screen is smashed. My feet race up the stairs towards his bedroom. A man's voice drifts towards me. Without considering the danger I am potentially putting myself in, putting Kieron in, I push open Connor's door just as shots are fired.

Instinctively, I cover my head before I realize the sound is coming from the war game blaring out of Connor's TV; whoever he was online with is still playing the game, unaware Connor has disappeared. His Xbox controller is tangled on the floor along with his headphones.

His bedroom is empty.

The Taken.

It's impossible.

'Connor?' He was here. He was safe. The front door was locked.

But he isn't here now.

Connor has gone.

PART TWO

CHAPTER FORTY-ONE

Ryan

When he was small, Ryan used to wake up screaming, 'night terrors' his mum called them as she scurried into his bedroom to comfort him. He'd be wrenched from sleep in the middle of a horrifying scenario where faceless figures and monsters were chasing him, immobilized by fright. That's when his mum would enfold him in her arms. Stroke his hair until his heart rate slowed, breathing settled. He'd drift back to sleep and in the morning he was never wholly sure if he had actually been awake, if any of it was real.

Now, he is waking again. He tries to move but his wrists and ankles are bound.

Three days.

It's been three long days since he was taken and although he's been given food and water and been allowed to go to the toilet he is still pinned to a bed.

Still rigid with fear.

It's like the worst hangover ever. Pain pulsing behind his temples, tongue swollen, mouth dry. He's exhausted, sick, sorry.

He shouldn't have accepted a lift that night, but why

wouldn't he? He didn't give a second thought to climbing into the car.

Stranger danger had been drummed into him from a young age but this wasn't a stranger.

His head is heavy, thick with memories he doesn't want to recall. He can't open his eyes. This isn't a nightmare at all. It was real, all of it. What happened when he was snatched and what had happened this morning when they had returned.

He doesn't want to remember but he can't help it.

'Ryan,' a whisper. A shake of his shoulder. 'I'm back.'

He had screwed his eyes tighter. He wouldn't look.

He wouldn't.

'Please, please.' He had babbled as he had each time before when they'd made fleeting visits to check on him as he'd sipped Evian from a bottle and forced down dried oatcakes that had clogged in his throat. 'I won't tell, I won't…'

'Shhh.'

This morning there had been something different in the tone of voice. Something even more terrifying as though something had snapped. He knew, undoubtedly, that he was trapped here with a monster, not a faceless figure like the ones he'd dreamt of when he was small. Someone ordinary. Someone he knows.

They told him what was going to happen later today and something inside him broke in two, and the compliant Ryan of the past few days, the Ryan who believed that if he was good he'd be set free, disappeared.

It was horrific.

Fear shook him hard and the word 'Help!' flew from his lips. He screamed over and over again, 'Help! Help!'

'Shhh.'

He couldn't stop screaming, jerking his body as a blindfold was again tied tight around his eyes. Tape covered his mouth.

He couldn't speak.

Couldn't see.

He didn't want to.

'See no evil, speak no evil.' The voice soft. Terrifying. 'I'll be back soon.'

He wishes he couldn't hear.

They couldn't really be planning to…

In shock, he had slipped into sleep.

Now he's awake again, alone again.

For how long?

CHAPTER FORTY-TWO

Connor

Sensations return. Pain throbs. Instinctively, Connor raises his hand and lightly presses his fingertips against his skull searching for a wound, wincing when he finds one. His fingers are sticky, coated with blood, although it's too dark for Connor to see it. Nausea rises, confusion, fear. He tries to manoeuvre himself to sitting but a sudden bang to his head explodes blinding flickers of light behind his eyes and he flops down onto his back once more.

He is disorientated. Scared. Panic hammering in his chest. Think.

Gingerly, he reaches out his hands, palms immediately connecting with a solid surface.

A coffin.

'Help!' His voice too loud in this tiny space. 'Help!' He bangs his fists on the low roof above him, tears leaking from his eyes. His chest heaving. There's a smell he recognizes. Something chemical?

Petrol?

A slam.

An engine.

The glow of lights.

A sudden movement.

He can hear the pattering of rain. He's in the boot of a car. He's not sure how long he's been unconscious for. Seconds? Minutes? Hours?

Where is he being taken?

He fumbles in his pocket for his phone but it isn't there. Vague memories charge towards him before disappearing out of reach. He's not sure if the bump to his head is preventing him from remembering or whether his mind is protecting him from the unimaginable.

Although he can't see, he covers his face with his hands and tries to recall the last thing he can remember.

Mum had asked him to go to the hospital with him but he'd said no. Not only had he refused but he'd hurled abuse at her. He is guilt-ridden over some of the things he said, accusing her of not loving him enough, screaming at her that it would serve her right if he disappeared. He wishes now he had gone to Kieron's appointment, but he hadn't wanted to spend the journey in awkward silence. Her, hurt. Him, ashamed. When he sees her again he'll tell her how sorry he is.

If he sees her again.

He'd spent the rest of the morning shut in his room with Kieron, playing on the Xbox, keeping out of Mum's way, trying to make silent amends. Although he didn't say so he knew Kieron was disappointed that Connor wouldn't be coming to the hospital so he'd asked Kieron to ring him straight after his appointment, promised he'd play with him again when he got home. Around lunchtime Mum and Kieron had left and then the doorbell had rung. Connor had bounded downstairs and opened the door to the postman, taken in a parcel. He'd locked the door and slung the package on the worktop in the kitchen, the kitchen where they sit and eat their meals together, as a family. Will he ever see them again? Connor wishes he had done things differently. Talked more. Listened more. Connor knew that Kieron was scared of dying, his brave face couldn't hide that. He should have been honest answering his brother's questions. Shared what it was like to kiss a girl. To love a girl.

His thoughts drift until he lurches forward as the car turns a sharp corner.

Focus.

After lunch, he'd felt trapped – ironic now – and considered going for a mooch around town, but the world scared him in a way it never used to. Tyler and Ryan were missing and a fear had settled over his skin that he'd be next. He was safer indoors, home.

Upstairs, he had fired up his Xbox again. Positioned his headphones over his ears.

Call of Duty – Mum hated it, of course.

'War isn't something to be glamourized.' She had been disapproving when Aidan had bought Connor a copy. 'Imagine how frightened soldiers are? The apprehension their families face each time they leave. The monstrosities the doctors and nurses witness as they piece them back together.'

'Chill out, Mum,' he'd told her. 'It's just a game.'

But he felt it now. The fear, the dread, the horror.

All of it.

Focus.

His thumbs twitched, reminding him the Xbox controller had been in his hand. He'd played for… he didn't know.

The doorbell had rung for a second time. He'd tried to ignore it, another parcel no doubt. They could leave it on the step – but then it had rung again.

Again.

Again.

Somebody keeping their finger on the button.

With a start, Connor realized that after he'd locked the door earlier he had left his keys dangling from the lock. It was probably Mum on the step, furious, assuming that Connor had locked her out purposefully. He hadn't. He stood, pulling his phone out of his pocket – had he missed Kieron's call to tell him they were on their way back? He sprinted down the hallway, virtually flying down the stairs, two at a time, three at a time, landing heavily in the hall.

He'd unlocked the door, pulled it open. Registered the face that greeted him, familiar and angry. He'd stepped back, wary, confused.

'Are you all right?' he'd asked, tentatively.

The response: 'Let's go.'

'Go where?' Connor had felt the anger coming towards him, had shaken his head, not quite sure what he was refusing, but he didn't want to leave the safety of the house. 'Mum will be back soon.' He'd watched for a softening of their expression.

Nothing.

Instead, a hand had grabbed his arm, pulled him forwards.

'Get off!' His feet skidded on the laminate floor, hip banging against the table. The smash of the vase. The splash of water from the flowers soaking into his jeans. All the while being pulled towards the open door.

'What the fuck?' Connor fought back. At seventeen, he was younger, stronger, but he lost his footing. Fell. His head slamming against the wall. His body going limp. And now there was here.

This.

Glowing in the darkness, a pinprick of clarity. Connor knows undoubtedly who had taken Tyler and Ryan now. Who has taken him.

He knows why.

CHAPTER FORTY-THREE

Lucy

'The Taken', the newspapers call them.

Tyler.

Ryan.

But Connor? How is it possible?

It isn't.

He was at home, safe. The door was locked. Still slumped against the wall, I cast my eyes around his bedroom again as though he might spring out from the wardrobe, from under his bed. I take in his crumpled duvet, his bin overflowing with scrunched-up cans of Pepsi. Empty tubes of sour cream Pringles. His shelf of books, untouched and unread since primary, gathering dust. Everything is normal. Horribly normal.

Where is my son?

I rush through the house, checking from room to room, calling his name. It's when I'm back in the hallway, back with the blood, that the breath is sucked out of my lungs as though I've been body-slammed by one of Kieron's wrestling heroes.

Kieron.

Running towards the front door, my feet crunch through pieces of broken glass, slip through water.

Sickness is hot in my throat.

Outside, Kieron is still on the passenger seat, covered with a blanket.

Still asleep.

I lock him in the car before rooting around my bag for my mobile. Snatches of past conversations with the police when Tyler and Ryan went missing spin a halo around my head.

'We don't have any leads right now'… 'don't believe there is an immediate threat to Connor'… 'doing all we can'.

But their best hasn't been good enough. I think of Melissa's distress. They haven't found the boys and I don't know if they will. The first twenty-four hours are vital – I've watched enough crime series to know that. After that, the chances of locating a missing person are drastically reduced. Something flutters furiously in my chest. Melissa has left Ryan's disappearance entirely to the police.

I will not do the same with Connor.

I do need to tell them though, but before that I want to tell my husband. My hands are shaking as I unlock my handset, press the photo of Aidan. It rings and rings but he doesn't pick it up.

It's odd. Generally, his mobile is always with him, never on silent. It's the only way either of us can bear to leave Kieron, knowing that we are contactable at all times. I know he's at a conference, but that wouldn't stop him answering. He'd reassured me again as he left: 'I'm always at the end of a phone.'

I cut the call and try him again.

Still nothing.

Where is he?

CHAPTER FORTY-FOUR

Connor

Connor remembers hearing somewhere that most murders are committed by someone the victim knows.

Murder.

It won't come to that, of course it won't but...

What's in store for him? He hardly dare speculate. His whole body is twitching, jerking, terror lifting and dropping his cells. What has happened to Tyler and Ryan? Were they shoved into this space, taken and...

He can't breathe. There's a rumble of thunder. He claws at the immovable surface above him, behind him, in front of him. Fingernails tearing.

Staying calm seems impossible, but Connor knows that he must.

Breathe.

He clenches his jaw to stop his teeth from chattering.

Think.

Journeys are never uninterrupted: roadworks, traffic lights, pedestrian crossings. They are gathering speed now, but Connor thinks if he can attract attention when the car slows, stops, all of this will be over. Doubt creeps in, the engine is loud, the roar of traffic deafening, but he pushes them away.

It is not a smooth ride. Each time there's a pothole, a speed bump, Connor is thrown around the boot like one of Kieron's WWE wrestling figures.

Kieron.

He has to stay strong for his brother. Renewed, Connor fumbles around his too-small prison. He'd seen a movie once where a billionaire was kidnapped and thrown into the boot of his car. There had been a release catch and the man was able to escape. Hopeful, Connor checks once.

Twice.

Nothing.

There is nothing.

He rolls over, checking behind him. Running his hands around blindly until he finds the divide of the back seats. Shaking, he tries to locate the mechanism to lower one of the seats, he could crawl through the gap, but then what? The car is moving and if Connor bursts out of his confinement he could cause a crash. If he waits until they stop there's the possibility he'd be able to open the back door, run away. But he might not have time. The child locks could be activated.

But.

But.

But.

There are too many things that can go wrong. Anyway, he can't find the button to release the seats. Should he try to kick them? He shuffles as far away from them as he can, testing his idea, but he can't get the angle right. There won't be enough force in his legs.

Curling onto his side, Connor shoves his hands in the space underneath him. There's some sort of hole. He digs his fingers into it and tugs. A false floor begins to lift. He can't move it too far because of his weight. He shuffles backwards until his spine is pressed painfully against something hard. He lifts it again with one hand, trying to loop his other arm over the top of the rising floor to feel whether there is anything that might help get him out of here. The car brakes, throwing Connor forwards. The floor slams shut trapping his fingers. He lets out a cry. Connor is face down, scrambling to free his hand, turn himself around, to take the opportunity to scream and shout and try to attract attention, but before he can do all of those things, they are moving again, slower, but gathering speed.

Frustrated, Connor wrenches the false floor open again. Biceps trembling with the effort of raising the panel while it bears some of his weight. His T-shirt clings to him, sodden with sweat. His hands swipe left, right, fingertips connecting with metal. Straining, he inches forward reaching, reaching, reaching. His fingers close around the object and he pulls it towards him, akin to the fairground grabber machines he and Kieron loved so much. Hopes rising and dashing as the metal claws released the cuddly toys they had coveted. The memory tightens his grip.

Don't let it fall.

Eventually, he has it firmly in his grasp and he lets the floor drop back down, panting, his prize tightly in his hands.

A wrench.

A weapon.

The car slows again and Connor has a flash of inspiration. Using the wrench he smashes the taillight. Pokes as much of his hand as he can through the hole, a shard of glass grazing his wrist. He wiggles his fingers. Somebody will see them and call the police.

Won't they?

The car jerks to a stop. Connor is thrust forward.

The engine stills. A door slams. Connor pulls his hand free and scrambles back as far as he can. Footsteps.

The release of a catch.

Tears build again and this time Connor allows them to stream down his cheeks unchecked.

Rain splatters into Connor's blinking eyes.

The face staring down at him.

Still familiar.

Still angry.

CHAPTER FORTY-FIVE

Lucy

My hair is sodden, rain dripping down my neck. I bounce from tears to anger as I wait for Aidan to answer the phone, all the while watching the reassuring movement of Kieron's chest. Aidan still doesn't pick up.

Instead of dialling 999, I call the local police station who are dealing with Ryan and Tyler's disappearance.

'This is Lucy Walsh, Connor's mum,' streams from me in a voice that sounds nothing like mine. I hear a sharp intake of breath on the other end of the line. The operator knows what's coming next. 'He's missing. He was at home. There… there's blood.' Light-headed, I lean against my car. Inside, Kieron stirs. How can I tell him his brother has gone? Not in the same way as Tyler and Ryan, disappearing from the streets, but nevertheless gone all the same. It is impossible Connor has been taken and yet somehow he has. It's unfathomable. I garble, 'I wasn't here but I thought he was safe. I had locked the door behind me. I had. He hadn't gone out, he was at home and he knows not to answer the door to strangers but…'

In my mind I hear us, shouting.

'How would you feel if I was missing?' Connor screaming in my face.

And now? Now I know what I feel. I feel all of it.

Everything.

The operator's voice drifts back into my consciousness, calm, reassuring.

'We're on our way, Mrs Walsh, stay exactly where you are.'

But I can't just hang around waiting, trying to make sense of the senseless.

Kieron stirs again. Everything is unravelling and I'm running out of time.

Where is Connor?

My body is out of control; heart pounding, blood speeding through my hot veins. Every cell twitching with fright.

Where is Connor?

I pinch the bridge of my nose, both trying to stem my tears and the fierce stabbing pain behind my eyes.

And then it comes to me.

In a starburst of clarity, impossible to ignore.

I know *exactly* what happened here today.

I get back in my car and start the engine. Squeal out of my driveway, hunched forward over the steering wheel as though my weight will tip the balance, propelling the car faster, glancing at Kieron to ensure he's still sleeping.

I know.

This fear. This uncertainty. Mothers terrified to let their teenage boys out of their sight.

The windscreen wipers swish.

Connor-Connor-Connor.

I know where to go. What to do.

I know.

It all has to end.

Now.

But my sense of courage pales in comparison to the fear I feel. My mind and my body detach from one another as I drive. I break away from myself, floating high above the car, watching the mother rush to save her son with a fierce determination on her face.

I can do this.

I can do this.

I can do this.

My heart hammers out a frenzied rhythm keeping beat with my words.

I can do this.

But I don't know if I can.

CHAPTER FORTY-SIX

Connor

The grey sky is momentarily brightened by a whip of lightning.

'Get out of the car.' The voice that had once spoken to him in kindness now growls with fury.

'Please.' Connor isn't too proud to beg. 'Please can we just go home? Talk about it there? Mum will—'

'Out.' One word, a thousand undercurrents of what might happen if Connor doesn't comply ripple through Connor's body – now, more than ever, he is terrified for Tyler and Ryan. He can't coordinate his limbs. It's an effort to rise to sitting. He wonders why he isn't being dragged out of the boot, the way he was forced in.

The calm before the storm, but the storm is already raging around him, rain lashing.

Connor wiggles his pins-and-needles toes and stretches out his hands, his fingers on cold metal.

The wrench.

Connor closes his hand around it and raises his head, stares into cold, angry eyes. Can he use it as a weapon? Should he? He imagines raising it high, springing forward. The crack of a skull. The crumple of knees. Blood spilling on the pavement.

He has hesitated too long. The wrench is spotted and torn from his grasp. Connor is disappointed but, more than that, relieved. He doesn't have it in him to hurt someone. Not purposefully anyway.

Connor swings his left leg out of the boot, his right, feet splashing in puddles as he glances around him; unbidden, his head gives a slight nod as he realizes where he is. The only surprise is that it has taken until now to get here. The building looks almost derelict, practically falling down, but it's as though it has been holding on until he arrived. Its windows are blank, soulless eyes watching him on his slow descent. He is biding his time, praying for an unlikely passer-by, someone, anyone who will see a boy climbing out of a boot and ask questions, but it is isolated here around the back, and besides, the foul weather will be keeping everyone indoors.

It's crazy that he was locked in a car boot and driven amongst the other traffic undetected. Connor knows that after this – for he has to believe there is an after – he will be more vigilant, more inquisitive. The car waiting at the lights, the one speeding in a residential area – who is driving them and what hidden cargo are they carrying? Connor will always wonder.

The pavement feels fluid under his feet. His brain not quite adjusting to being back on solid ground, sensing movement although he's standing still.

'This isn't fair on Kieron, or Mum—'

A short sharp push to his shoulders causes him to swallow the rest of his words. Momentarily, he considers running, but where will he go? Where can he go that he doesn't have to face this horrible, terrible thing he did. Unless he never returns home again there is no way he can be free and, honestly, Connor knows he is far from free now, his mind a mass of thoughts and regrets that he does not want. That he should not have at his age.

Home.

Connor's throat swells at the thought of his mum.

'How would you feel if I'd gone missing?' he'd screamed, but he knows how she'd feel. Terrified. There's a pang as he envisions her arriving back to an empty house – an unexplained absence – he can't imagine how frantic she'll be when she realizes where he is, what is happening…

Perhaps she will be proud of him for facing up to his past. She thinks it's her fault. He shouldn't have let her believe that because it isn't. It never was.

Slowly, he walks towards the door, knowing who will be waiting inside, part of him eager to see them but mostly all he feels is dread.

It is time for retribution.

CHAPTER FORTY-SEVEN

Lucy

The windscreen wipers swish. Scenery whirls by the car window, a blur through the streaking rain, speeding green gardens and shopfronts that merge together into one solid mass. Every now and then I glance at Kieron, his pale skin, his troubled sleep. I slow down – the last thing I want to do is crash and hurt him – but then I remember that time is running out and my foot squeezes the accelerator.

If I'm right about my theory then I know that Connor will be in turmoil, confused and scared, and I'm certain I am right.

Hurry.

The needle gauge on the petrol tank has slipped into the red and is hovering dangerously close to empty. I can't afford the time to fill up.

My eyes flicker between the gauge and the road. I recall Aidan telling me once that cars use less fuel at a lesser speed and I don't know if that's true but still I slow down by 5 mph.

Minutes tick by and dark thoughts creep in. What if I am too late?

Hurry.

Again, my foot presses the pedal to the floor and we are roaring ahead.

CHAPTER FORTY-EIGHT

Aidan

Aidan hasn't been able to focus on the lecture since her text.

Ignore me & you'll be SORRY

He had turned his phone off but now it's the coffee break he worries that Lucy might need him and so he switches it back on. He was right to be concerned, he sees the missed calls from her. Has something happened at Kieron's appointment?

He tries to call her back but it goes straight to voicemail.

Something is wrong.

He calls her again, again. No reply. He tries Connor. Kieron. None of them answering.

His handset beeps a text alert.

I have something you want. Clock is ticking. I'll let u know where & when

It's a slow and sickening dawning that *she* won't ever leave them alone until she's destroyed his family. How far will he go to protect them? The muscles in his jaw tighten painfully, his back teeth grind together. He knows how far he'll go.

As far as it takes.

He's only half an hour from home and, as Aidan speeds

away from the hotel, he intermittently redials Lucy's number, reaching her voicemail each time.

His quiet cul-de-sac is a flurry of activity. Police cars, a tangle of blue and white crime-scene tape sectioning off his front garden. He feels, he actually feels, his heart plummeting, free-falling into his boots, landing with a thud. He can't get onto the driveway and so he screeches to a halt, half blocking the neighbours' drive and almost falls out of his car. Outside the surrounding houses, occupants cluster on steps, huddling under the shelter of porches or umbrellas speculating about what might have happened inside this red-bricked four bedroom with its neat flowerbeds and double garage.

There's a sense of detachment – a sense of this-can't-be-real as Aidan ducks under the tape and pushes aside the policeman who demands his name and tells him he can't go inside.

'Try to bloody stop me.' Aidan splashes through the puddles on his driveway as he sprints into his house. It's a short journey, not more than eight steps, but during those eight steps myriad scenarios burn through Aidan's brain, macabre images scorched onto his retinas that he'll never be able to shake. It can't be Kieron, there'd be an ambulance otherwise, possibly Lucy – his heart hurts at the thought of his wife beaten and bloody – but he knows, he knows before he's told that it's Connor.

The Taken.

I have something you want. Clock is ticking. I'll let u know where & when.

How can she have taken Connor? He is seventeen – to all intents and purposes still a child – but his height equals Aidan's five foot ten, he's strong – his love of sports has shaped his muscles. It doesn't seem feasible she'd have been able to overpower him. Could she have taken the other boys? Tyler and Ryan? She must have tricked Connor somehow. Drugged him? She's a stranger to him – Connor wouldn't have gone with her willingly, would he?

A wash of shame heats him from the inside out. He should have been here to protect his son, protect them all. After Tyler and Ryan had disappeared he had known there was a risk but Connor stayed off school today. He should have been safe. But the array of walkie-talkies, the crackle of radios tells a different story.

What exactly has happened here? Where are his family?

'Connor!' The word is painful, torn from Aidan's throat. Breathless, he runs into the hallway. Sickness clumping in his stomach when he catches sight of the blood on the walls. Wherever Connor is, he didn't go willingly.

'Mr Walsh. It's PC Leighton, do you remember I asked you some questions regarding the disappearance of Tyler and Ryan?'

'Where's my wife? My sons?'

'That's what we're trying to ascertain. You can't be in here. Don't touch anything.'

'This is my… Lucy!' he calls frantically up the stairs.

'Mr Walsh, please.'

Aidan shrugs free the hand that grasps his elbow.

'Connor!' he shouts, not expecting an answer but hoping for one all the same.

'Come with me.' He is ushered through to his kitchen like a guest, a visitor in a strange place, full of strange people talking in a language he doesn't quite understand. He drops onto a stool at the breakfast bar. Cradles his head in his hands. Sifting through the black and white, the shades of grey in between. Should he tell PC Leighton about the text? But that would mean sharing the whole shameful mess and he isn't convinced Connor is with *her*. She doesn't have the strength. He is certain it must be a man. A man who is strong enough, powerful enough to wrestle his son out of the door. To leave a trail of blood.

Blood.

Aidan bites down on the urge to cry.

Who has his son?

'I'll make you a cup of tea,' PC Leighton offers.

'Are they…' Aidan can't bring himself to say it. He rises to his feet.

'We've no reason to believe that anyone is seriously hurt…' The bubble of the kettle cuts off the rest of the sentence. Water is sloshed into mugs.

'The blood…' Aidan can't stop moving, adrenaline forcing his feet to pace, his fingers clench into fists.

'That's not as bad as it looks. It's only a small amount, but it is obviously a cause for concern. There's no sign of your family, but one of the neighbours has reported seeing Lucy come home and leave again several minutes later. She telephoned us in the time that she was here. As far as we know she's okay, but we think she's gone to look for Connor, which may hinder our investigation. She'd be more use to us here, answering questions. We've tried to reach her of course but she isn't answering her phone. Can you try?'

Aidan pulls out his handset, but his hands are shaking too much to hold it. He places it on the workbench and jabs at buttons until it's on speakerphone, calling Lucy.

Again, she doesn't answer. When her answerphone kicks in, he cuts the call and chooses Connor's name from his list of contacts instead.

A hand gently stops him. 'We have Connor's phone here.'

If Aidan was scared before, now he is terrified. Connor's mobile is permanently in his possession. What happened here?

The Taken.

'Where have you been today, Mr Walsh?'

'At the North Star Hotel in Highbrook. I had a conference.'

'When did you last see your wife?'

'This morning.'

'And your children?'

'Last night. I cooked carbonara for everyone,' he says as though this is important.

'And what were their movements today?'

'Kieron had a hospital appointment after lunch. He's seriously ill. He shouldn't be out there.'

'What's wrong with him?'

Aidan explains about PSC.

'And which hospital is Kieron under?'

'Wheatfield General.'

'I'm just going to let the team know this and be prepared that Kieron may need medical attention. I'll be back in a few moments.'

Aidan is left alone. His body taut with nerves, sitting here, doing nothing seems so… helpless.

He drums his fingers on the top of a parcel that has been delivered.

Has *she* taken Connor? He has to find out.

Aidan hears the murmurs of the officers coming from the

lounge as he creeps towards the back door. Gently turns the key and eases down the handle. With one last, guilty look over his shoulder he pads outside, crouching as he runs under the lounge window. He wrenches open his car door and before he can be stopped he drives away from the house – from the crime scene – as fast as he can.

CHAPTER FORTY-NINE

Lucy

Hurry.

I'm driving too fast for this road.

Forty.

Fifty.

My heart thuds painfully in my chest, my throat, my ears. My whole body pulsating with each and every noisy beat. I am incredulous that it hasn't woken Kieron up yet.

Hurry.

My foot squeezes down on the accelerator as I watch the needle on the speedometer creep higher and higher.

Sixty.

Seventy.

I'm in a frenzy.

What if I'm wrong about Connor? Should I have stayed and explained my theories to the police? But it was so frustrating, the slow, methodical way Mel had said they questioned her over Ryan's disappearance. The endless cups of tea and empty reassurances and they haven't found him yet. I don't have time for that.

Hurry.

Seventy-five.

Eighty.

From the centre console my phone begins to ring. Periodically, Aidan has been calling. I glance at the screen to see if it's him again or if it's the police with news of Connor. As I momentarily tear my eyes away from the road the car begins to weave. It pulls violently to the left, dragging me into the oncoming traffic. I press my foot hard against the brake and the car begins to spin, into the path of an oncoming truck.

My hands are tight around the steering wheel.

Connor the only thing on my mind.

Headlights loom towards me.

The blare of a horn.

A bang.

My body jerking forwards.

Kieron's body jerking forward.

I thrust my arm across his chest to protect him.

Spinning. Spinning. Spinning.

Silence.

CHAPTER FIFTY

Aidan

Aidan pulls up outside her house. It's shabby and run-down. Most of the other houses on this street have been boarded up and the ones that haven't have metal shutters on their windows. Connor is here. He has to be.

I have something you want. Clock is ticking.

Her battered white car is parked outside.

He could creep around the back – the element of surprise – but she might have noticed his car is here. It's time to stop playing games.

I'll let u know where & when.

Here.

Now.

He raps on the door.

No reply.

'I know you're there,' he shouts through the letterbox, 'and I'm not leaving.'

He thumps the door with his fists until it opens. She stands before him, there's a slouch in her spine, her usual confidence missing.

'What are you doing here? I told you—'

'And I'm telling you.' He pushes into the hallway and slams the door behind him. 'That I want my son.'

'Your… What are you on about?'

'Connor?' Aidan runs into the lounge – there's a dip in the battered beige sofa cushion where she's been sitting, a spiral of smoke curling from the cigarette which smoulders in an ashtray balanced on the arm. There's scarcely any other furniture. He can see immediately that Connor isn't here. He checks the kitchen with its dated dark wooden cabinets, the avocado bathroom. The whole house feels oppressive. She trails after him, tugging at his arm. 'Aidan, stop. I haven't… I don't…'

He ignores her. Climbs the stairs two at a time. The first bedroom is a mess. Dark purple wallpaper peeling from the walls, double bed crumpled with stained sheets. Clothes heaped onto the worn hessian carpet.

'Aidan, please. We can talk about this.'

He pulls the door to the second room. The last room.

It's locked.

'Open it,' he demands.

'I… Connor isn't here. I don't—'

'Open. It.' He slams his palm against the wood. Glares at her. He's never come close to hitting a woman before but… 'Now.'

Her hand shakes as she pulls a key out of her jeans pocket.

His hand is trembling too as he silently takes it.

CHAPTER FIFTY-ONE

Connor

Connor is inside the house. He turns and meets the ice-cold eyes of his captor; it all seems so obvious now who has taken Ryan and Tyler. Who has taken him.

'Please…' Connor isn't sure what to call him now. Sir? Stephen? Mr Marshall?

His headmaster.

His kidnapper.

His girlfriend's dad.

Except Hailey isn't his girlfriend anymore, is she? Because of what he did, what he, Tyler and Ryan did – she will never be anyone's girlfriend again.

CHAPTER FIFTY-TWO

Lucy

It hurts to breathe.

My chest burns as I gasp for air in short, sharp bursts.

We're okay.

I've never had a blown tyre before and the experience was terrifying.

Slowly, I draw my arm back from Kieron's chest.

He's okay. Briefly, he wakes.

'Are we nearly home?'

'Nearly,' I whisper. 'Go back to sleep.'

Lulled by the rain pattering on the roof, his eyelids flutter and then close.

We narrowly missed an oncoming truck when we spun onto the verge but not one single car has stopped to see if we are okay, if we need help.

Traffic streams past, tyres swooshing over the wet tarmac.

Frustrated tears rise and I swallow hard. There is no time to cry.

My head is woozy, I can't think clearly, stress and fear have rendered me useless.

I could call my breakdown service but how long might they take to arrive? I can't afford to wait. It's all on me.

Connor.

Kieron.

Aidan.

I'm the one who can bring our family back together.

I click open the door, rain gusts into my face as I head to the boot, pull out the jack. My hands curve around the spare tyre. It's heavier than I thought. My arms ache as I drag the tyre out of the boot. I begin to roll it towards the front of the car, my heart is racing, my chest heaving by the time I drop it onto the grass. On my knees, my jeans soaked, I loosen the wheel nuts.

Quick. Quick. Quick.

This delay could be crucial.

Vital.

Life and death.

CHAPTER FIFTY-THREE

Connor

Mr Marshall – for Connor still can't address him as Stephen – turns and locks the front door before pocketing the key.

'You can't just keep me here. Where are Tyler and Ryan? My parents will be looking for me.' His desperate words spew from his lips, his voice ranging from high to low the way it had when he'd reached puberty. He clears his throat. 'You can't just fuc…' He trails off. Ridiculously, he still can't bring himself to swear in front of this man.

Connor draws three discreet breaths, trying to calm himself the way Mum had taught him. Mr Marshall stares at him as though now Connor is here he doesn't quite know what to do with him, or maybe he is savouring it: Connor's fear. Taking some perverse pleasure that Connor is as scared as Hailey was that night. Connor glances around this house which has always made his skin crawl with unease. Years ago, the local kids would freak each other out with stories of the witches they believed lived in this tumbledown Victorian house with its draughty sash windows, the front garden a tangle of weeds as high as their knees. Later, when Mr Marshall had bought it and renovations began on the inside, rotten floorboards piled up outside of the house, the old stained bathroom suite was taken away. Still, no matter how much the house was updated Connor could never relax here, not for fear of monsters but fear of Mr Marshall catching him here on the occasions Hailey had snuck him in. Once he had very nearly been caught.

They had been lying on Hailey's bed. 'Turn the music down,' he had whispered. 'Did you hear something?'

'Dad won't be back for hours.' Hailey's fingers slipped under her bra strap, she slid one down her shoulder, and then the other.

'Seriously.' Connor sat up, reached for his top.

'Chill!' Hailey laughed and padded over to the window. 'There's no car on the drive. Just relax.' She cranked up the volume on her phone. 'Lady Marmalade' streamed from the speakers. She danced for him. Turning her back and glancing over her shoulder. Flashing him a suggestive grin as she raised her arms towards the ceiling, closing her eyes as she swayed her head, feeling the rhythm. This is Connor's favourite memory of her, full of life. Loving life.

Loving him.

There had been a creak.

With a gasp, she cut the music, her eyes wide as they met his. They listened to the footsteps on the stairs. Heard Mr Marshall call, 'Hailey? I'm home.' His voice softer than it was at school but still terrifying. He had dived under the bed and had lain there, limbs stiff, muscles aching for hours until Hailey could sneak him out.

Now, the stairs stretch in front of Connor carpeted in a dark green swirl. Hailey's room is at the back of the house on the right. He wonders what it looks like now. Whether all the posters of *Stranger Things* and *Orange Is the New Black* have been removed. The glittery nail polish and pale pink lip glosses that were strewn over her chest of drawers packed away. There's the lounge to his left. At the back of the house a dining room and a kitchen with steps leading down to the basement. Everywhere has a musty smell. The hallway is gloomy. One of the light bulbs is out. Cobwebs hang from darkened corners. Despite the photos of Hailey still hanging from the walls, it is no longer a home and Connor knows that he and he alone is the cause of this.

He has broken this family.

Now, Connor thinks the monster might be him.

He could run. Shove Mr Marshall out of the way and race towards the back door. Unlock it, smash it even. Scream for help as he pelts across the garden, heading towards the gate. He is younger. Fitter.

He could run.

But he doesn't want to.

Connor turns to face Mr Marshall. Whatever is coming to him is no more than he deserves. His courage catches in his throat as he wonders if Tyler suffered. Ryan. A deep-rooted primal instinct whispering to him, *Find a way out*.

But too late, Connor's shoulder dips under the weight of Mr Marshall's hand and he is propelled forwards. Towards the back of the house.

Towards the basement.

CHAPTER FIFTY-FOUR

Ryan

Now as he lies in the blackness wondering if anyone will ever find him, he casts his mind back to three days ago and one thought, just one thought, whirls around Ryan's head, faster and faster, until he's dizzy with it.

It didn't matter that he knew the driver. That he was cold and tired and was grateful for a lift.

He shouldn't have got in the car.
He shouldn't have got in the car.
He shouldn't have got in the car.

CHAPTER FIFTY-FIVE

Connor

The basement entrance looms – a black hungry mouth – but instead of being propelled down the stairs Mr Marshall gives Connor a short, sharp push between his shoulder blades. The door to the dining room is ajar, from the other side, a soft moaning sound. Connor stops, tries to shuffle backwards, not wanting to confront what he knows awaits him.

Afraid.

'You don't get a choice.' Mr Marshall speaks in the same low tone that he uses in his office when rowdy pupils are sent to him for misbehaving. The steel in his voice far more intimidating than shouting. There had always been an authoritative air surrounding him that made only the most disobedient kids defy him. Connor wasn't one of those kids, but still he doesn't want to obey the command, stretching out his arms, the velvety texture of the deep red wallpaper soft under his fingers.

'Please.' Connor leans backwards, is pushed forwards.

The moaning comes again.

'I want to go home now.' Connor has changed his mind. He doesn't want to be punished. He doesn't want to see what is on the other side of the door.

Who is on the other side of the door.

He wants his mum. Tears bubble in his throat. Tears of sorrow and guilt and a longing to turn back the clock. He swallows and swallows but they keep rising.

Mr Marshall reaches past him and pushes the door open.

The world stops.

Connor is no longer aware of the hand on his shoulder, the breath against his cheek. Black speckles obscure the edges of his vision. He is looking through a telescope of fear, in its centre one perfect round image and it's all Connor can see in the room.

Her.

Hailey.

CHAPTER FIFTY-SIX

Lucy

Am I doing the right thing?

My shoulders scream in pain as I pull the wrench to tighten the wheel nuts. Swollen clouds scud across a slate sky. Rain slaps against my face. I'm sweating. Shivering. Hot and cold.

I bundle the jack back in the boot. Kieron stirs again as I open the door and slip into the car.

Hurry.

I feel so lost.

So scared.

So completely out of my depth.

Am I doing the right thing?

I try to call Aidan, I need him. I can't do this alone.

I just can't.

This time it's him who doesn't answer.

Hurry.

I turn the key in the ignition.

I cannot wait.

I have to save my son.

Am I doing the right thing?

I'm not sure that I am.

CHAPTER FIFTY-SEVEN

Connor

The dining room no longer houses a table and chairs, instead a hospital bed with a solitary seat beside it – waiting for a visitor who never comes.

Him.

Connor stands still.

Sad.

Ashamed. It is painful to look Hailey in the eye but he knows he must face her. Face what he has done.

He is suffocating. It's stifling. An electric heater plugged in next to the gas radiator.

'We have to keep it warm,' Mr Marshall says, noticing Connor wiping his forehead with his sleeve. 'Hailey gets cold. You do when you can't freely move around.' His voice sounds bitter. Sad. Heartbroken. Angry. Everything Connor is and more. Rightfully so.

He takes a step towards her.

Another.

He skirts around the wheelchair, barely aware of the hoist above her bed.

Hailey.

His beautiful, brave girlfriend. She'd rushed into the lake

during his stupid dare when he got into trouble and released his foot from the tangle of weeds and in return the next day he'd... he'd...

Hailey.

He says her name in his head and then under his breath. It no longer tastes sweet upon his tongue.

Her eyes brighten as she sees him. The soft moaning sound spilling from her lips replaced with.

'Conn-Conn-Conn.'

He hesitates. Uncertain and afraid. Unsure whether she is calling him or calling him out. Either way, he turns to Mr Marshall.

'Is she... Can she...' He is met with a silence so solid he can almost touch it. Mr Marshall is not going to make this easy for him and for that he cannot be blamed. Connor should have visited. It shouldn't have taken being shoved inside a boot to bring him here to the girl he had loved with all of his heart. The girl who now causes him to feel... conflicted. Confused.

Responsible.

'I'm so sorry.' Connor states simply the words he should have said weeks ago, but he knows he owes her so much more. He knows she deserves more. He crosses to her and takes her hand. It is heavy in his, dry. Connor remembers the coconut body butter she used to rub into her skin.

'It smells like sun cream,' Connor had once said.

'We should go to the beach,' Hailey had said. 'After our exams. Barbados. The Maldives. Fancy seeing me in a bikini?' She waggled her eyebrows.

'I do fancy seeing you in a bikini.' Connor had nibbled her neck. 'And out of one.'

'Nah. I'm more of a one-piece girl.' Her hand fluttered to her stomach. Connor lifted it away and kissed her fingertips.

'You. Are. Not. Fat,' he said gently.

'Whatever,' she said. 'But shall we go somewhere?'

'Spain is more our budget but what about your dad? I can't see him agreeing.'

'You leave Dad to me. He's a softie, really.'

Connor sees the softness now in Mr Marshall's eyes as he adjusts Hailey's pillows. Picks up her glass of water and gently places the straw between her lips. Hailey jerks her head away.

'Conn-Conn-Conn.'

'She's been asking for you,' Mr Marshall says. 'It's the first thing she's tried to say since…' He clears his throat.

'You could have just told me rather than shoving me into the boot of your car.'

'I didn't exactly plan it. I should be at school, working, but… I don't know, it just all got too much. Would you have come if I had simply asked you?'

'That's not the point. You don't have the right to—'

'My right as a parent is to try to make my child happy—'

'Not by basically kidnapping someone from their own home and—'

'Would. You. Have. Come. Otherwise?' Mr Marshall has his teacher voice back.

Connor looks at Hailey, at his shoes, back at Mr Marshall. 'Probably not.'

'Probably? You've purposefully stayed away.'

'You still went too far.'

'If ever you become a parent, Connor, you'll understand that there is no too far when it comes to your child, but admittedly I was angry Hailey was asking for you and I knew you'd never come. I may have been too rough. That's not an apology though.'

'I didn't expect one.' In truth, Connor didn't feel he deserved one. 'And you're right.' Connor nods. 'I wouldn't have come.' It is a day for honesty.

Finally. He wants to tell the truth. But first there are things he wants to know.

'Are Ryan and Tyler here?' He is certain they are.

'Here?' Mr Marshall casts his gaze around the room. 'Why would they be here?'

'I thought you'd taken them, the way you had me. To punish us. For that night.'

'What, so you think they're locked in the basement or something.' Mr Marshall draws a sharp gasp as he studies Connor's expression. 'You do think I've got them locked in the basement. What do you take me for?'

Mr Marshall fetches the landline and bangs it on Hailey's bedside table. 'You can call the police and tell them what I did to you and they can come and search for Ryan and Tyler again, but I can promise you they are not here. Have never been here.'

Hailey had flinched at the sound of the phone slamming down and Mr Marshall gently leans into her with a smile. 'Sorry. It's okay. I'm not angry.' He curls his fingers and strokes her cheek until her worried face relaxes. He turns back to Connor, this time speaking calmly.

'You're the one Hailey wants. That Hailey needs. You're the one I wanted to come. Hailey should be able to communicate in some form, her medical team can't understand why she isn't, but it's something to do with you. Protecting you, perhaps? She doesn't want to answer my questions. But... that doesn't excuse what I've done so report me if you must.'

Connor stares at the phone but he makes no move to pick it up.

'I just wanted her to see you. For you to see her. To see if she might... Can you just...' Mr Marshall's voice brims with emotion. He crosses to the chair in the corner and straightens a cushion that doesn't need straightening. He tugs the curtains open wider before drawing them closer together again. He pinches his thumb and forefinger against the bridge of his nose before he lowers his hand and turns to Connor again.

'Can you just spend some time with her. Nobody visits anymore. Amber did once, but she found it too hard. People of your age, it's...Well, it's hard for us too. Me. Your mum. She came, of course.'

Connor isn't surprised. He knows Mum blames herself, not for what happened, but for what came after. He didn't know she'd been to see Hailey, but there had been times she'd asked him if he wanted to visit, offering to drive him, but Connor had felt overcome with the weight of expectation. Would a decent boyfriend have stayed? A decent human being?

Yes. He believes so.

'What should I...' Connor sits on the chair.

'Just talk to her. It's so quiet here. Too quiet. Those first few weeks in hospital were easier. It was busy. Always someone coming and going. Now it's just Aileen, her nurse – she's gone for lunch – and me and... I... I was going to give up work, but then I'd be here all day, seeing her. Remembering her. Hoping she'll change back into the person she was, trying to come to terms with the person she is now. Connor. I shouldn't have dragged you from your house but...'

'I needed dragging,' Connor says. 'I've been a coward. Not just because I've avoided Hailey, but I've blamed everyone. I blamed Mum.' He looks directly at Mr Marshall. 'I am so sorry. I want to tell you what happened that night. All of it.'

'And I want to hear it, but first...' Mr Marshall looks pointedly at Hailey. 'I'll give you two some space.'

He leaves the room.

Anxiety nips at Connor. What should he do? Say?

Tentatively, he sits on the edge of the bed and meets the eyes he has lost himself in time and time again.

'Do you... Do you remember the first time we went out?' He recounts the story. They had been studying together at his house when Hailey's stomach had grumbled.

'Got anything to nibble on?' she had asked.

He'd pounded downstairs and opened the fridge. Dad had been shopping the day before and it was laden with food.

'Sorry.' Back upstairs, he'd hovered in his doorway. His fingers nervously pulling the neck of his T-shirt away from his throat. 'The cupboards are bare... Do you fancy going into town and grabbing a pizza or something?' He casually spoke the words he'd been rehearsing all the way up the stairs. *Please say yes. Please say yes.*

'Yeah. I could do with a break.'

His heart swelled.

'Kieron?' He stuck his head into his brother's bedroom. Kieron was sitting on his giant black beanbag, the sides curling around him as he watched *The Big Bang Theory* for the millionth time. He looked so small. Connor hesitated. 'I… I'm going into town for pizza. Do you want…' Kieron's eyes lit up. Connor had been about to ask whether he could bring back some food for his brother, but instead he invited him to come along.

'Cool. Can we have dough balls?'

'You can have what you want.'

'As long as Tyler doesn't eat them all!' Kieron pulled on his hoody.

'I'm not going with Tyler and Ryan. I…' Connor felt his cheeks redden. 'I'm going with Hailey.'

'Like a date?' Kieron fastened his zip.

'Yeah. Well, I dunno. Maybe.'

Kieron sat back down. 'You can't take me along then, idiot.'

'But I…'

'I'm pretty tired anyway.' Kieron faked a yawn.

'Liar.'

'Takes one to know one.' Kieron aimed his remote at his TV and switched it back on. 'It's totally a date. I'm not that hungry anyway.'

Connor lingered for a moment longer. 'I won't be long then.' He sped down the landing, calling to Hailey it was time to leave, before Kieron changed his mind.

They walked into town. Connor deep in thought. Luigi's had candles on the tables. Was that overkill? He wouldn't order garlic bread in case he kissed her later. He would order garlic bread so she didn't guess he was planning on kissing her. It wasn't until they reached the town centre that Connor became aware of the silence between them. The chill of the wind on his arms. Shit. In his haste leaving the house he'd left his jacket at home, his wallet still in its pocket. He patted his jeans. There was a chink of coins. Not enough for a restaurant, not even McDonald's.

'Dunno if I fancy a pizza,' he said. 'How about sharing a bag of chips?'

'I can pa…' Hailey trailed off as she read his embarrassment. 'Sounds great. I'll buy the drinks.'

They sat on the wooden slatted bench in front of the church, large bag of chips hot in Connor's hand, the smell of salt and vinegar mingling with the damp air, the fizz of the Coke as he pulled open the tab.

'Here.' Hailey held out one of her earbuds. 'Don't laugh but this is one of my favourite songs. Blame my dad.'

Connor expected something boring. Slow. Instead, he began to tap his foot; he raised his eyebrows at Hailey.

'It's Ray Charles. "What I'd Say". Dad's a blues fan.'

It surprised Connor that Mr Marshall was a music fan. That he was human.

He placed another chip on his tongue. Wiped his greasy fingers on his jeans. When the song had finished he offered Hailey one of his earbuds. Swiped through his music.

'This is my favourite song. It's old but… not as old as Ray Charles, I guess, but…'

'Oasis!' She nodded approvingly as 'Don't Go Away' began.

They sat on the bench long after the chips had been eaten. Long after the sun had begun to set. Taking it in turns to share their playlists. Getting to know each other through music and lyrics.

Hailey introduced him to Etta James' 'I'd Rather Go Blind'.

Had Connor heard it on the radio he wouldn't have listened, wouldn't have appreciated it, but now, with the sky tinged with pinks and reds, he fell into the soothing tones. Then watched anxiously for Hailey's reaction as he followed it up with The Verve's 'Bittersweet Symphony'.

It is hard for Connor to carry on talking. Remembering. Hailey's face is more relaxed than it had been when he arrived. He wants to share with her the memory of their first kiss. He had walked her home after the batteries on their phones had died but his head, his heart, had still been filled with music. On the corner of her street, she'd raised her face to his expectantly and he had grazed his lips gently against hers, asking a question she had answered by winding her arms around his neck and pulling him closer. He wants to share it all with her but he doesn't. Conscious of Mr Marshall in the next room.

Instead, Connor pulls out his earbuds, untangles them, before realising he doesn't have his phone.

Hailey's eyes flicker to the iPad on the dark mahogany table. He opens the cover and an app opens up. He sees it is to help Hailey communicate. He opens YouTube and searches for the song he has listened to endlessly since that first night.

'Don't Go Away'.

Her lips flutter a brief smile as he finds it.

Gently, he holds an earbud against her ear, taking the other for himself. They listen together, in silence, his hand on hers.

After the song has ended, her fingers gently squeeze his and this one small gesture brings tears to his eyes. He stands but doesn't move towards the door, his feet reluctant to walk away from her. Away from the hope he feels for the first time in such a long time.

'I'll see you soon,' he promises, knowing that he will come back, not as her boyfriend but as something else, if he is still welcome once he has told Mr Marshall the truth.

It is time.

He walks slowly down the hallway. Eyes flickering towards the entrance of the basement. How could he ever have thought that Tyler and Ryan were down there?

'Mr Marshall?' he calls. 'I'm ready to talk.'

CHAPTER FIFTY-EIGHT

Ryan

Ryan cannot see. He cannot speak.

But he can hear.

He's been listening to the rhythmic drip-drip-drip for what seems like hours, days even. He wonders if a tap has been left on or if it's raining. It could be sunny or stormy, day or night, he has no way of knowing.

Drip.

Drip.

Drip.

He remembers Tyler telling him and Connor about water torture. There was this experiment where water was dripped onto a victim's forehead with an intent to wear away the skin, the brain, to cause death.

It didn't work.

But he remembers what came after, when they randomized the fall of the drops creating an inconsistent pattern. This induced a psychotic break in less than twenty hours.

He wonders if that would have been the case if the victim could have only heard them rather than felt them. If, left for long enough, he'll eventually go insane.

Drip.

Drip.

Drip.

Ryan's body begins to shake with a silent laugh.

He's already going mad.

And then he's shaking with sobs he can't release.

Drip.

Drip.

Drip.

He doesn't know how much more he can take.

CHAPTER FIFTY-NINE

Connor

Connor leaves the warmth of Hailey's room. Shivers as he reaches the kitchen.

Mr Marshall is sipping tea from a mug with 'World's Best Dad' written on it. Connor doesn't want to face this broken man and tell him what really happened to his daughter, but he tells himself that he can.

He must.

There's an empty chair opposite Mr Marshall – Hailey's chair – and Connor slides onto it, uninvited. What he has to say won't be quick and nerves have turned his knees to rubber. Mr Marshall takes another sip of his drink and Connor sees the tremor of his hand.

'Is Hailey—'

'No questions.' The dulcet tone Mr Marshall had used in front of Hailey has vanished. 'It's time for answers.'

Connor's throat is dry but he isn't offered a drink. He closes his eyes, travelling back to that night. The memories good and bad tumble into the forefront of his mind and Connor is unsure where to start so he begins at the only place he can.

The first dare.

Mr Marshall doesn't speak. Doesn't react as Connor relays

Tyler's and Ryan's dare. Then Connor falteringly speaks of his own experience, of Hailey braving the freezing water to save him, of his fear when she disappeared under the water, his desperation as he tried to find her. The relief when she broke free of the surface coughing and spluttering and he realized she was okay.

Then she was okay…

Mr Marshall's hand tightens around the handle of his mug. Connor touches his throat – he can almost feel the man's hands there. He wouldn't blame him. Still Mr Marshall doesn't talk. He is waiting, waiting for Connor to get to the point. And at last he does.

It was the final evening of the residential. Next to Connor, Hailey's thigh pressed against his under the table. She speared one of his chips with his fork and he rolled his eyes although he wasn't annoyed.

'Stop ordering salad and nicking my chips.'

'The only thing I want to steal is your heart.' Hailey fluttered her lashes.

'Gross. Get a room.' Tyler mimed sticking his fingers down his throat.

'Speaking of rooms…' Connor glanced around the room, placing the teachers. 'We wouldn't mind the dorm to ourselves for a bit tonight.' Now they'd all completed their dares, Connor wanted the final night to be just him and Hailey.

'How long did you want the room for? Five minutes okay? Or didn't you want to do it twice?' Tyler gave a cartoon waggle of his eyebrows.

Connor placed his hand on Hailey's knee and gave it a squeeze that said 'sorry my mate is a dick' and in return she placed her hand over his and pressed a 'that's why he's no hope of ever getting laid' into his fingers.

'Anyway, it's our last night,' Tyler said. 'Hailey's turn.'

'Hailey's turn for… no! Not after last night. We could both have drowned. Don't be a prick, Tyler.'

'I'm not! She's an honorary member of our little gang—'

'We're not a gang. You make us sound about six. Or the Mafia. She—'

'Can you stop talking about me as though I'm not here. I'll do your stupid dare and then you let us have the room. Deal?'

'Deal.' Tyler shook her hand.

Already Connor felt uneasy, a sense of foreboding looming.

The inky sky was popping with stars, the moon casting enough light to see the entrance of the cave gaping its carnivorous jaws wide. Connor stared into the blackness.

'So, how do you fancy being underground without a light?' Tyler asked.

'No fucking way.' Connor yanked Hailey's hand.

'You haven't even heard the rest yet!' Tyler said.

'She's not doing it.'

'Enough with the "she".' Hailey pulled away from Connor. 'I can make up my own mind.'

'I don't like this either,' Ryan said. 'There's one hundred and twenty metres of tunnel down there. Doing something for the buzz is one thing but this is reckless, Tyler.'

'It isn't. I don't expect Hailey to wander through the caves alone.' He turned to Hailey. 'Your challenge, my lady, if you choose to accept it, is for us to lower you down on a rope, without a head torch. After fifteen minutes we bring you back up.'

'No.' Connor was adamant. Hailey was scared of the dark.

'Wait.' Hailey touched his arm to silence him. 'So… I just reach the bottom and stay there?' she asks Tyler. 'I don't need to go into the caves?'

'Nope,' Tyler said.

'And you three will wait here?'

'Yep.'

'And if I want to come back up, you'll fetch me out.'

'You have my word.' Tyler placed a palm across his heart.

'It sounds pretty simple to me,' Hailey said, but there was a touch of apprehension in her voice.

'It is.' Tyler grinned. 'What could possibly go wrong?'

Tyler was more safety conscious than Connor had expected him to be. For all the talk of treating Hailey as one of the boys, he took extra care fastening the rope around a tree. Making sure Hailey had her harness on correctly. Still, Connor didn't want Hailey to do it.

'Where's the helmet?' he asked.

'I couldn't get one but she's not going into the tunnels so there'll be nothing for her to bang her head on.'

Connor wasn't happy. They stood apart from Ryan and Tyler. 'Listen.' He placed his hands on her shoulders. Could feel the tremble in her body. 'You have nothing to prove.'

'Not to you maybe.' She flashed a glance at the other boys. 'Not to anyone.'

'I want your friends to like me. I know you're not spending as much time with them because of me and—'

'They do like you, and even if they didn't, I wouldn't care. I. Like. You.' Connor rubbed his nose against hers.

'Just like?'

Connor hesitated. He felt the words, he felt them in his heart, but he'd never said them. 'More than like. Look, Hailey. We're not kids and this stupid dare stuff is just something we did when we were bored and now… I'd rather just be with you. Don't feel pressured.'

Hailey's face was pale, worried.

'Decision time!' Tyler said. Ryan's eyes were fixed on her. She turned to him. 'I'm not sure I can do this,' she whispered.

'You can.' He believed she could do anything. 'But that doesn't mean you should. Let's just go—'

'Fifteen minutes.' She huffed out air. 'Fifteen minutes and then we get the room. And then you—' she touched his chest with her index finger '—get me.'

A slow smile crept over Connor's face.

'Are you sure?'

'Yes. Right, let's get this done.' She wrapped her arms around Connor's neck and pressed the body she had promised him against his. 'I love you,' she whispered in his ear.

Oh God. Why hadn't he said that back to her? The memory haunts him over and over. He replays it a million different ways. Sometimes he takes her hand and runs. Sometimes he goes down the tunnel with her, but always, always he says, 'I love you,' back to her because those words, he really, really felt them.

Connor's breath had escaped his mouth in a tiny white cloud. He wrapped his arms around his chest and stamped his feet.

'You okay, babe?' he shouted down the hole. 'She must be freezing. We should bring her up before she gets hypothermia.'

Tyler checked his watch. 'Chill. She's only got three minutes left.'

'I'm fine.' Hailey's faint reply echoed towards them. Connor was still annoyed that Tyler had pressured Hailey into this, disappointed with himself for allowing it to happen, but amongst his simmering anger was a pride that Hailey hadn't shown any fear as she was lowered down the hole, her eyes locked on to his.

'Okay. Let's get her up,' Tyler said. 'Well done, Hailey.'

Now, Connor pauses in his story. Fiddles with the neck of his T-shirt, all the time avoiding Mr Marshall's eye. That should have been the end of the events that night. They should all have gone back to the dorm and slept. As Tyler said to Hailey, it should have been all over.

But it wasn't.

He takes a deep breath and continues to talk.

CHAPTER SIXTY

Aidan

This is the only room he hasn't been into in her house and Aidan is certain Connor will be inside it. The key is stiff in the lock, it squeaks as Aidan twists it. His palm is slippery as he turns the handle.

'Wait.' Her fingers enclose his arm before he can push the door open. 'Don't judge me,' she implores. He's never heard her sound so… desolate and this amplifies the fear that's already squirming around his stomach.

His mouth is dry. It's hard to swallow as he steps inside the room.

The curtains are drawn, blocking out all the light except a thin vertical strip where the material doesn't quite meet.

His fingers fumble around the wall until he finds a switch and bright, electric light fills the room.

For a second he can't move. He's shocked.

Angry.

Scared.

Everything.

His eyes drawn to one thing only. In a mound in the corner of the room.

'My God. What have you done?' He rushes inside.

'Please.' She's right behind him. 'I know I've done a terrible thing but… don't tell anyone.'

He picks up a top from the pile on the floor.

A top he recognizes.

'What have you done?' he asks again as he turns to her. It is only then he notices what else is in the room.

Who else is in the room.

CHAPTER SIXTY-ONE

Connor

Hailey had completed her fifteen minutes in the dark and the boys were pulling the rope when there was a catch. A muffled shout. Connor loosened his grip but Tyler and Ryan yanked harder.

Connor yelled at the others to stop pulling. Simultaneously, they obeyed, the rope sliding through their hands, Hailey plummeting back down inside the hole.

A scream.

Connor can still hear that scream.

Her pain.

Her terror.

Freaking out, he reached for the rope. Began to pull her up again. Fearing she was badly hurt but taking an odd comfort from her crying. If she was conscious she had to be okay.

Didn't she?

A screaming Hailey emerged from the hole. Her tear-streaked face deathly pale. She was wailing. Connor's fear intensified. She'd never show emotion in front of Tyler and Ryan unless something was really wrong.

'What's happened?' Connor dropped to his knees and took her hands in his.

She couldn't speak through her hiccupy sobs but when Tyler shoved his hands into her armpits and dragged her the rest of the way out, she howled in pain. It was then Connor noticed the flop of her right leg.

'Wait!' Gently, he stroked her hair. 'Tell me where you hurt.'

'My… my leg.'

'Anywhere else? Did you hit your head?' It was stupid to have sent her down there without a helmet. It was stupid to have sent her down there at all.

'No.'

'Can you stand?' Ryan asked.

She tried to move, vomited.

'Hailey?'

Her eyes rolled, the whites bright in the darkness. She was drifting in and out of consciousness.

'I don't have a signal to call for help.' Ryan stuffed his phone back into his pocket. 'I'll run back to the dorm. Find my dad or Mr Marshall.'

'He's going to kill us,' Tyler moaned.

'Hailey.' Connor patted her cheek. 'Stay with me.'

Her eyes flickered open. But she didn't speak. Couldn't speak. She'd stopped crying. Connor knew she was in shock.

'Help will be here really soon.'

Her eyes flickered open. 'Connor.' Her voice was rough.

'Shh. You don't have to talk.'

'God, I am so sorry, Hailey.' Tyler was close to tears. 'I'm such a dick. I—'

'Take… take the harness off me.' The pain was etched onto

Hailey's face as she spoke falteringly. 'Dad will have a fit if he knows what happened. We can say we were all out for a walk and I caught my foot in a pothole and fell.'

'Shh.' If he could, Connor would have traded places with her in an instant. 'Don't worry about that now, it doesn't matter.'

'It matters to me. I won't be allowed to see you again if you get the blame and we'll miss the end-of-year ball.'

'Hailey…' Connor's throat closed. She must be in unimaginable pain but she was still thinking of him. Of them.

Tyler was already gently unfastening the harness, easing it off. She winced although he was barely touching her. 'Right, we're agreed we're going to stick to the same story. We took a walk after dinner and Hailey stumbled and fell awkwardly. I'm going to dump this.' He held the harness in his hands and ran.

And then there were two.

'Hailey…' Connor swallowed hard. Saw she was slipping away again and knew he had to speak quickly. Three words. How long could it take to say? How much it would mean. 'I lov—' But there was a shout. A flash of torchlight. The sound of footsteps on damp grass.

Connor shifted to make room for Mr Marshall as his knees seemed to break and he almost fell to the ground.

'Hailey!' His usually calm voice was frantic. 'Hailey!'

She opened her eyes. 'Daddy… we went for a walk and I tripped over a pothole. My leg…'

He felt Ryan watching him, gathering the gist of what was going on. Fergus standing beside him, a worried expression on his face.

Hailey had vomited again by the time the ambulance arrived. Flashing blue lights intermittently illuminating the hills. Connor told the paramedic he thought she was sick from the pain; she hadn't hit her head. She was swiftly, efficiently placed in the back of the ambulance and Connor was left alone, the blackness swallowing him whole as the blue flash of light faded away.

Back at the dorm he made a phone call. 'Mum?'

'What's happened?' She detected the distress in his voice.

'It's Hailey, she's… she's hurt. Mum, it's all my fault, we—'

'Is she breathing? Have you called for help?'

'Yeah, she's gone off in an ambulance. It's her leg. I'm pretty sure it's broken.'

'She'll probably be brought here. We're the nearest orthopaedic department to the residential centre. I'm just clocking off. Do you want me to come and fetch you?'

'No. Can you stay there and look after her?'

'Of course. Connor, why don't you get a cab here? I'll leave you some cash on A and E reception.'

The hospital was exactly the same as it had always been. Hot. Noisy. Smelling of bleach and disinfectant although no amount of cleaning could hide the shabbiness. The years of wear and tear. St Thomas's was due to be closed at the end of the month and it already had an aura of decay and neglect. Many times Connor had sat on one of the hard, grey plastic chairs waiting for his mum to finish her shift, which often overran. He'd never really thought about the people surrounding him, anxiously waiting for news of a loved one.

Praying that when it came it would be good, expecting the worst. Now he was the one with the cup of hot chocolate his mum had thrust towards him, forming a skin as he left it to grow cold, not aware if he was hungry, thirsty. Not needing anything but news that Hailey was, or that she would be, okay.

His mum had reassured him when he arrived. 'She's broken her femur, that's the thigh bone. It's a transverse fracture so the break is a clean horizontal line, which is relatively uncomplicated to repair, but we need to insert a rod into the length of the bone with screws above and below to hold it into place.'

'Will she...' Dance. Run. Still love him.

'She should be fine, in time. It can take up to six months to set properly but she's young and healthy. Too young really to have sustained an injury like this purely by falling over a pot-hole.' His mum waits for Connor to fill in the gaps. He doesn't.

'Usually it takes a fair bit of strength to snap a femur.'

Like being dropped from a height, Connor thought, but he remained silent. Mum went on, 'They're pretty strong. We'll check if Hailey has any underlying problems that might have weakened her bones. She shouldn't have at her age but it's not unheard of.'

'But it will heal?'

'Yes. There's a chance that if it isn't set properly one leg will become shorter than the other which can cause an imbalance in the skeleton and lead to hip or knee pain later but I'm carrying out the surgery so...'

Relief flooded through Connor. Any doubts he had that something might go wrong vanished.

His mum was calm. Capable. Confident.

She'd never let him down.

It was hours of waiting. Time bent and blurred. Occasionally, Connor went for a walk to burn off his nervous energy but never too far in case news of Hailey came.

Once, he passed the visitors' room. He hesitated. Through the Venetian blinds he could make out Mr Marshall hunched in a chair, elbows on knees, his head in his hands. Fingers of pity strummed Connor's stomach muscles.

'I'm sorry, I'm sorry,' he blurted out to Mr Marshall as he entered the room. Snot and tears had clogged his throat. His eyes, two swollen slits. 'I'm sorry.'

Mr Marshall glared at him and it was Connor's dad who led him away, throwing a glance over his shoulder at the man who stood broken and alone.

'I can't imagine…' Dad shook his head. He didn't say anything else. Connor had no idea whether he was angry or sad. Resentful or relieved. Whether Dad felt all of it or none of it.

But still, Connor had had the childish faith that his mum could fix this. His mum could make everything better. It was a leg.

A broken leg.

Nothing more, something easily fixed, so Connor didn't know why he felt a morbid apprehension when his mum finally stood in front of him, but he did.

CHAPTER SIXTY-TWO

Lucy

I'm here.

Am I doing the right thing?

Slowly, slowly, I climb out of the car. Above me the dark grey sky is bursting with heavy rain clouds. Autumn leaves whirl around my feet as a chill wind whips my hair around my face. I barely register the cold because my blood is anxious-hot, running through my veins. My heart bouncing wildly in my chest. Fight or flight. But I have to do this.

I have to.

For my son.

Am I doing the right thing?

It is hard to put one foot in front of the other, as though my feet are no longer controlled by me. My body numb with fear.

Am I doing the right thing?

I'm here.

And I have never felt so scared.

CHAPTER SIXTY-THREE

Connor

'Surgery went very well.' Connor's mum gave a tired smile. 'You won't be able to see Hailey tonight, she needs to rest, but perhaps you can visit tomorrow, depending on whether her father let's you see her.'

'Does he… Is he…' Connor wasn't entirely sure what he was trying to ask.

'He's with her now. Refusing to go home. Connor… I've had to be honest and tell him it would be quite rare to break a femur in the circumstances you've described.'

'So… what will happen now?' Connor expected the cold steel of handcuffs on his wrists. He was unsure what his crime was but he felt the guilt nevertheless. 'Will the police…' He can't finish his sentence. He shouldn't be thinking of himself right now.

'The police haven't been called. They won't be unless a law has been broken. If you're all saying, including Hailey, that she stumbled over a pothole then no one is at fault. If she changes her story, if it turns out you were able to easily access somewhere you shouldn't have been, then the centre will potentially be investigated for breaching health and safety regulations, but I really can't see it being taken any further. I'd say in the great scheme of things you've all been very lucky.' She gave Connor that look. The look he'd seen a thousand times before. The 'I know you've been eating biscuits before dinner' look. The 'I know it was you who broke my favourite mug' look. The look that told him she knew that he was lying. The look that always shamed him.

The following morning, Mum took his hand. He couldn't remember the last time she'd done that, not since he'd begun shaking her off after he'd left primary.

'Mum?'

He looked to her to tell him everything was all right even though he knew from the expression on her face, from the way she was squeezing his fingers, that it wasn't.

'Mum?' he asked again, more urgently this time.

'I'm so sorry, Connor. There's… there's no easy way to say this.' But she didn't say anything.

He searched his mum's face for a clue both wanting and not wanting to know.

'Hailey…' Mum faltered. 'Hailey had a stroke last night. She had an underlying condition that I didn't know about—'

'But she's okay, right?'

'It was quite severe, Connor.'

'She's… she's not…'

Mum's hand was clammy around his. 'She's alive, but in intensive care. She's unconscious right now. It's hard to ascertain the extent of any… damage until she wakes up. If she wakes up. Connor, I am so, so sorry.' Connor couldn't remember the last time he'd seen his mum cry. She swiped away her tears.

'Why are you so sorry? Is this your fault?' He lashed out, angry and afraid.

'No. But… she had high blood pressure and I didn't know at the time that hypertension ran in her family. It's usual for patients scared and in pain to have high blood pressure. I didn't think it was odd. Had I known that Hailey had a family history of hypertension I might have… but unfortunately there's no predicting this sort of complication.'

'It's not a fucking complication! This is Hailey's life!' Connor snatched his hand away. 'You were her surgeon!' Connor passed the baton of blame, unable to bear the weight of it any longer.

'Connor… I… I did everything right. I promise you—'

'Did you, though?' He narrowed his eyes. Lowered his voice. 'You were tired. You should have finished your shift. You chose to stay—'

'You asked me to!'

'You could have said no.'

The words hung between them.

Mum's eyes were bloodshot, ringed with dark circles. She looked awful, but she could never look as awful as Connor felt in that moment. His relationship with his girlfriend was irrevocably altered. His relationship with his mum irrevocably altered. In his mind, she was no longer someone he could rely on and he felt furious at her for that, for shattering his sense of childhood safety as much as anything else.

'If she dies, it's your fault. Some fucking doctor you are. I should have known better than to ask you to look after Hailey. Just look at Kieron! You can't even save your own son. You couldn't even save your own—'

'Stop. Please.' Mum held up a hand as though she could prevent the vicious words from reaching her but it was too late. Connor had said things that could never be unsaid. Mum had immediately resigned and he'd felt even worse. He had so much to apologize for. So many people to apologize to. He had tried to start with Hailey.

'I write to Hailey sometimes,' he tells Mr Marshall now, thinking of the 'I have a confession' messages he'd send on Facebook Messenger despite knowing she can't read them, can't answer. 'I tell her I'm sorry and I tell her that if I hadn't asked Mum to operate she might have been okay. The accident was my fault and the operation was too. I asked Mum to be her surgeon.'

Mr Marshall shakes his head. 'We could hardly have left her with a broken femur, could we?'

'Suppose not. But…' Connor doesn't know how to express all the things he wants to say. If he's honest with himself, it isn't only the guilt of knowing it is all his fault that has kept him away. He'd watched victims of strokes on YouTube. Seen drooping faces, slurred speech, jerky movements, and he couldn't handle seeing his beautiful Hailey like that. Despite Mum's concerns that Hailey might not wake up, she did and Connor had felt a skip of elation before Mum explained that she was unable to talk or walk. There would be a period of time where she'd improve but she couldn't predict to what extent. What lasting damage there might be. He'd come once. Stood outside of the house, hand fisted, poised to knock, but he couldn't. He just couldn't.

'Will she get any better?' Connor asks.

'I'm always hopeful,' says Mr Marshall. 'But the weeks roll by and it looks less likely she'll improve. There's only so many times I can be told "Don't get your hopes up" but I do. I read something into everything. Did she smile? Try to sit up?' He lowers his voice. 'I blame myself; if the trip had been better supervised...'

'We'd still have found a way to get out. We wanted to.'

'And that,' Mr Marshall says, 'sums everything up really. Hailey wouldn't have been forced into doing something she didn't want to. Were you stupid? Yes. Irresponsible? Yes. Did you make her agree to that preposterous dare? No.'

For the first time in months, a smidgen of weight lifts from Connor's shoulders.

'We all have things we are guilty of,' Mr Marshall says. 'How's your head? I... I apologize for being so rough with you.'

'I'm glad you brought me here,' Connor says, truthfully. 'I'm glad I've told what happened that night.'

'Me too and, if anything,' Mr Marshall says, 'it sounds as though you tried to stop her.'

'Yeah but... I didn't try hard enough.'

'That daughter of mine is strong-willed.' He clears the emotion from his throat. 'She was pleased to see you today. I could tell.' He looks expectantly at Connor.

'I will come back,' he says.

Before Mr Marshall can answer, the doorbell rings.

Connor leans back in his chair. Listens as Mr Marshall traipses down the hallway, creaks open the front door. He hears the low murmur of voices. The close of the door. Voices growing louder, he recognizes one of the speakers as PC Amin who had interviewed him after Ryan went missing.

'This is the door to the basement?' He hears the policeman say. 'Last time you said it was being damp-proofed and we couldn't look down there. We'd like to look now, Mr Marshall.'

'It's still—'

'We could come back with a warrant.'

'On what grounds? I don't—'

'Could you open the door please?'

A ripple of heat shuddered through Connor.

What has Mr Marshall done?

CHAPTER SIXTY-FOUR

Ryan

Footsteps. Ryan hears footsteps.
Please save me. Please save me. Please save me.

CHAPTER SIXTY-FIVE

Connor

Connor grasps the edge of the table waiting for a 'We've found the boys!' cry to drift up from the basement. But it doesn't.

Instead, after a period of silence, voices approach the kitchen.

'Thanks for letting us have another look around, Mr Marshall,' says a woman. 'Sorry your basement is in such a state.'

'That's what you get with older properties,' Mr Marshall replies. 'Least of my worries, really.'

'Of course. PC Amin won't take too long looking upstairs. I'm sorry but with Ryan still—'

'Don't apologize. Look, here's Connor. Safe and sound.'

Connor loosens his fingers.

'Connor.' The policewoman's voice is soft but her eyes are hard as they flicker around the kitchen before settling on him. 'I'm PC Leighton. Your mum reported you missing. Your dad's been going frantic. Can you tell me what you're doing here?'

'I came to see Hailey.' Connor doesn't hesitate.

'And you came here of your own volition?'

'Yes.'

'You weren't forced in any way?'

'No.'

'Right.' She doesn't believe him, Connor can tell.

'You left a bit of a mess at home.' She studies his face.

At first, Connor thinks she means his bedroom. His face flames – there are dirty socks, his boxers strewn over the carpet. The half-empty pizza box abandoned on the floor. But the side of his head throbs a reminder of the scuffle in his hallway: the broken vase; his smashed phone.

'I was running for the door, a parcel was delivered, and I knocked over the table and hit my head. I should have cleared up the mess. I'm sorry if I worried anyone. Wasted your time.'

PC Amin pokes his head into the kitchen. 'Nothing upstairs. I'll radio in.'

PC Leighton nods as she steps out into the hallway before turning back to Connor. 'You must have left in a hurry. What was the urgency?'

Now Connor has told his story once he thinks he should again. It will be easier this time. 'I wanted to tell Mr Marshall the truth that—'

'The truth is…' Mr Marshall cut in. 'Is that Connor hasn't visited Hailey since the accident and suddenly had the urge to. He rushed here before he could change his mind. I've told him not to blame himself. It's been difficult for us all, but I don't hold him accountable, any more than he holds me accountable.'

Connor's eyes meet his head teacher's and he knows that this is more than Mr Marshall saving his own skin. More than him not wanting Connor to relay how he really came to be here. He really doesn't blame Connor and Connor wonders whether he should stop blaming himself. Certainly he should stop blaming his mum. He's made it so difficult for her and after everything she's been through. He wants to see her. To tell her how sorry he is. She has so much to worry about with Kieron. So much guilt over Hailey. He shouldn't have added to it.

'Is my mum angry?' he asks.

'Worried like any mother would be. You didn't leave a note? No, of course you didn't.' She sighs the sigh of a parent. 'I'll ring your parents, tell them you've been found safe and sound. It's all going on today.' She sighs again as she punches numbers into her phone, presses it against her ear. She leaves a message for his mum, and then his dad.

'Neither of them are picking up. We'll take you home in a few minutes.'

PC Amin clatters into the kitchen. 'I saw… in the next room… your daughter. How is she?'

'She's better for seeing young Connor. She's been scant of visitors, I'm afraid.'

'You couldn't persuade her mum to come then?' PC Leighton blurts. 'Sorry, I didn't meant to mention—'

'But Hailey's mum is… dead. She's dead,' Connor says with certainty. Hailey wouldn't have made up anything so awful. 'Mr Marshall?'

Mr Marshall averts his eyes and Connor notices the red flush travelling up his neck. Doubt niggles at him. 'She is dead, isn't she?' But this time it's a question, not a statement. Hailey can't have lied to him. She just wouldn't.

'No. She isn't,' Mr Marshall says quietly.

'But… but…' Connor flounders, trying to make sense of it all until a thought occurs to him. 'Does Hailey know she's alive?'

'No.' Mr Marshall fixes Connor with a stony stare. He's back. The gentle father disappearing and in his place the stern headmaster Connor knows and fears. 'Don't judge me, boy. You've no idea what I've been through.'

'What you've been through?' Connor doesn't check himself. He doesn't care that his voice is raised. That his fists are clenched. 'You've let Hailey believe her mum died.'

'It was kinder that way.'

'I don't know ho—'

'It's none of your business.' Mr Marshall takes a step towards Connor but Connor stands his ground, fury rooting him to the spot.

'Let's all calm down.' PC Amin steps between them. 'Connor, Hailey's mum was… troubled.'

'A junkie, if you must know. She had a choice between her child and drugs.'

Connor turns this over in his mind. Today he'd learned a lesson that he'd always been too quick to judge. To blame.

But still he says, 'You could have helped her?'

'The only person who can help an addict is an addict. They have to want to change. She could have cleaned up. Come back. But she never did.'

'But now?' Connor gestures vaguely towards the wall separating them from Hailey. 'Does she know about… now?'

'Yes,' Mr Marshall says. 'PC Leighton helped me to track her down.'

'I have a daughter,' PC Leighton says. 'And I can't imagine not being in her life. I wanted to help.'

'I saw her,' Mr Marshall says. 'And she played the concerned mother, asking questions. I thought… I thought she was interested in Hailey but all she was interested in was who was at fault.'

'She must be angry.' Connor knew if anything happened to him his mum would fight for the truth. Fight to do whatever she could to help.

'It isn't anger, Connor. It's greed. She's bitter about the way her life has turned out and wanted to know if we could claim compensation. Place the blame on somebody. Me. The school. She didn't care if I lost my job, if I couldn't support Hailey. Still, for all her talk she hasn't started proceedings. She'll never pull herself together enough to convince a solicitor to take the case. There isn't even a case. Every now and then I see her car parked in front of the house and I think she wants to see Hailey but then she drives away and I get another message about money.'

'But…' Connor can't process this. She doesn't want to see her own daughter.

'Hailey's mum didn't once go to the hospital or even telephoned to ask how she is,' PC Leighton says gently. 'It might be hard for you to understand but sometimes there are things we are better off not knowing. Telling Hailey her mum was alive, living close by but choosing not to be part of her daughter's life. How do you think she'd have felt?'

Rejected.

Angry.

Sad.

'Suppose.' Connor says. 'Could she have had something to do with… you know, Tyler and Ryan?'

PC Leighton shakes her head. 'No, Connor. We have spoken to Julie. She has an alibi and we checked on CCTV that her car is where she said it would be. We really don't think she's capable.'

'Her car…' A thought occurs to Connor. 'What colour is it?'

'White. Why?'

Connor's stomach sinks. 'Do you have a picture of Julie?'

PC Leighton fiddles with her phone before she produces a photo.

It's the woman from the graveyard.

The woman who had approached him after finding his scarf. Connor remembers the flicker of recognition when he had met her. He'd thought he must have seen her there before but it wasn't there, he recognized her from the grainy, tattered photo that Hailey kept in the bottom of her drawer. She was older, of course, ravaged by time and drugs but her eyes… Hailey's eyes. The same green.

'Connor?' Mr Marshall clicks his fingers and Connor drifts back to the now where Hailey's mum is still alive and she had befriended him and Tyler and Ryan. He can hear his own heartbeat, the ringing in his ears as though he's back in the lake, back underwater.

She must have taken them.

She must be planning on taking him next.

'Have you met Julie?' he is asked.

'Yes.' He feels a stab of hot fear. 'Yes. We all have.'

CHAPTER SIXTY-SIX

Ryan

Three Days Ago

The rain was sheeting down harder, water seeping through Ryan's thin jacket. He increased his pace, feet splashing through puddles, the bottom of his jeans sodden. It was early but such a miserable evening that everywhere was deserted. Still, he didn't mind getting wet, it would be worth it to see Kieron back at home, happy. He'd been almost as worried as Connor while Kieron had been in the hospital.

The houses stood stiffly at the side of the pavement. Streaks of light shining through the gaps in the curtains. Rooms awash with the blue glow of TVs. It was like the depth of winter, not September. Yesterday had been glorious, T-shirt and shorts weather, now he wished he had his thicker coat, gloves. Ryan hated autumn. It felt like the end of something. He liked the sunshine. Long summer evenings hanging out with Tyler and Connor. Sitting in the beer garden of the Dog and Duck, whose staff had stopped asking for ID once Tyler hit six foot last year, sipping too sweet cider, the fizz of bubbles in his nose, the stickiness coating the inside of his mouth. Hands dipping into bags of Scampi Fries, fingertips tinged orange.

At the thought of Tyler, a shiver snaked down his spine.

Not only from the cold, but the thought that his friend had been walking these same streets days ago, but he had never made it home. Where was he? It was difficult to believe he'd been snatched, Tyler was the biggest of their friendship group. Tall. Solid. Ryan recalls movies he has seen, children bundled into the back of vans kicking and screaming. Nobody would mistake Tyler for a child.

What had happened to him?

Suddenly the rain turned to hail. Dozens of tiny balls of ice striking Ryan's neck – miniature hammers – with force.

Ryan sheltered in the doorway of Waterstones. The window displayed the latest best-selling serial killer novel. Why would anyone want to read anything so dark? Ryan looked at the cover while he waited for the hail to slow, the glint of the serrated knife dripping blood. He turned away but his head was already full of thoughts of knives and vans and blood.

What had happened to Tyler?

He shoved his hand inside his pocket for his phone. He'd call his mum to pick him up.

Before he could dial, there was the shine of headlights coming round the corner, the splash of tyres on tarmac, the dark shape of a car, which passed him, slowed.

Stopped.

Its reverse lights glowed as it backed up. Ryan pressed his spine against the doorway. Looked away, determined not to make eye contact.

The buzz of the window lowering.

'Ryan?'

He looked up.

'Thought it was you. You okay?' she asked. 'Want a lift?'

He wiped the rain from his eyes. 'Umm. Yeah.' He dashed to the car and clicked open the door. 'Thanks.'

There was a song playing, he didn't take much notice until it ended and began to play again.

Odd.

'Here.' She passed him a blanket. 'Dry yourself off a bit.'

He leaned forward and draped his head in the blanket. Rubbed furiously at the freezing dampness. He dabbed the back of his neck, his chest, trying to absorb as much of the water as he could.

The song finished.

He turned to her but before he could make a joke about it, it started again.

She softly sang along and he didn't know why, but unease crept down his spine.

He looked out of the window. 'This is a weird way to come.'

'There's a diversion. So how was your day at school?'

'Was all right.' He shrugged. 'Got an essay to do but I've already finished it.'

It was hot in the car. Steamy. He stared out of the window, his breath misting the glass. Fleetingly, he thought about writing 'HELP' on the window but then swallowed down a laugh at his own ridiculousness. He'd freaked himself out with the novel cover, the dark, Tyler going missing. Since he was small his mum had told him not to get into cars – stranger danger – but this wasn't a stranger.

Why was he so uncomfortable? He couldn't pinpoint a reason. He sat back. Tried to relax.

They turned left. Even if there were roadworks, surely they should be going right?

He glanced at her. There was something very odd about her. Very wrong.

The car made an abrupt stop.

'A flat tyre. That's all I need. Help me change it?'

She got out of the car and Ryan did the same. The rain pelting down. While she rummaged in the boot, he squinted through the gloom at each tyre in turn.

'I don't see that any of them are flat?' he said, puzzled.

'No. They're not.' He hadn't heard her footsteps behind him. He turned.

Suddenly, he knew what madness looked like. He was staring it straight in the eyes.

CHAPTER SIXTY-SEVEN

Aidan

Seven weeks before

It had been gloriously hot the first time Aidan met Julie, Hailey's mum. Sleeves-rolled-up-shirt-soaked-through-with-sweat weather. Clear blue skies and a beaming sun lulling him into a false sense of security that things were going to get better.

Aidan had left the practice through the fire exit at the back. It was a busy time of year for a vet. Clients not realizing that for animals heat could be fatal. The weather could be cruel. Dangerous.

Not as dangerous as Julie.

Aidan had just got into his truck when she clambered out of her car and strode across the car park, climbing onto his passenger seat as though she belonged there.

'Sorry, I...' Aidan stared at her in confusion. 'Can I help you?'

'I'm Julie.'

'If you have an appointment, you—'

'Hailey's mum.'

'Hailey?' Aidan couldn't work out what was happening.

'Hailey. Stephen Marshall is my ex.'

'But Hailey said…' Aidan trailed off. It seemed wicked to tell a mother that her child had declared her dead and, then, Aidan felt compassion towards her. Sympathy. Not knowing that she knew all about being wicked.

He wasn't sure if he believed she really was Hailey's mum but still he said, 'I'm sorry about Hailey.' He felt more sorry than she looked. 'We all are.'

'Ah yes. Your son, the boyfriend. Connor, isn't it?' Something in the way she said his name made Aidan raise his guard.

'I have to get to an appointment now.'

'And your wife, the doctor. Lucy.'

'You need to get out of my car.'

'And you, the vet, you've all done very well for yourselves, haven't you? I thought, that's a good family my girl got herself involved with but you aren't good, are you?' She narrowed her eyes.

Cold, cold fingers trailed across the back of Aidan's neck. What did she want? 'We… we… try to be decent people. That's all any of us can do, isn't it?'

'And I'm not decent because I left my child?'

'I don't know the circumstances of you leaving and I certainly don't judge you, but I'm going to ask you again to leave my car.'

Julie didn't move, instead picking at a loose piece of cotton hanging from one of the paisley squares on her shorts, tugging at it until it unravelled, the patching lifting at the corner revealing a glimpse of pink skin underneath.

'I'll go when I've said what I came to say. Were you young when you met Lucy?'

Aidan remained silent. Unwilling to divulge anything

personal to a complete stranger. How could he get her to leave? He couldn't physically force her, the minute he laid a finger on her the implications could be astronomical.

'I was young when I met Stephen,' Julie said. 'I saw him walking through town and I followed him. There was something about a man in uniform. We saw each other a few times and by the time he was deployed again I were pregnant. He married me, of course.' She glances at him before staring into her lap. 'It was… hard. Lonely. We moved around a lot and the other wives were older than me, cleverer. I didn't fit in. I missed my mum, we'd been so close. One day, someone offered me something to take the edge off. I'm not proud but I felt I had nothing to lose.' She met Aidan's disapproving gaze. 'Don't judge me.'

'I'm not.' But he was, although he knew babies were hard. He could imagine the desperation of a young mum far away from home.

'A quick hit every now and then turned into a regular thing and by the time Hailey was three… when Stephen figured out why I'd changed he…'

Aidan could imagine, the anger, the threats.

'He cried,' she said simply. The one reaction Aidan hadn't been expecting. 'He took some leave, brought us home, and… things got better for a while. With Mum to help out it seemed almost manageable, the periods Stephen was away weren't so lonely, but then Mum…' This time tears spilled down Julie's cheeks. 'Mum had a heart attack. Hypertension.'

It runs in families. If only Lucy had known.

'I couldn't cope. Turned to… my mechanisms again.' She wiped her face with the heel of her hand. 'I felt… I was suffocating. I couldn't manage without Mum. Hailey was so demanding. Stephen was abroad. I… When he came home I told him I were going to the shops and…' She huffed out breath. 'It wasn't planned but I couldn't face going back.'

Aidan didn't know what to say, why was she telling him all of this? Didn't she have any friends to talk to? It was disconcerting. His fingers rested on the car keys, desperate to leave.

'I rang once… a few years later, but Stephen… Stephen had said they'd waited in limbo long enough. He had told Hailey I'd died so she'd have some closure.'

'That's incredibly sad, but I really do have an appointment to get to. Why don't you go and see Hailey? It's never too late for a fresh start.'

'Yeah it is. It is for me. I haven't got a soul anymore.' She holds Aidan with a steely stare. 'If I had, I'd fucking sell it.'

Despite the air conditioning blasting out of the vents, sweat pooled under Aidan's arms. Rolled down his forehead.

'I don't know what you want—'

'I. Want. You. To. Listen.' Julie pulled out her mobile.

Aidan knew that whatever she wanted to play him was bad. He had the urge to snatch the phone out of her hand, throw it across the car park, but it was an older model, sturdy, and even if he threw it away she might have a copy of whatever it was.

There was a crackle. Hissing. Despite not wanting to know what the recording was, Aidan automatically leaned closer to hear.

'God, Mel.' It was Lucy speaking. Aidan's hands tightened into fists. This woman had been near his wife. 'I can't believe that Hailey…' There was the chink of china drowning out her next words. They must have been in a coffee shop. He could picture Lucy, her hands wrapped around a mug of steaming cappuccino sprinkled with chocolate. 'Connor will never get over this. Never forgive me.'

'There's nothing to forgive. What happened with Hailey is tragic. Terribly sad, but it isn't your fault.'

There's a muffled sound. Lucy is crying.

'I never should have operated. Her blood pressure was high and...'

'Blood pressure in patients is usually high. White coat syndrome. You weren't to know that hypertension runs in her family. She's a little overweight but...'

'But what if I missed something?' Lucy's voice is high and anguished. 'I was tired. Exhausted. I should have finished my shift but Connor wanted me, begged me... oh God.' Again tears. The spurt of a coffee machine. 'Did I miss something?'

Julie clicks off the recording and watches him. Waiting for a reaction. Inside, Aidan's organs twisted and writhed and fought to be free but on the outside he was impassive.

'Get out. I'm leaving.' He pulled his seatbelt across his body. Put his hand on the gear leaver and hoped that Julie did not see the tremble of his fingers. 'Get out,' he said again when Julie made no move to do so.

'I won't.'

Aidan's heart galloped out the rhythm: *'I won't-I won't-I won't-I won't'.*

'What...' Aidan's mouth was incredibly dry. His tongue felt incredibly thick. He eyed up his bottle of water in the centre console but wouldn't give her the satisfaction of knowing she had unnerved him.

Unnerved wasn't strong enough.

He was petrified.

'What do you want?' He loathed to think. 'Money?'

She cocked her head to one side, he could almost hear her thoughts slipping around.

'Because you're not getting cash from me. Recording my wife is... immoral, probably illegal and proves nothing. Hailey's stroke was a terrible, terrible accident. Lucy wasn't at fault.'

'But she thinks she was,' Julie said. 'And so do I. High blood pressure runs in the family. What kind of doctor doesn't even pick that up?'

'When people are anxious, distressed, in pain, their blood pressure rises. I see it every day with the animals—'

'We're not animals,' she threw at him.

'Well, Hailey isn't,' he bounced back. 'Where did you record that anyway?'

'The hospital canteen. Stephen let me know about Hailey, God knows how he found me, and I went in to see her. I... I do... I am fond of her, despite how it seems. I looked through the window and she was... just lying there and I couldn't... Fuck!' She slammed her palm against the glove box. A stinging slap that Aidan felt in his own hand. 'Anyway, I went to get a coffee and overheard your wife and her friend and realized they were talking about my daughter and so I recorded them.'

'With the intention of what? Blackmailing her? Go ahead. Give it your best shot. There's no case for misconduct here.' He watched her expression change. 'Oh but you know that! You've talked to a solicitor then? What, a no-win, no-fee one?' Her features hardened and Aidan knew that he was right. That he was gaining the upper hand.

'Maybe she's done nothing wrong, but does your family need the stress of an investigation?'

'The board wouldn't call an investigation on the grounds that a doctor was upset over a patient suffering an episode like this and had questioned herself. It's natural. Normal. We all wonder whether there is more we could have done. But... there's no grounds... surgery was textbook perfect. I'm sorry.' Aidan wasn't. 'But you're barking up the wrong tree. Barking mad. Get out.'

Confidently, his fingers clutched the ignition key, began to twist it.

'Would Connor look at it that way?'

Aidan froze.

'I can imagine he's pretty upset? Was in love with my girl. How will he react if he heard his mum saying that she was too tired to operate. Exhausted. Thinks she made a mistake. Would he think there was grounds for blame. Would he forgive her?'

'If you...' His voice was even. 'If you try to blackmail me I will tell the police.'

'Fucked if I care.' She shrugged. 'The damage will be done once I've spoken to your boy. Speaking of your boy, that isn't all by the way.' Julie pressed play again. Lucy's voice filled the truck once more. 'What do you think really happened to Hailey?'

'The boys said—'

'I know what the boys said,' Lucy interrupted Melissa. 'But a broken femur, stumbling into a pothole. I don't buy it. They're lying. And… if we stay silent we're helping them cover whatever really happened up, but if we report them… goodness knows what trouble they could be in.'

'I think they're lying too. Ryan can barely look at me. Fergus keeps asking him what really happened, he feels so awful he was supervising and didn't realize they'd left the building. Ryan sticks to the same story though, and Tyler. We have to stand by them,' Mel said. 'Publicly and privately.'

Julie snapped off the recording. 'Hear that, Aidan? Your wife knew they were lying and said nothing. What did your boy do? There were four of them there that night, Stephen said—'

'Connor didn't do anything. Hailey fell. It was an accident.'

'So they're not to blame. Your wife isn't to blame. Somebody has to be. Somebody.' Julie slammed her palm against the glove box again emphasizing each word. 'Has. To. Pay.'

'No,' he said quietly.

'Suit yourself.' She flashed him a sudden smile.

Aidan felt his intestines knot together. Everything inside of him squirming. 'I can't give you money, Lucy would notice. Please. Connor has been through enough. My wife has been through enough.'

'Okay.' She nodded and Aidan thought she had seen sense until she said, 'Not money, though. Something else.'

'What?'

'Tramadol. Diazepam. Ketamine. Whatever you've got in there. I know you treat animals with the same drugs as humans.'

'I can't. It's illegal and besides, my receptionist Donna orders the stock. She'd notice if suddenly I was supplying a dealer—'

'I'm not a dealer! It's for me. Personal use. To numb the pain of what your wife did to my daughter.'

'My wife—'

'It will relax me. Soften my anger. So I don't speak to your son or report him.'

Aidan drummed his fingers on the steering wheel.

Think-think-think.

Lucy did blame herself although it wasn't her fault. If Connor hears Lucy on the recording their relationship might never recover. What if the hospital did find out that Lucy had known she was too exhausted to operate? It's not a cut and dry case. A no-win, no-fee solicitor rarely takes things on without it being almost certain they would win, but nevertheless, there could be grounds for an investigation at the very least.

Not only that but if Connor realized that Lucy didn't believe him, called him a liar… What if Julie played that recording to the police? Mr Marshall? What had happened that night and what might the consequences be? Donna had cut her hours, was retiring to look after her grandchild. He could take over managing the stock. Nobody would know if the drugs went missing.

'I'll give you what you want. But it's a short-term offer. I'm not risking my licence for you. My family. My freedom.'

But Aidan knew that once he handed over the first box of pills she would have another hold over him, but what could he do? He would do whatever he could to protect his family, but he hadn't envisaged then that her demands would become so frequent, so ruinous. Long after she had left his car, his skin crawled as though she had physically touched him. Dirty. He felt dirty.

That day when he foolishly said yes, the sky was still cornflower blue. The sun still beat down.

But although oblivious of what was to come, Aidan felt a chill that had never left him since.

CHAPTER SIXTY-EIGHT

Connor

PC Leighton places a hand on Connor's shoulder as he gulps down the water he has been given. The icy liquid travels down his throat and into his stomach, but it still doesn't eradicate the hot fear that bubbles deep in his gut.

'Julie... Julie must have...' He is light-headed. Struggling to breathe. To speak. 'Tyler...'

'Tyler's been found today,' PC Leighton begins.

'Oh God. Oh no.' Connor digs his fingertips into his scalp.

'Shh. Sit. It's okay. Tyler's fine, I promise.'

'Did she... who...'

'He ran away,' PC Amin says.

'No way.' Connor shook his head. 'He would have told me or Ryan. He—'

'He lost his phone. He couldn't have contacted you, he didn't know your numbers without his mobile. He's been sleeping rough for the past few days. He turned up at a police station in Brighton, hungry and cold and told them what had happened.'

'What do you mean? What did he say?'

The officers exchange a glance. PC Leighton gives an almost indiscernible nod.

'His mum's boyfriend, Liam, had been selling knock-off gear.

317

Tyler had been taking his money and when Liam caught him stealing, he hit him, not just once this time. Gave him a black eye. Bruised ribs. A split lip. Tyler had reached breaking point. It was a spur of the moment decision to run away. He thought he'd be able to find a hostel. Pick up work. He looks far older than seventeen but it hasn't gone as he'd hoped.'

'Where is he now?'

'We've sent an officer to speak to his mum. It's up to her. We'll charge Liam but we can't detain him until the court case. If he stays, Tyler can't return there. There are other options though. Social Services have a duty of care—'

'He can stay with me.' Connor doesn't hesitate. They have an empty fourth bedroom and he knows that despite Kieron being so sick and his mum having a lot to deal with, she would welcome Tyler in. She always wants to save everyone.

'What... what about Ryan? He'd never have run away. He gets on well with his mum.'

'We're still making inquiries.'

'But you don't know where he is?'

'Not yet but we're hopeful he'll be found soon. Try not to worry.'

Connor opens his mouth to say of course he's worried – The Taken – but he closes it again. Tyler hadn't been taken. Perhaps something else had happened to Ryan, but what?

There's the ring of the bell, a key in the lock.

'That'll be Aileen, Hailey's carer,' Mr Marshall says. 'Do you want to go and say goodbye, Connor?'

Connor slips into the dining room, avoiding Aileen's eyes as they pass. What must she think of him?

Hailey's eyes are closed. There's a split second when Connor fears the worst and it is like losing her all over again, but then he sees the rising of her chest as she inhales.

He stands over her. In rest, she looks the same. Perhaps paler, skin a little looser, and wearing a nightdress she'd never be seen dead in, but unmistakably Hailey. He crouches down. Kisses her fingertips. Her nails are no longer neatly filed and coated in varnish and stickers. He will ask Amber to come back. Give her a manicure. That might give Hailey a lift; already before he has left he is planning how he can make her feel better.

The clouds have broken and the rain has stopped pouring down. Everywhere looks fresh. A new beginning. The guilt that has burdened him these past few months is dissolving.

Out of the window, the shops flash by, red and pink flowers bunched in buckets outside the florist, wooden crates stacked with rosy apples and vibrant oranges and lemons outside the greengrocer. The colour is coming back into the world in sharp focus. Connor's mind travels back to the journey to Mr Marshall's house. How scared and small he felt inside the car boot. He is a different person now. He wishes he could tell Ryan that Mr Marshall has forgiven them, he feels the need to talk. Where could he be? Connor can't imagine but then he'd never thought Tyler would run away so perhaps he should try not to worry. Stay positive. He wonders when Tyler will be home, when he'll get in touch. In the meantime, though, there is one person who will listen, who is always around to listen.

Connor leans forward. 'Can you drop me somewhere?' He says where and if PC Amin is surprised he doesn't show it.

'We really should take you to your house, your parents—'

'You've left them messages. I thought you said Mum hadn't been at home when you arrived and Dad had left?' Connor talks quickly. Convincingly. 'I won't be long, I promise, and then I'll head straight home. They'll need time to calm down anyway.'

The officers exchange a look.

'Please.'

There isn't a direct acquiescence but PC Amin indicates left instead of right and Connor knows they are going to the church.

Connor has been coming here since as long as he can remember, but still it is always a surprise to him that once he steps through the black wrought iron gates that thunder doesn't rumble, lightning doesn't clap. That everything inside the cemetery is exactly as it is on the outside of the fence. The sun still shines. People smile. Talk. Walk their dogs. It's wrong somehow. Everything about her being here is wrong.

Still.

Always.

He settles himself cross-legged in front of her headstone. Absently pulls grass before letting it fall from his fingers.

'So, today I got locked inside a car boot.' He waits. 'Seriously! Yeah. Mr Marshall…' Again a pause. 'Yeah, I totally deserved that.' It was second nature to him, these one-sided conversations, her replies only in his head. In all the places he feels self-conscious, the classroom, home, pretty much everywhere, here is never one of them.

'I saw her,' he says quietly. 'Hailey. She looked… she looked like her but not. I've been a dick, blaming everyone, Tyler,

Ryan, Mr Marshall, Mum. Myself. I still blame myself, I guess, but he… Mr Marshall told me that nobody could have made Hailey do anything she didn't want to and… basically I'm not saying it was her fault but maybe it wasn't anyone's. Maybe it's time to let go. Move on.'

This time when he waits for her voice to tell him that he is right, it doesn't come.

'What? Tell me. Please.' His presses his palm against the stone butterfly, wanting to feel the connection that is strong and broken and impossible to be free of.

'Yeah. I should apologize to Mum. To everyone.' This time he wonders whether perhaps it is his conscience telling him this.

'Anyways, I'd better shoot. Kieron's been to the hospital today and I want to know what they've said. He's sick… sicker. I'm scared that he won't make it… that he'll…' He can't bring himself to say the word, not here, in the cemetery, when he is surrounded by it. He swipes his hand across his stinging eyes. The emotions of the day are building up in tears that he won't release. Not here. It wouldn't be right to be crying for his life when so many people have lost theirs.

He turns.

Squints.

The sun bright in his eyes.

Is someone watching him?

CHAPTER SIXTY-NINE

Aidan

Aidan can't pull his thoughts together as he drinks in the contents of the locked room. The walls plastered with fuzzy A4 photos of Hailey. Hundreds of them. The same three images, over and over, creating such a presence it's as though she's here, with them. Although there is only him and Julie here it is Hailey who fills the space.

He gently touches a picture with his fingertips.

'They're the only ones I had,' Julie says. 'I photocopied them in the library.'

On a small table is a candle, melted wax hardened around its rim.

It's a shrine.

It's incredibly sad.

'I keep the room locked so I don't come in here often, it's too… much.'

'You do care?' he whispers.

'Of course I care, she's my daughter.'

'But why then? Why don't you build a relationship with her? Why the blackmail? The threats?'

'Because I need…' She covers her face with her hands to compose herself, before dropping her arms to her side and looking Aidan in the eye. 'Because I need the high more than I need her. More than I need anything.'

'But... what are you doing with Lucy's clothes?' He is still clutching the crimson top dotted with yellow stars he'd pulled from the pile in the corner. 'How did you even get them?'

'From your washing line.'

'You've been following her? You're the white car she keeps seeing.' Aidan holds the top to his chest as though he is holding his wife, saying sorry he hadn't believed her.

'When you told me a few days ago that you weren't going to meet me anymore, I had to... I was angry. Thought if she were scared, you'd be scared and you'd change your mind.'

'But after you left those knickers under the car seat I gave you more pills.'

'It was... I felt I was doing something for Hailey. I keyed your wife's car. I felt so angry. I knew you wouldn't keep supplying me for long. When I heard on the radio your lad's friends had gone missing, I thought sending that "eye for an eye" letter would unnerve you.'

'I thought you'd taken him. I thought you'd taken them all. That's why I came here. That text you sent – "I have something you want. Clock is ticking"– I thought that was Connor.' He was wrong. Blood rushes to Aidan's head and he begins to sway on his feet. 'He's not here, is he?'

'No. I was referring to the recording of Lucy.'

A battle rages inside of him. Fury pitted against relief. She's put him through so much, but Connor isn't here. She hasn't hurt him. Fear fights against a fleeting sense of freedom.

Connor is still missing. But this… these weeks of hell where she'd been intent on destroying his family is over.

He wants to yell at her, hurt her, oddly thank her. The shake in his legs spreads to his torso, his whole body convulsing.

'This is the end,' he says with finality, trying to pull himself together, but he can't.

He must.

He has to find his son.

'What are you going to do?' she asks.

'I could press charges for blackmail. I can't go on with this,' Aidan says. 'With you.'

'I know,' she says quietly.

There's so much he could say in this moment, but she is not his priority, his son is.

He turns and stalks away. She doesn't tell him that she is sorry, he doesn't think she is.

Aidan is confused all the way home. He'd been so sure Connor would be there. He clings to the hope that he'll be back at home but he isn't. The police have gone. In the kitchen, he idly picks at the tape sealing the parcel as he wonders what to do. There's a tear, the tape loose in his hands. He scrunches it up and tosses it to one side, opens the flaps of the cardboard.

When he looks inside, he knows.

Oh, Connor.

He is putting two and two together and he is making four but he hopes he has made six, eight, ten.

He has to be wildly wrong, doesn't he?

He glances at the parcel again.
He hopes he has time to stop this.
He prays it's not too late.

CHAPTER SEVENTY

Connor

All the way home from the cemetery, Connor throws glances over his shoulder as he runs, but he doesn't think he is being followed.

He's paranoid and that won't change until Ryan is found. Where is he? Could he have run away too, gone to find Fergus?

His house is empty. A mess. The table is still on the floor, he can see one of the legs is broken. The lilies have been cleared up but there are still fragments of the green vase that smashed. On the wall, a streak of Connor's blood. Mum must have been so frightened when she saw it, still believing Tyler to be missing, Ryan having not yet been located. He knows she is out looking for him. She has never been one to sit around and wait; impatient and fiercely protective, she wouldn't have left finding him to the police. Dad isn't here either and Connor wonders if they are together.

In the kitchen are mugs half-full of tea, coffee. Too many mugs for his parents. Perhaps the police were drinking from them when the news came in that he had been found.

Connor runs up the stairs and pushes open the door to

Kieron's room. His duvet is smooth, pillows plumped. He can't have been back here since his hospital visit.

Back in the kitchen, Connor picks up his mobile from the worktop. Its screen is broken but it is still switched on. He calls his mum. His dad. Both numbers go directly to voicemail. He leaves a message that he is okay. That he is at home.

He opens his Find My Friends app that his parents made him install. He sees where Dad is and is puzzled but it isn't far away. He can run there in ten minutes.

As he's leaving, he remembers PC Leighton's scathing 'Didn't you leave a note?' and so he scribbles his destination on the back of the shopping list and then he slips out of the front door. Eyes scanning for Julie.

Fear pushes his walk to a jog, to a run.

He can't wait until he's back home again with his parents and Kieron.

Until they're all safe.

CHAPTER SEVENTY-ONE

Ryan

Ryan hears the drift of a voice.

He holds his breath as he waits to hear it again, not sure if he'd imagined it.

Through the blackness, the dull thump of footsteps.

He begins to rock his body from side to side; if he can cause himself to fall, make a loud noise, he might be heard.

Saved.

His muscles shake with exertion but still he is held firm.

Sightless.

Voiceless.

Trapped.

CHAPTER SEVENTY-TWO

Lucy

Hurry.

Walking, running, things I've always done without conscious thought, but not now. My legs don't feel like my own, cumbersome and difficult to control. My heart and my head fighting against each other, my body not knowing quite what to do. My hands and feet leaden.

I need to go inside.

I have to.

But I have never felt more terror-stricken than I do right now.

Hurry.

I'm light-headed as I creep forward. I have to keep reminding myself to breathe.

Hurry.

Faster, faster, until I'm standing outside a door. Softly, I push it open, my eyes darting around.

Inside the room, he's there.

'Ryan!'

On the bed. Tied up. Motionless.

Fearing the worst, I run towards him. My heart is hard

and weighted in my chest, sinking into the pit of my stomach.

With unsteady fingers, I search for his pulse.

CHAPTER SEVENTY-THREE

Aidan

Aidan is here.

He reaches the building with the razor-wire fence and the 'Danger. Do not enter' sign and fear bellows in his ears.

He has to be wrong.

Has to be.

But even as he thinks that, he knows that he doesn't believe it. He wouldn't have come otherwise.

The gates aren't padlocked and he pushes against one and slips through the gap. Scouts around the outskirts of the building. At the back is the car park. Ashes of a bonfire, scrunched-up cans of fruit cider, empty Big Mac boxes. Kids must have started hanging out here at night, undisturbed, away from the prying eyes of adults.

Parked close to the door is one solitary car.

It doesn't cross his mind to call the police, God knows how long he's got.

He still hopes that he is wrong.

Tyler.

Ryan.

Connor.

Aidan can't afford to hang around speculating. His theories can't be any worse than the truth? Can they?

He tries the door, half expecting it to be locked.

It isn't.

Taking one last breath of fresh air, he steps inside and breathes in decay and neglect.

He breathes in fear.

His.

Theirs.

CHAPTER SEVENTY-FOUR

Lucy

Oh God. Oh God. Oh God.

Panic grabs hold of me, twisting my stomach into a tight, hard ball. I fumble at the ties around Ryan's wrists, snagging my nail. Blood trickles down my thumb but I don't stop, working the knots free.

Hurry.

'Ryan? Are you okay?'

The rope loosens.

Thank God.

Hurry.

CHAPTER SEVENTY-FIVE

Ryan

Once more Ryan hears her voice and the sound of it causes his teeth to press together painfully. His whole body rigid.

Before, when he'd heard her, she was just… normal. Now she is anything but.

Oh God. He should never have got in her car.

He should never have got into Lucy's car.

CHAPTER SEVENTY-SIX

Aidan

Aidan runs through the twisty corridors of the old hospital. The hospital Lucy had spent much of her career working in. 'Lucy?' he shouts. 'Lucy?'

CHAPTER SEVENTY-SEVEN

Ryan

Ryan hears another voice again. As much as he wants to warn Aidan to run, to save himself, it's impossible.

It's too late for both of them.

CHAPTER SEVENTY-EIGHT

Lucy

Ryan stiffens when he hears Aidan call my name. He's awake, this I know not only from his muscles, but from his laboured breath. From the sweat that trickles down his forehead, his hair damp against his scalp. I didn't mean to scare him, really I didn't. It crosses my mind that I should give him something to help him relax. Sleep. But I don't.

I hadn't meant to take him.

I'd gone to lie down after bringing Kieron home from hospital after his terrifying bout of sepsis and had fallen asleep. I'd woken up at 8.30. Both Connor and Kieron were asleep. Aidan was nowhere to be seen. I'd missed dinner, hadn't wanted chips when everyone had eaten, but my stomach had growled and I'd slipped out of the house to pick up a ready meal from the garage.

Ryan wasn't far from our house, saturated in the pelting rain.

'Do you want a lift?' I shouted from the window.

'I was coming to see Kieron. Is it too late?'

'It is a bit. He's asleep, I'm afraid. I'll drop you home.'

He got into the car, dripping wet and, I swear to God it was

337

like the streak of lightning that lit up the sky. An epiphany, you might say. I knew exactly what I had to do.

I pretended the car had a flat tyre and when he got out I injected him with something to make him sleep – I still carry medical supplies in my car. He was heavy to move, but I got him back into the car and then outside here there was a trolley which made moving him a little easier. Once we were inside, I ordered what I needed from the black market. I've had a notification that it's been delivered.

It's almost time.

Aidan is nearly here.

And then we can begin.

Kieron is asleep. That is because of me. I've given him a mild sedative, not wanting him to be confused. Frightened.

Footsteps echo through the empty corridors. The hospital is so different to when I worked here. A ghost ship. Soon the solid walls will be knocked down. Houses built on the land where lives were lost. Saved. Where relatives grieved. Rejoiced.

My memories here are both good and bad. This wasn't solely my place of work. It was the place where Catherine…

Wait…

Outside doors open, bang shut. He has come straight to the area where he knows I will be.

He knows me so well.

'Hello, Aidan,' I say as he dashes into the room. 'You found me.' Not that I'd been hiding. Not from him.

I need him.

'I knew you'd be here, Lucy. I found the parcel.'

I knew he would. I knew he'd figure it out.

'What are you playing at?' he asks.

Our eyes lock. His are full of fear.
But he knows what I'm doing. That's why he came.
He knows I am not playing.
This is not a game.

CHAPTER SEVENTY-NINE

Aidan

The smell of bleach hits him first, the second he pelts into the room.

'Where's Connor?' Aidan looks frantically around, rushing over to Kieron when he spots his youngest son lying flat on a trolley. He lifts his limp hand. Presses two fingers against his wrist.

'He's fine,' Lucy says. 'I've given him a little something to help him sleep.'

'Ryan?' Aidan glances across the room, not wanting to leave his son's side.

'He's fine too.' Lucy soothes him in the same voice she has used over the years when he's lost an animal at the practice, but this... this woman standing in front of him may sound like his wife, may look like his wife, but he knows from the calm detachment in her eyes that the Lucy he loves has been hidden. He has to find her. Appeal to her as a parent. A mother.

'Melissa has been going frantic since Ryan went missing. Imagine how you'd have felt if it had been Connor. Is he here?'

'No. He's all right though.'

'How do you know? I got home to find the house swarming

with police, there was blood on the wall, the table knocked over. They think he's one of The Taken'

'I know he hasn't been taken because I'm the one who did the taking. Not Tyler, I don't know where he is. But Ryan.'

'But Connor is missing—'

'We had a row. It was vicious. He accused me of loving Kieron more than him. He was upset. Out of control. Screaming at me, asking how I'd feel if he went missing like Ryan. You know how angry he's been since Hailey's stroke. How he blames me. He's staged his own disappearance to teach me a lesson.'

'But the blood—'

'Was only a smidgen. You know blood loss always looks more severe than it is. He probably pricked his finger with a needle and smeared it against the wall. He thought I'd believe he'd been taken by the same person that took Ryan, but…' She gestures towards Ryan with one hand.

'Lucy.' Aidan doesn't quite know what to say. Do. He needs to get Ryan out of here, but he's already consumed by what comes after. The police. The charges.

The thought of Lucy in prison wounds him. 'I don't know what you're thinking—'

'But you do. That's why you're here. You opened the parcel of anti-rejection drugs I've bought. What did you think I was going to do? What was running through your mind as you came here? Really?'

'I thought that you'd decided to carry out a living liver transplant, taking a lobe of Connor's liver to save Kieron.' It's sickening saying the words, sickening that she doesn't deny them, but he knows it is possible. It was something they had discussed as a possibility when they first realized that one day Kieron would need a transplant.

'Partial liver transplants from a live donor are becoming more common,' Lucy had told him one night as they'd sat in bed not long after Kieron had been diagnosed. She'd spent sixteen years training as a transplant surgeon and she was one of the best. Aidan often thought it a shame she'd walked away, retrained in orthopaedics after the time it took her to qualify but he understood why she did. Why she felt unable to carry on the life or death operations, not that any surgery was without risk, of course. She idly ran her forefinger down his wrist. 'Although the first partial transplant was carried out more than a decade ago it's still not standard practice but when they're used it's generally for kids rather than adults so...'

'Kieron?' Aidan had felt a smidgen of excitement. He'd tried not to dwell on what would happen when his son reached transplant stage, but it was hard not to allow dark thoughts to creep in. Although he'd be so grateful if Kieron received a new organ, the inevitability of explaining to Kieron that somebody had died which had enabled him to live was something of a heavy weight on his chest. 'Are they as effective as a full transplant?'

'Yes. Probably more so. It's useful knowing when the surgery will take place so the recipient can be as best prepared as possible, and the donor and the recipient are in the same place so the donated liver portion is transported within minutes. The liver regenerates so quickly, within eight weeks generally it returns to its original size.'

'So why don't we use this method all the time?' But as Aidan asked he knew the answer. 'Who are the donors?'

'That's the thing. Would you donate a piece of your liver to a stranger? Most donors are family members or friends. Unlike heart and kidney transplants, livers don't need to be tissue matched, although both blood groups need to be compatible.'

'I'll do it!' At last, something positive Aidan could do, but Lucy shook her head.

'You wouldn't be able to. Not only do livers need to be roughly the same size – an adult's liver would never be used in a child – but you have a family history of diabetes.'

'And your liver is too big as well?' Aidan guessed it would be.

'Yes, but anyway, I'm a blood group B which isn't compatible with Kieron's O.'

Aidan fought to keep his next question contained, but it sprung from his lips anyway. 'But Connor's blood group is O. He could do it?'

'In theory, he's fit and healthy, but you can't donate in this country unless you're over eighteen.'

'Even if—'

'No exceptions.'

They hadn't discussed it anymore. They hadn't needed to. Kieron didn't require a liver then, unlike now.

This is why, when he saw the parcel of anti-rejection drugs, he had thought she'd snapped and brought both his sons here, to St Mary's, the operating theatre where she'd been based until Wheatfield General opened. To take a piece of Connor's liver for Kieron.

He knows he's got the right scenario.

Right scenario. Wrong donor.

CHAPTER EIGHTY

Lucy

All my emotions brew and churn but I can't afford to fall apart. I need the steely calm of my surgeon persona. To explain the facts to Aidan as I would to any relative of a patient.

'I knew Kieron should have gone on the transplant list weeks ago.' Dr Peters wouldn't agree. Yes, I know that statistically Kieron shouldn't have needed a transplant for years, but I had an inkling. A knowing. Mr Peters should have listened to me but he dismissed my career as a transplant surgeon as too brief. Too long ago. He knows the circumstances I left under and he doesn't trust me to make a detached, unbiased decision, but I was right. 'It's taken until now for Kieron to go on the waiting list.' The space in my throat grows smaller as I think of how large that list is.

The amount of people that die waiting.

'But if Kieron's now on the waiting list, then why…' Aidan gestures to Ryan.

'I can't hang around anymore, watching Kieron grow weaker. Disappearing in front of my eyes. When Kieron had sepsis, I thought… I thought…'

'Lucy, you're not well. You need help. I know it's scary waiting…'

'You don't understand!' I'm really not convinced that he does.

'I do,' he says. 'You don't want to lose Kieron. Neither do I. You're scared. So am I. Utterly terrified, but you cannot use Ryan to...'

'But it's fate.' I really believe it is.

'Why? You're not making any sense.'

'Catherine.' I utter just one word before the sadness of remembering what happened eclipses my ability to talk.

CHAPTER EIGHTY-ONE

Aidan

It is clear in Aidan's mind, in his heart, every single detail of the day Lucy told him she was pregnant. The carpet of orange and brown leaves crunching underfoot as they tramped through the woods with their old Labrador, Brady. The smell of damp earth. The sky, a hopeful blue despite the chill in the air. Her gloved hand in his – there had been no Indian summer that year. The emotions that overwhelmed him, snatched his voice: pride, joy, love. A fleeting doubt that caused his stomach to hop – he was going to be responsible for a family.

'Are you…' Lucy couldn't quite meet his eye. They hadn't exactly been trying, but they hadn't exactly been careful either.

'Bloody ecstatic!' Aidan's arms had encircled her waist. He picked her up and spun her around before setting her gently back down with an, 'Oh God. I'm sorry. I haven't hurt you… the baby?'

'I'm not made of china,' she had laughed.

But to Aidan she felt suddenly fragile. Breakable. He wanted to treat her like a treasured heirloom, wrapping her up and guarding her.

A baby!

'But how did you... when did you...?' Aidan's mouth stretched into the widest smile, couldn't form any more words.

'My boobs are sore.' She cupped them with her hands, laughing again at the disapproving stare of an elderly lady walking past, although Aidan noticed her husband taking a second glance. 'I thought I'd do a test just to rule it out and...'

'Have you seen a doctor?'

'I am a doctor! I can diagnose a pregnancy.'

'I meant, I don't know, scans and all that.'

'Not yet. Do you want to do it?'

'Make an appointment?'

'The scan. I could come into the surgery and you could use your ultrasound.'

'I am not scanning you with the equipment I use for the animals...' He trailed off as she pushed him lightly on the shoulder and he realized she'd been joking.

'But I could totally handle the labour. When I was training, I delivered a litter of nine spaniels. Nine!'

'Christ, the poor mother. One will be enough for us.'

'For now.'

'Don't start all that football team talk again. It's not going to happen.'

They'd left it late to start a family because of the length of time of Lucy's medical training.

'Is this a good time for a career break?' Aidan asked. Lucy had worked so hard to qualify as a surgeon. Young and female, she'd felt she had to prove herself to the older men who believed the only place in an operating theatre for women was passing surgical tools, swabbing the blood.

'I don't know if any time is the right time, but I do know that I am very, very happy.' As she spoke her smile slipped.

'Melissa and Fergus?' Aidan knew what she was thinking. Their best friends had been trying for two years and it seemed cruel almost that they'd fallen pregnant without making a conscious effort.

'They'll be happy for us.' Aidan knew that this was true. 'Everyone will be happy for us, including you.' Aidan bent down to rub Brady behind his ears. 'You're going to have a human brother or sister, Brady. What do you say about that?'

He lowered his ear near the dog's mouth. 'He says he wants a boy, how about you?'

'It's such a cliché to say "as long as it's healthy",' Lucy said. But… you know. What sex would you prefer?'

Aidan shrugged. 'Genuinely, I'd be delighted with a boy or girl.'

It turns out they were expecting both.

'Twins!' The twelve-week scan brought the unexpected but welcome news. It was both happy and daunting. They were still adjusting to the thought of life as a three, now they'd be a four. Catherine and Connor.

Although they loved their two-bed Victorian cottage with the tangle of roses under the bay windows and their view of rolling fields, they hurriedly sold and moved into a larger new-build with enough bedrooms for the twins to have one each and a spare for a future sibling.

The twins were identical, sharing the same placenta. Extra checks were needed as a shared placenta could lead to complications, but Lucy sailed through without any problems. Until week twenty-two.

'The girl is growing at a slower rate to the boy,' Dr Chandra told them. 'I'd mentioned this previously, but although we'd hoped she'd catch up, she hasn't. You have Intrauterine Growth Restriction – IUGR.'

'What does that mean?' Aidan was baffled. 'What's caused it?'

'It means there's an increased risk to the smaller of the babies—'

'Catherine.' Lucy placed her hand protectively over her bump.

'To Catherine. This is caused by a failure of the placenta.'

At the word 'failure' Lucy and Aidan exchanged a glance, each of them feeling it keenly, but they were medically trained. Knew the quicker these things were picked up, the better.

'Why?' Aidan asked.

'There's no specific cause. It's nothing you've done or haven't done.'

'So what happens now?' Aidan asked.

'A placenta failure could have disastrous consequences for both babies. But of course we'll be monitoring you closely and hopefully it won't come to that. We'll make another appointment—'

'Disastrous?' Aidan asked.

'Please,' Lucy said. 'Be frank with us.'

'Okay. Well, Catherine's receiving less blood flow than Connor. There's a chance she could die in the womb. If she does, Connor would attempt to revive her by transferring blood back to her.'

'But that's good? He'd save her?' Aidan asked tentatively,

although the look on the doctor's face indicated it wasn't good at all.

'That would mean Connor would die too,' Lucy said flatly.

'We'll monitor you twice a week.'

At twenty-four weeks, the doctor's voice was grave.

'Connor has grown as expected but Catherine hasn't caught up and the difference in their sizes now is outside what the NHS considers acceptable.'

Lucy crushed Aidan's hand between hers but she was outwardly calm as she said, 'Go on.'

Only he could detect the terror in her voice.

'We could deliver the babies now—'

'It's too early.' Lucy immediately dismissed the idea. 'What about surgery?'

'Well... There is a relatively new procedure that could split the placenta but it needs to be performed by twenty-five weeks. If you could get to London—'

'We'll go now.' Lucy was already standing.

The following day found Lucy being scanned again but they were told that due to the position of the placenta the surgery was not an option.

At thirty-one weeks, 'I'm sorry. The flow of blood has reversed,' the doctor revealed. 'Blood's now flowing away from the babies to the placenta. Spontaneous death in the womb is a likelihood so we're going to deliver you later today.'

Spontaneous death.

Aidan had never felt so helpless. So hopeless.

When Lucy had first fallen pregnant they'd talked of a natural birth. Of classical music and mood lighting. As relaxed and unobtrusive as labour could be. Instead, Aidan was draped in a gown and cap, under the harsh lights of the operating theatre, stroking Lucy's furrowed brow as first one twin was lifted shrieking and wailing, and then the other. They were perfect, although small.

Connor was the largest at 4lb and Aidan thought how impossibly small he looked until Catherine was delivered.

There was only a brief snatch of time to see his children before they were whisked away.

'Go with them,' Lucy had cried.

The heat in the special baby unit pushed Aidan back as he entered the room. It was bright, lights flashing, the silence broken by beeping monitors. Aidan was surprised to see so many incubators. Some were empty, but others contained tiny babies. He had felt he and Lucy were the only couple in their situation. He followed the nurse.

'Here we go. Boy and girl – do we have names?'

Aidan's throat was dry. 'Connor and Catherine,' he barely scratched out, before coughing and trying again. 'Connor and Catherine Walsh.'

Emotion beat at his chest, his shirt clinging to the perspiration that dampened his skin. Although he'd known they were likely to be premature, whenever Aidan had pictured his babies they'd resembled the ones from the adverts for nappies or milk. Ruddy-cheeked and podgy arms.

He gazed in wonder through the plastic dome. Connor and Catherine were tiny. Their skin almost translucent. Downy hair covering thin limbs. Aidan felt a surge of love. A fierce desire to protect them as he counted their miniature fingers and toes.

'Are they…?' His questions were stuck to his tongue. Impossible questions with no answers. There were so many things he wanted to know. Are they going to be okay? Happy. Healthy. Live long and fulfilling lives.

'They need extra help breathing and feeding. Catherine more than Connor. They are also at a greater risk of infection because their immune systems are developing.'

It was terrifying. All of it. Aidan hadn't realized he was hyperventilating until he was gently led to a chair. Given a paper bag to breathe into. A soothing hand rubbed his back and Aidan wanted to weep. He should be the one doing the comforting, not being comforted. He lowered the bag.

'I need to get back to my wife. Can I take a picture of the babies?'

'Of course. Tell her we will take very good care of them. She'll be brought down in a wheelchair to see for herself soon.'

Aidan took one last, long, lingering look at his children. And it took a superhuman amount of strength to wrench himself away from them.

Lucy was hooked up to a catheter and a drip. His whole family surrounded by tubes and wires. He thought she might be asleep, but although groggy with painkillers, she was alert and agitated. Her hands protectively over the still visible bump of her belly as though the babies were still there.

'I've brought you pictures.' Aidan settled himself in the chair next to her bed. He pulled his digital camera out of his pocket.

'The first ones are of Catherine.'

Lucy's head bent over the screen. Immediately, her hand

fluttered to her throat, as a small cry escaped her lips. She lingered over each picture. Zooming in the images. Her fingertips tracing each tiny feature, delicate noses and pouting lips.

'They're beautiful.' Tears streamed unchecked down her cheeks. Aidan slipped his arm around her and let her rest her head on his shoulder so she couldn't see his face. She couldn't see that he was also crying. And if she felt his sorrow dampen her hair, she didn't say.

'I need to be with my babies,' she said raising her tear-stained face to his. 'I'm not just a mum, I'm a doctor, I can... I can...' Sobs caught in her throat, hiccups spilling from her mouth. 'You have to get a wheelchair. I can't feel my legs properly. Please, Aidan, please. There might be something they're not doing in the NICU—' She pressed her fists against her chest. 'I'm a doctor, I'm... I'm...' Lucy gasped for breath. Her face glowing red in the whip of lightning outside of the window.

It was then the unimaginable happened.

CHAPTER EIGHTY-TWO

Lucy

As I watch my husband, I know that he's remembering exactly the same painful memories as I am. It all slips across his face. The hope. The despair. But he still doesn't understand why I have chosen Ryan and I know this because there is one emotion I'm looking for that isn't there.

'Remember, Aidan,' I say. 'Remember it all.'

And he does. I see it all in his grief-stricken eyes. Every shameful secret that sits between us.

Unforgiven.

Unspoken.

Until now.

CHAPTER EIGHTY-THREE

Aidan

'Lucy. Aidan.' Dr Chandra hovered at the foot of the bed. The storm continued to rage, but nothing outside of this room mattered. 'I'm so sorry.' When the doctor broke eye contact, Aidan knew his life would never be the same again. 'It's Catherine. We did everything we could, I can promise you—'

Lucy's scream was primal, slicing through Aidan – that scalpel through her skin – he was just as raw and bloodied.

'I am so sorry,' Dr Chandra said again. 'Her heart stopped beating.'

'But I can give her a new heart… I can…' Lucy threw back her covers.

'It's too late.'

'No! I can save her, I can…' Lucy's legs were still numb from the anaesthetic but she somehow managed to swing them out of bed. 'I can…'

Aidan held her while she beat his chest with her hands, tried to push him away.

'I. Can. Save. Her.' She glared at Dr Chandra. 'I'm a doctor. I demand that you take me to my daughter.'

'We can arrange for you to see her, of course, but Lucy, Catherine was so small. The team did all—'

'But she didn't need a team. She just needed me.' Lucy covered her face with her hands. 'She just needed me.' She wept.

In the hours that passed, Lucy and Aidan were able to hold Catherine. Lucy carefully dressed her in the premature baby sleepsuit dotted with yellow daisies that despite being small, still swamped her. A nurse took photos of them all. Faces stiff, hearts breaking, a family of three, not four, and it occurred to Aidan that's what they'd be now. The double buggy waiting in their hallway, the two cots, it was useless now. All of it. He turned away from his wife then, from his child who he would never strap securely into the seat they had bought with the duck print to drive her home. She would never leave the hospital with them. Lucy's emotion filled the room, her grief enormous. There was no place for his. His would come later when alone, he would shout and scream and shake his fist at the sky.

A nurse helped them take handprints and footprints of Catherine, impossibly small and they would remain forever so.

Time stretched slowly but all too fast. Lucy, in between bouts of tears, crooned 'Hush little baby' to her daughter, but it was all a lie. She would never buy Catherine a mocking bird, a diamond ring or a looking glass, but she sang it over and over, voice cracking, as though if she stopped singing for one single second she would have to let her daughter go.

Nevertheless, eventually it was time to say goodbye.

Time for Lucy to meet Connor. Her first sighting of her

son was forever imprinted on Aidan's mind. It was bittersweet watching her emotions slide across her beautiful face. She'd aged today. Her skin grey and looser than it had been yesterday. The love she instantly felt for her son was marred with sorrow for the loss of his twin. Guilt that she hadn't been there when his sister had slipped away.

'If my body had just—'

'Shh.' Aidan shook his head. 'You are not to blame.'

'I save lives every day.'

'And sometimes you lose them too.'

Lucy was both grateful to and hostile with the staff of the NICU. Her anxious eyes following their every movement. Reading Connor's notes. Making them explain again and again how frequently they were checking him. Telling them what to look out for as though she was their supervision doctor and they her trainees.

The staff were kind. Patient. Genuinely saddened to have lost a baby.

At last Lucy was sleeping. The nurse told him she'd be out for hours. He ran a hand over his chin, felt the bristles underneath his fingers. There was so much to do. He wanted to pack away all of Catherine's things before Lucy came home later that week. There were so many people to tell, he didn't know where to start. They thought they'd be arranging a christening, instead he needed to plan a funeral. He stood and swayed on his feet. He couldn't remember when he last slept. Ate. He doubted he'd ever feel hungry again. Nothing could fill the void of loss inside of him.

Legs leaden, he stumbled out to his car. Not knowing if it

was the same day. Unaware of the time. He peeled a parking ticket from his windscreen and tossed it onto the back seat.

He drove. He still couldn't cry, but he felt it all inside of him. He reached their road but he didn't turn into it. Not wanting to go inside and face the double buggy as soon as he pushed open the front door. Not wanting to be alone when he called his mum, Lucy's mum. Instead, he drove to Fergus's house, thumping his torment onto his front door. Falling into the hallway as Melissa let him inside.

'Aidan?'

But he couldn't speak. All of his words knotted inside of his throat.

Melissa led him into the lounge and settled him on the sofa, crouching in front of him in her candy-striped pyjamas, her hands on his knees.

'Is Lucy okay?'

Aidan shook his head. Opened his mouth and then closed it again.

'Aidan,' Melissa said. 'I need you to tell me what has happened.'

There was a gentleness about her. Her eyes. Her voice. But he didn't want gentle. He wanted hardness. Anger. Someone to tell him it wasn't fucking fair.

'Where's Fergus?'

'He's on a long-haul flight. He isn't due back until tomorrow. Can I get you something? A drink?'

'Whisky.'

'Aidan, it's eight o'clock in the morning.' But still Melissa fetched a glass. Ice. A bottle.

The first gulp burned his throat. Warmed his belly. He

knew that he needed to stay sober. That he had too much to do. He wanted to be back at the hospital before too long. But still he slugged a second glass of the amber liquid and swallowed it down in one go. He wiped his mouth and collapsed back against the cushions. Melissa eyeing him warily.

'What's wrong, Aidan?'

'Are you and Fergus still trying for a baby?' he asked.

'Yes but… it's been two years now. We need to look at other options but Fergus won't admit—'

'Don't,' Aidan said gruffly.

'Don't explore our options?'

'Don't have a baby. It's too… It's too…' He reached for the bottle again. This time Melissa held out a second glass and joined him, coughing as she drank. Aidan had never seen her drink spirits before.

'Aidan, tell me what's wrong.'

'Are you happy?' Aidan asked.

Melissa swished the dregs of her whisky around her glass. 'I don't know. We used to be but trying to create a family, me trying to fall pregnant has put such a strain on us. Sometimes I wonder if we're broken.'

'Lucy falling pregnant has broken us.' Aidan closed his eyes. 'Connor's okay but Catherine… Catherine didn't make it.'

The sofa dipped as Melissa sat next to him and scooped him into her arms. He tried to push her away but she held him fast.

'Shh.' She soothed as he would eventually soothe his son. As he should have been able to soothe his daughter.

His muscles grew limp. His shoulders began to shake. Still he tried to keep his grief inside.

'Shh.' Her fingers stroked his hair. 'Let it all out.'

The force of his sobs shook his bones as they hurtled from deep in the pit of his belly, travelling up his throat before he propelled them out of his mouth. A guttural sound, filling the quiet room. He couldn't stop them. He needed them to stop. He needed to be strong but he felt weak. Melissa's body trembled next to his. He raised his face. She was crying too. She cupped his cheeks with her hands.

'I'm so sorry, Aidan. For you and Lucy. But you will get through this.'

'How?' His desperation spilled out in that one word.

She shook her head, unable to answer. Their eyes still locked. A torrent of tears built again and he just couldn't bear it. He pressed his lips hard against hers. Immediately, she pushed him away, but his hand snaked around the back of her head. He drew her to him again. Kissed her firmly. His other hand creeping under her T-shirt. He grew hard. It wasn't that he'd ever fancied Melissa. It wasn't that he wanted her, but he wanted to feel something, anything, other than the crushing grief.

He wanted it to stop, if only for a few moments.

Melissa relaxed, her fingers tangled in his hair, raising her hips as he tugged at her pyjama bottoms. Her breath sour with whisky and sleep but he didn't care. He didn't care about anything except the here and now.

CHAPTER EIGHTY-FOUR

Lucy

It's displayed on Aidan's features, carved into the lines that now furrow his brow; his guilt. His entire face wracked with pain.

He has read my thoughts.

All of them.

Now he knows why I want it to be Ryan.

A complete circle. A repeat of the past.

A truth.

Will he agree? I want to believe that he will. Sometimes hope is enough.

It's all I have.

I wait. Teetering on the brink. The brink of what, I am not sure.

What is he thinking, my husband?

Why doesn't he say something?

Anything.

Yes.

CHAPTER EIGHTY-FIVE

Aidan

Sex with Melissa was quick. Animalistic.

Pleasure-less.

It was something they had never, ever talked about again and three months later when she and Fergus had come for lunch and told them they were expecting, he hadn't questioned who the father was.

He hadn't wanted to know.

He doesn't now.

'Ryan is a perfect donor for Kieron,' Lucy says.

Aidan takes a step back – out of reach from the words that hang in the air, snaking towards him with their poison.

'He isn't. He can't be.'

But Aidan knows, deep down Aidan has always known.

'How… how did you find out?'

'I had lunch at the hospital with Fergus the other day. I kept asking him what had happened and why he was leaving. He wasn't going to tell me, but as he was walking away, he turned back. He asked if I was sure I really wanted to know, warned me that what he was about to say could ruin my life. My friendship with Mel. My marriage. He discovered the truth after he and Mel took Ryan to give blood for the first time. When Ryan was in the loo the nurse made a flippant remark about Fergus being his stepdad. Fergus questioned why she'd say that and she apparently was mortified, but told him that his and Ryan's blood groups are incompatible. She'd backtracked. But Melissa confessed. Said it had been haunting her for years. Ryan is an O. The same as you. The same as Connor and Kieron.'

'No! I'm not… Melissa would have told me. He… he can't be mine!'

'He is.' There's an almost ethereal quality shimmering around Lucy. A calmness that is frightening.

'I don't believe it. It was a one-off. A mistake. A—'

'Aidan.' Lucy slowly shakes her head. 'It only takes one time. You must have questioned it when Mel fell pregnant. Thought about the dates.'

Aidan's head is stuffed with a nothingness. He can't process what is happening. 'Of course not. I tried not to think about… any of it. I was such a mess over losing Catherine, having to be strong for you. Connor. I… Have you asked Mel about this?'

'No. I don't need to. I believe Fergus. Do you remember the night he left? How frightened she was on the phone that he had come round to ours? She was scared he'd tell me. She didn't want me to go round. She couldn't face me. It. Her shame. She's virtually avoided me ever since.'

There's a beat. The smell of bleach burning his throat. Tears burning his eyes.

'Aidan, siblings save each other. Connor thrived while Catherine didn't. I had to have an emergency section because

Connor would have reversed the blood flow in the womb to try to save Catherine. Ryan could save Kieron now.'

Aidan glances at Kieron and then at Ryan. He doesn't feel the same level of protectiveness with Ryan that he does with Connor and Kieron. He doesn't feel love.

What he does feel is the burden of guilt and he knows that this will never leave him. For the first time he has a glimpse into how Lucy must feel each day, so knotted up inside, regret swimming fast as tadpoles through her mind.

His wife feels guilty about many things that aren't her fault. He thinks it's driven her mad.

CHAPTER EIGHTY-SIX

Lucy

All that I have left of Catherine is her tiny hand and footprints on the mug Aidan made me on my first Mother's Day. I glance at Kieron, so young, so innocent, so much like Catherine. If I'm going to lose another child, I want it to be on my terms. I left it up to nature before and look what happened.

I'd trained as a transplant surgeon. It wasn't originally what I wanted to specialize in when I began my degree in medicine, but by the time I graduated five years later, I knew without a doubt it was what I wanted to do. It was another two years to get my postgrad and a further six of specialist training before I realized my dream, but my dream turned to ashes the second I returned to work after losing Catherine. My first patient was a baby with cardiomyopathy who needed a transplant and the thought of losing her on the table, of her tiny heart stopping beating the way Catherine's heart had, caused my hands to shake so violently I had to walk away. I couldn't bear being responsible for another life. For months I stayed at home. Concentrated on raising Connor but after a two-year break I was itching to go back to work. I thought I'd have a complete career change, but nothing excited me in the way medicine did. I thought of the intricacies of Aidan's pelvic surgery when he was in his twenties, how he'd likely have never walked again if it wasn't for his orthopaedic surgeon, and after weighing up the pros and cons in depth, I decided to retrain. To offer hope, a new beginning, the way that Aidan had been.

'Are you sure?' Aidan had asked. 'It's another four years' residency. Is it what you really want?'

What I really wanted was Catherine, but I couldn't have her and I needed to do something.

The hospital was supportive, people move about in medicine all the time and they don't want to lose their staff. They didn't want to lose me. After I'd finished my residency, I was pregnant with Kieron and then after my maternity leave I returned to the hospital.

Mostly, I love what I do, but sometimes it's harrowing. It isn't all hip replacements and sports injuries or degenerative diseases that we're understanding more about every day. We treat people after near fatal accidents, repairing their musculoskeletal system, giving them back their mobility even if we can't fully take away their pain. Last year I operated on a little boy with a tumour near his spine. I'd thought of my boys then and it was the hardest surgery I've carried out, but it was a success and those successes stayed with me.

Until Hailey.

Life is so fragile. If I'd stayed with her things might have been different. Her life, in my hands.

Catherine's life was never in my hands, she was taken away from me. This theatre is where she was born. This hospital is where she died. I could have saved her, I know I could. It seems right that this theatre is where Kieron will be given back his health, his life, by me.

I really can't trust anybody else with the life of my child. I had once before and the first, and last, time I held my daughter she was cold, still, silent.

I begin to hum 'Hush little baby' and I am singing to her, to Kieron, to Connor and Hailey and my cheeks are wet but I don't know why I'm crying.

I pick up a scalpel. It's been months since I held one but it still fits perfectly into my hand.

I can save them all.

CHAPTER EIGHTY-SEVEN

Aidan

Aidan watches the light bounce off the scalpel as Lucy twirls it around in her hand.

Catherine.

The rawness of loss never fades. His only daughter, his little girl who will never grow. He'll never see her graduate, marry. Will it be the same with Kieron?

'I know you miss Catherine – we all do,' he begins.

'Do we? We never talk about it?'

'That doesn't mean we don't care. I think about her every single day. Connor visits her – I've often seen him coming out of the cemetery – but this isn't the answer.'

'What is the answer? Taking a chance with Kieron's life?'

'Waiting. It's all we can do. If we don't find a donor and his condition deteriorates even more then…'

'Then he'll be too weak to operate on. Now he's strong enough.'

'Ryan is someone else's child. Melissa's child. She'll—'

'It's not like he's going to die. A lobe of his liver. He'll be fine.'

'Even if he's fine physically, he'll never recover emotionally. This. Is. Wrong. Lucy, please. We need to take Ryan home.

Tell Melissa what you've done. Tell the police you aren't in your right mind. Explain about Catherine. How the stress of Hailey and now Kieron has pushed you past your limits.'

'Hush little baby,' Lucy sings. Aidan starts to cry. 'A woman was singing that in the hospital last time Kieron was in,' Lucy says when she's finished the song. 'It broke my heart.' Lucy begins to sob. 'Aidan, I am broken. Kieron is broken. But we can fix him. Please.' As quickly as she softened, she turns stone hard. 'It's all right for you. If Kieron dies you will still have two sons. Two children. I'll have one and I should have three. Three.' She is crying harder now.

'Even if I agree to this, which I don't, it's impossible. You can't carry out surgery here.'

'I've got everything I need and I've scrubbed everything multiple times. It's as sterile as it was when it was in use as a theatre. It's safe. I've thought of it all. Everything.' She strokes Kieron's face gently and plants a kiss on his forehead. 'I did it all for you,' she whispers.

The tenderness in her gesture causes Aiden to falter until he catches sight of Ryan again. This may be all for Kieron, but that doesn't make it right.

'You can't possibly perform a transplant on your own. Without a team. It would be crazy.'

'At weekends, with a skeleton staff, I've carried out a transplant with only four other people assisting.'

'That's still three more than you have now.'

'Not true. Agnes is on her way. She's going to help.'

'Agnes?' Aidan struggles to place her. 'The nurse who was struck off?'

'Yes. Because she has lost a child. She knows. She wants to help.'

'This is illegal! I can't believe... how much did you offer her?'

'Ten thousand. She isn't working and can't pay her mortgage, but it isn't about the money, for her. It's about saving a child's life.'

'Oh, Lucy.' His wife is breaking his heart. 'You're a brilliant surgeon and I don't doubt Agnes was a fantastic theatre nurse before she was grieving but... I'm a vet...'

'The anaesthetic is the same. Propofol. Exactly the same. Please. You could anaesthetize. You know how much I love Kieron. I wouldn't suggest this if I wasn't confident I could operate with minimal risk.'

Minimal risk is still too much.

'It is... wrong.'

'Children getting sick is wrong, Aidan. Children dying is wrong.'

'Two—'

'Don't you dare tell me two wrongs don't make a right. I can promise you that Ryan will be fine. I promise.'

'Both boys could die.'

'They won't.'

'Either way we'd go to jail.'

'I've thought about that, of course, but Aidan, I'd rather be locked up for the rest of my life knowing my boy is healthy than have my freedom but watch him die, wouldn't you?'

Aidan looks his wife in the eye and gives her his answer.

CHAPTER EIGHTY-EIGHT

Ryan

Yes.

He can't believe Aidan has said yes.

He can't believe Aidan is his father.

He listens to the squeak of a trolley. Lucy softly singing 'Hush little baby' the way she had over and over in the car the night she'd taken him, and he's never heard anything more chilling.

The chink of something metal.

Hot breath near his face.

'Relax,' Lucy says. 'It'll all be over soon.'

CHAPTER EIGHTY-NINE

Connor

Connor doesn't get why the Find My Friends app has shown his dad at the old hospital, but according to his mobile he's still here so Connor finds a way inside. The building is huge, but it's also dusty and there is a clear line of footprints for Connor to follow. He winds through the corridors until he pushes open a double door and there they are. His parents.

'Connor. What are you doing here?' He hears the panic in his dad's voice. He glances over to Mum, who doesn't say anything. There's an odd expression on her face, a sense of calmness he hasn't seen in such a long time. 'You need to leave.' Dad is pacing towards him. 'Now.'

'What's going on?' Confused, Connor takes a step back, his eyes searching the room.

Then he sees Ryan.

'You've found him!' Excited, he runs over to his friend, skidding to a halt as he sees the way he's blindfolded. Gagged. Vomit rises in his throat and he swallows it down. Why aren't his parents helping? The walls closing in, the ceiling pushing down. Light-headed, he clings to the side of the trolley Ryan is lying on.

What is going on?

'Is he…' He can't say the word. But he gently touches Ryan's chest with one hand, reassured by the movement of his ribcage.

'Mum?' Tears pour from Connor's eyes. 'Mum, help him. You're a doctor, for fuck's sake. Dad?' It is when he turns to face his father that he sees his brother on a second trolley.

'Oh God. No.' His knees buckle as he stumbles towards Kieron.

He runs towards him and like Ryan, he looks as though he is asleep.

'What the fuck!' Terror is knocking his heart against his ribcage. He doesn't understand this. Any of it. Why aren't his parents moving? Speaking. Where are the police?'

He pulls out his phone.

'No!' his dad says sharply. 'Don't call anyone.'

'But… what? Why…?' Connor has lost the ability to think coherently.

'It's okay,' his mum says. 'We're going to use a small piece of Ryan's liver to save your brother.'

Connor looks to his dad. Waits for the punchline. It doesn't come.

'What the fuck?' he says again.

Aidan can't look him in the eye.

'If we wait for a donor on the NHS there is a chance that Kieron could die. This way he won't. Ryan won't either, don't worry.'

'That's… insane. Dad?'

'I know it sounds crazy. It is crazy. But Mum knows what she's doing. She's a skilled surgeon.'

'Great. The prison will probably appreciate a new doctor or haven't you thought that far ahead?'

'Whether we do or don't do the op, I'll be going to prison now anyway,' Lucy says. 'But it won't matter because Kieron will be okay.'

'He won't be okay.' Connor's voice shakes. 'I won't be okay. I need you. We both do. You're our mum.'

'And I was Catherine's mum too but she died and I should have—'

'Oh, so you think that was your fault? It was mine and let me tell you I have lived with that every single day.'

'Of course it wasn't your fault!' Aidan says.

'Oh right? Because I grew in the womb and she didn't. I had all the nutrients and she didn't.'

'It doesn't work that way—'

'This.' Connor sweeps his arm around the room. 'Doesn't work this way. You can't just pick a random—'

'Ryan isn't random,' Lucy says.

'Okay, a friend.'

'He isn't just a friend.' She walks over to Connor and takes his hands. They are cold. She is cold. 'This is going to be hard for you to hear. Connor, we love you so much.'

'I made a mistake. Once,' his dad cuts. 'With Melissa. Ryan is my son. Your half-brother.'

Connor shakes his head. Pulls his hands out of Mum's grasp. Why are they saying these things? Dad isn't… he isn't Ryan's dad. Fergus is. And yet Fergus isn't here, he left. Did he leave because…

Connor shakes his head again. It's too much.

'I don't believe you.' It can't be true. Melissa and Fergus and Mum and Dad have always been such good friends. How can they be if… Unless they're into some weird swinging shit.

'Am I… me and Kieron…You're our dad, right?'

'I am. But I am also Ryan's father.'

'You can't be. Kieron is my brother. Catherine was my sister. We should be a family of five but we're four. You can't have another son, you… you just can't.' Connor's pulse races. He feels sick. Scared. Nothing is as he thought it was. His parents are… fucking insane. His best friend is his brother?

'You've lied to me. All these years. All the times Ryan's stayed over.' Connor's tears come now, falling freely. He remembers the times his dad would kick a football around with them in the garden. Praise Ryan who was infinitely better at sport than Connor.

'Do you… Do you love him more than me?' He wipes his nose with his sleeve as though he's five years old. Stupid being jealous but Ryan… not just his brother but Kieron's too. Connor should be the one to save this family. He had volunteered for a living transplant. It should be him.

'Connor. I love you more than anything, you and Kieron,' Dad says. 'I didn't even know Ryan was mine until today but now I do, we have a real chance here…'

They all fall silent.

'I wanted to help Kieron.' Connor is the first to speak.

'I know but you're not eighteen yet.'

'I know all that but as soon as I am I want to help. I weighed up all the options and I made a choice. Ryan hasn't been given a choice. This… this isn't right, Mum.'

'But Connor, we can't wait until next year.'

'No.' He holds up his hand. 'No. All of my life I have felt responsible for Catherine. These last few months I have felt responsible for Hailey. I lied about what happened. She didn't fall during a walk. We'd snuck out to do a dare. It went wrong. I have to live with that. Don't make me live with being responsible for Ryan if something goes wrong. Don't make Kieron feel responsible for Ryan, for you being in prison. He… He might have a new liver but he'll have lost a parent. I'll have lost a parent. Please Mum, please. Don't do this.'

He knows how to make her change her mind.

CHAPTER NINETY

Aidan

It is like being pulled out of a dream for Aidan. He wades back to reality. He can't believe that he almost agreed to help Lucy operate on Melissa's son – his son.

'Mum.'

He sees Connor run towards Lucy.

He sees what is going to happen.

He is too slow to stop it.

CHAPTER NINETY-ONE

Lucy

It is a heartfelt speech from Connor and I'm wavering. Split with indecision. That Stretch Armstrong doll again. But what he said strikes a chord and suddenly I am incredulous that I ever thought this was a good idea. I am ashamed. Mortified at what I have done. Desperately searching for a way to put everything right. Wondering if my children, my husband, will ever forgive me, trust me.

Love me.

Connor has stopped speaking and is crying. Calling my name and rushing over to me with his arms wide open to hug me. I raise my hands to hug him back but he has reached me before I can position myself correctly. Before I have realized that I am still holding the scalpel in my hand. There's a slight pressure against his skin, a tear.

His blood is warm as it spills over my hand.

Connor crumples to the floor. I raise my face to Aidan who seems to be moving in slow motion towards us.

I hear someone screaming.

I think it is me.

PART THREE

CHAPTER NINETY-TWO

Connor

Eight months later

The pain in his side makes Connor wince, the stitches have dissolved and he is healing but it still throbs. It was worth it though, to donate a piece of his liver to his brother. The second he had turned eighteen, Connor knew that was what he wanted to do and the surgery went well. Kieron is recovering and will be healthier than he has been for a long time. For that Connor is grateful.

He will have two scars now. The one from the operation and the one from the scalpel that had pierced his skin. It wasn't Mum's fault but still, he was lucky it missed his vital organs. Connor barely remembers it, the blood, the confusion. He has blocked it out.

'Hey.' There is a banging on his bedroom door. It's Tyler. Tyler's mum chose to stay with Liam, her boyfriend, and so he has been living with them – it's almost like having another sibling. Not a replacement for Catherine – Tyler's too butt ugly for that – but he brings a warmth to the house. A new sense of home.

Connor will miss Tyler when he heads off to uni in September. Connor has deferred his own place for a year. He thought about giving up completely on his dreams, but after everything that happened with Mum, he is more determined than ever to one day find the cure for diseases so no one feels the fear and the desperation his mum must have felt to even contemplate performing a transplant.

He's trying to forgive her.

But often he wakes in the night, nightmares raking him with sharpened nails. A chilled voice whispering in his ear, *The Taken*.

And he has to remind himself that he is safe. His friends are safe, although Ryan isn't solely his friend now, is he? He's his half-brother and that's been a lot to get his head round. They hadn't spoken for months after it all went down, but lately they've been gaming online together again, though not speaking about what happened. He hopes someday that they will, but slowly, they are repairing their broken relationship. Ryan and Melissa live in Scotland now, not with, but near Fergus. Fergus had rushed back the minute he had heard what happened, assuring Ryan that he couldn't love him any more if he were his biological son. Realizing he should never have left him.

Connor pulls open his door.

'Want to play *Forza* with me and Kieron?' Tyler asks.

'Nah. I'm going to FaceTime Hailey.'

The past eight months, Hailey has made so much progress in her recovery. She's still weak, particularly on one side, but she can walk now, although only with a stick. Her speech is returning to normal. She told Connor that it wasn't exactly that she couldn't speak, she didn't want to. Couldn't face the questions she knew she'd be asked. Had wanted to protect him.

They're not back together. Connor wants to be but he knows he has a lot of making up to do first. He deserted her, his first love, when she got sick. Although they've spent hours talking it through and Hailey understands that it wasn't her being ill that had turned him away but the guilt he felt that it was his fault.

He's not worthy of her.

Yet.

He visits her several times a week and talks to her most days.

Mr Marshall is so grateful about her progress he... not exactly welcomes Connor in with open arms, but he makes him tea and offers him the odd biscuit. It's a start.

He's about to call Hailey when there's a knock on his door again, this time Aidan.

'Time to go and visit Mum,' he says.

Connor doesn't want to go and see her – she just isn't the same.

She frightens him. She frightens Kieron. And... that place. It has a smell, a taste, it seeps into every pore so that long after he's arrived home and scrubbed his skin in the shower, it's still with him.

She's still with him

It hurts to call her Mum after what she did but he can't call her Lucy.

He just doesn't know who she is anymore.

Dad calls him again and his legs tremble as he stands. Still, he has to be the strong one. He has to be the one to stand by Kieron's side and reassure him that everything is all right.

But it isn't all right at all.

CHAPTER NINETY-THREE

Aidan

It's almost time to go and see Lucy. Connor tramps down the stairs, trailed by Kieron. They look so alike, his two sons.

Even now it is hard to think of having three.

The last time he saw Ryan, Aidan had gently untied and ungagged him, before the police came.

'I'm so sorry,' Aidan had said.

'It wasn't your fault, it was Lucy's,' Ryan replied. His face was white. His voice shaking. He was scared, still scared, but adamant.

'No, I...'

'Didn't know anything. Didn't agree to anything. That's what I'm going to say. Someone has to stay out of jail to look after Connor and Kieron.' Ryan was crying, wiping tears away. 'Is my mum coming to get me?'

Aidan had sent a text to Melissa explaining Ryan was safe and telling her that he'd ring her in a few minutes while he deliberated what he should say. Not just to her, but to everyone, not wanting to throw his wife under the bus, but Connor agreed, his palm pressed against his side, blood spilling everywhere. 'Please, Dad, you haven't done anything wrong. Don't leave us too.'

And Aidan hadn't.

Ryan, perhaps out of loyalty to Connor as his best friend, or as a brother, after discovering they were siblings, or just because Aidan was his father, had omitted to tell the police about Aidan's part in it all when he gave his statement. Aidan was grateful, even if he hadn't seen Ryan since he moved to Scotland. Fergus had sent him one message – **I never want to hear from you again.** Some things you can't forgive.

But everyone deserves a fresh start.

Aidan had met with Agnes shortly afterward. She was genuinely sorry she had offered to help. Wanted to give him back the money. She hadn't begged him not to report her, but he hadn't anyway, on the condition she went for counselling. He'd only taken half the money back too, knowing how she felt, losing a child. Wanting her to get back on her feet.

Second chances.

He hasn't heard from Julie since. She's moved away. Aidan explained to Connor about the recording, the way that Lucy had blamed herself and Aidan saw something in his son's eyes. Understanding. Maturity. Since he's been visiting Hailey he's been... not the old Connor but a newer, wiser, kinder one.

Life is different. There's the relief that Kieron is now healthier than he has been in years thanks to Connor's generosity. Aidan had taken him to a therapist before he signed the consent form. He'd wanted to make sure Connor wasn't agreeing to something out of some misplaced sense of guilt, but he'd done his own research. Was just as knowledgeable about the operation, and the recovery, as well as the emotional implications as anyone. Mr Peters was certain Connor was sure he'd known what he was agreeing to. Still, Aidan had been a wreck when both boys were in the theatre, thoughts of losing Catherine, fear of history repeating itself never too far away.

Now they are both recovering well, he is relishing the time with his boys while his wife is away. Thankfully, Kieron can't remember anything that happened. Aidan has promised them both he will take them riding. They've already visited the stables and met the horses he will hire. He is no longer scared of being back in the saddle. He won't be scared of anything again.

They are almost there.

It's hard for the boys seeing Lucy in this facility, catatonic. Not understanding why she won't – can't – speak to them. Her doctor says it's the trauma. Encourages them to talk to her in the hope that one day she might reply.

Aidan hopes it is today.

CHAPTER NINETY-FOUR

Lucy

I want to come back. I do. I hear everything my family say to me even if I don't reply.

I can't reply.

Kieron has had his transplant and I no longer have to live in fear that he will die like Catherine, but the weight of responsibility to keep everyone safe is too heavy for me to bear.

A nurse fills up my favourite mug with tea; Aidan had brought it from home. 'Your husband and kids will be here in a minute.'

I look at those tiny hands and feet on the side of my mug – Catherine's hands and feet – and Connor and Kieron come to mind, once equally small and needy. I want to say something today, even if it's only hello.

I want to test my voice to see if it works – it's been so long since I heard it.

I open my mouth, but instead of words, out slips a tune.

'Hush little baby, don't say a word.' I sing it over and over again.

One day I'll come back to them.

One day.

But not today.

THE FOLLOWING LETTER
CONTAINS SPOILERS

Hello,

Thank you so much for reading my seventh psychological thriller. If you enjoyed it and have a spare moment to pop a review online, I'd hugely appreciate it. It really does make a difference to an author.

This story came about, as many of my stories do, following a conversation with my youngest son, Finley.

'Mum,' he had said one night over dinner. 'Do you know that you can buy an organ on the dark web?'

'What's the dark web and why are you looking for organs?' I was puzzled. 'We have a piano.'

'Not that sort of organ,' he had said.

For a crime writer I'm really not very crime.

Thus ensued a discussion on how far we'd go to save somebody we loved, my husband and I debating the wrongs and rights over a bottle of wine long into the night. Our opinions, polar opposites.

My initial thought was to put two parents in the position

of being able to buy an organ for their child, and observing them as they anguished over whether or not they should.

Lucy and Aidan wouldn't fit in that mould, and as much as I tried to shape their story, they had their own tale to tell. A story that touched me deeply.

I know the fear of almost losing someone, of watching helplessly as they battle with a health condition.

I know loss.

The grief Lucy and Aidan feel, I have felt.

I became so fond of this family who are bound together by secrets and lies, but at their core, they love each other completely.

I really hope you rooted for Aidan, Lucy, Connor and Kieron. Do let me know. You can find me at www.louisejensen.co.uk and https://twitter.com/Fab_Fiction and https://www.facebook.com/fabricatingfiction/ and https://www.instagram.com/fabricating_fiction/

Louise x

ACKNOWLEDGEMENTS

So many people to thank! This is my seventh thriller and I never feel any less grateful to everyone involved in turning my idea into a book.

Firstly, importantly, Lisa Milton and the entire team at HQ, in particular my fabulous editor Manpreet Grewal who really helped me shape this story into what it needed to be. Melanie Hayes, marketing and PR and the production team. Thanks to Sandra Ferguson for the copyedit.

My forever calm agent, Rory Scarfe, and the rights team at The Blair Partnership.

As ever, a BIG shout out to all the book bloggers who champion not only my books, but stories everywhere. The Fiction Cafe Facebook group and Book Connectors – a safe space for me to hang out online and everyone who chats to me on social media – writing can be such a solitary affair. Of course, I couldn't publish books if it weren't for readers – thanks to everyone who has spent time with Lucy, Aidan, Connor and Kieron.

I owe huge gratitude to Darius F Mirza MA FRCS, the Professor of Hepatobiliary and Transplant Surgery at QE Hospital and Birmingham Children's Hospital. You were so generous with your time both over email and on the telephone, answering my many, many questions. I have had to take artistic licence with this book for the sake of fiction but I remain in awe of the life-changing and life-saving work you carry out every single day. By simplifying the details I am in no way depreciating the skill of you and your dedicated expert team.

Louise Molina, thanks for your nursing expertise. Any mistakes are purely my own.

My friends and my family who have put up with me locking myself away while I wrote another book, particularly Natalie, Sarah, Mum, Karen, Bekkii, Pete and, of course, Glyn who I think of often.

Tim, my husband, who has yet again supported me through my first-draft angst.

I'm ridiculously proud of my exceptional children, Callum, Kai and Finley, who will ALWAYS remain the centre of my world.

And Ian Hawley. With all my love.

BOOK CLUB QUESTIONS

1) Who did you think had taken the boys? Did your opinion change as the story progressed?

2) 'His generation don't have the innocence of those before. They don't believe people are inherently good. They've grown up with Twitter, Facebook, YouTube, the worst of humanity streaked across their screens.'

   Connor refers to the negative impact of social media on his generation. What do you think the positives are? Discuss.

3) Everyone in the book has a secret. Do you think this is true of most families?

4) '"Chicken." Tyler had tucked his elbows into his waist and flapped his arms like a bird.
   '"I'm not scared," Connor said. But he was.'

   Connor has been involved in an incident that has left him with a huge amount of guilt and regret. What are your thoughts on peer pressure? Can you understand why people, particularly children, succumb to it?

5) Which character did you have the most empathy for and why?

6) 'When the boys were small they had a Stretch Armstrong action figure. They'd each tug on an arm, laughing as the limbs grew and grew, wondering if he would snap. I feel like that toy now. Wishing I could snake one arm out around Connor and keep the other one here around Kieron.'

Lucy feels torn between her children. When Tyler went missing do you think she should have left Kieron in hospital and gone to Connor?

7) 'This is not just Kieron's illness. It's everyone's.'

Discuss the impact a sick family member can have on the rest of the family. Do you think this family could have communicated more effectively?

8) 'Connor knows that after this – for he has to believe there is an after – he will be more vigilant, more inquisitive. The car waiting at the lights, the one speeding in a residential area – who is driving them and what hidden cargo are they carrying? Connor will always wonder.'

If the news is to be believed, crime is all around us and yet we very rarely see it. Why do you think this is?

9) The local radio station asked people to tweet their thoughts on the missing boys using #TheTaken. What are your opinions on social media being used in this way?

10) Were you satisfied with the ending?

Turn the page for an exclusive extract
from *The Stolen Sisters*, the gripping and
unputdownable thriller from Louise Jensen

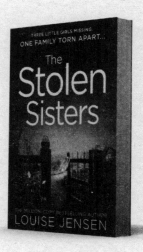

Sisterhood binds them. Trauma defines
them. Will secrets tear them apart?

Available to buy now!

Chapter One

Carly

Then

When Carly looked back at that day the memory was in shades of grey; the trauma had sucked the blue from the sky, the green from the freshly mown grass. She had sat on the back doorstep, the coolness of the concrete permeating through her school skirt, the late-afternoon sun warming her bare arms. Carly remembers now the blackness of a beetle scurrying down the path before it disappeared into the soil under the rose bush. The stark white of the twins' socks, bunched below their knees.

Inconsequential details that later the police would jot in their notebooks as though Carly was somehow being a great help but she knew she wasn't, and worse than that, she knew it was entirely her fault.

It had all been so frustratingly normal. Leah and Marie had shrieked in mock disgust as Bruno, their boxer, bounded towards them, drool spilling from his jowls. But their screams then still carried an undercurrent of happiness, not like later when their cries were full of fear and there was nowhere to run to.

The things that have stayed with Carly are this.

The way her fingers gripped the cumbersome Nokia in her

hand as though she was clutching a secret. Her annoyance as she angled her screen to avoid the glare, never dreaming that soon she would be craving daylight.

Fresh air.

Space.

The pounding in her head increasing as the girls bounced a tennis ball between them across the patio. The way she had snapped at the twins as though it was their fault Dean Malden hadn't texted her. Of all the things that she could, that she should, feel guilty about, she had never forgiven herself that the last words she spoke to her sisters before they were all irrevocably damaged was in anger rather than kindness.

Although in truth, she had never forgiven herself for any of it.

'Shut up!' She had roared out her frustration that the first boy she loved had shattered her thirteen-year-old heart. Crazy now to recall that she once thought the absence of a text was the end of the world. There were far worse things. Far worse people than the floppy-haired blond boy who had let her down.

Her younger sisters turned to her, identical green eyes wide. Marie's sight trained on Carly's face as she chucked the ball for Bruno. Carly's irritation grew as she watched it fly over the fence.

'For God's sake.' She stood, brushing the dust from the back of her sensible pleated skirt. 'It's time to come in.'

'But that's not fair.' Marie looked stricken as her gaze flickered towards the fence.

'Life isn't fair,' Carly said, feeling a bubbling resentment that at eight years old the twins had it easy.

'Can you fetch our ball, please, Carly?' Marie pleaded.

'Fetch it yourself,' Carly snapped.

4

'You know we're not allowed out of the garden on our own until we're ten,' Marie said.

'Yeah, well I'm in charge today and I'm saying you can. It's not like we live in a city. Nothing ever happens in this dump.' Carly was sick of living somewhere so small where everyone knew everyone else's business. Where everyone would know by tomorrow that Dean Malden had rejected her. 'Be quick and shut the gate *properly*.'

She turned and pushed open the back door, stepping into the vast kitchen that never smelled of cakes or bread. It never smelled of anything except freshly roasted coffee. Carly clattered her phone onto the marble island and yanked open the fridge door. The shelves, which were once stocked with stilton and steak and that had groaned under the weight of fresh fruit and vegetables, were woefully bare. There was nothing except a shrivelled cucumber and some out-of-date hummus. It was all right for her mum and stepdad out for the evening at yet another corporate function. They spent more time on the business than with their children nowadays, although Mum had assured her it wouldn't be for much longer. She'd soon be at home more but in the meantime it was left to Carly to sort out tea again. She had loved her half-sisters fiercely since the day they were born, though sometimes she wished Mum still paid the retired lady down the road to babysit, but since Carly had turned thirteen, Mum felt that she was responsible enough.

She sighed as she crossed to the shelf above the Aga and lifted the lid from the teapot. Inside was a £10 note. Chips for tea. She wondered whether the money would stretch to three sausages or if they should split a battered cod.

Minutes later the twins tumbled into the kitchen.

'Yuck.' Leah dropped the tennis ball coated with slobber into the wicker basket where Bruno kept his toys.

'Wash your hands.' Carly checked her phone again.

Nothing.

What had she done wrong? She had thought Dean liked her.

Marie perched on a stool at the breakfast bar, swinging her legs, the toes of her shoes thudding against the kick board. How was Carly supposed to hear her text alert over that? Marie had her chin in her hands, her mouth downturned; she hated being in trouble. Carly could see the way her lip trembled with upset but she couldn't help yelling again.

'Shut. Up.'

Marie slid off the stool. 'I… I left my fleece in the garden.'

Carly jerked her head towards the door in a go-and-get-it gesture before she clicked on the radio. The sound of Steps flooded the room. Marie paused and momentarily their sisterly bond tugged at them all. '5, 6, 7, 8' was one of their favourite songs. Usually they'd fall into line and dance in synchronicity.

'Let's do this!' Marie flicked her red hair over her shoulders and placed her hands on her hips.

'It's childish,' Carly snapped although inside her shoes, her toes were tapping.

'It doesn't work unless we *all* do it.' Marie's voice cracked. 'We *have* to be together.'

Carly pulled the scrunchie she'd been wearing like a bracelet from her wrist and smoothed her long fair hair back into a ponytail. The twins got into position. Waited. Carly reached for her phone and tried to ignore the pang of meanness that flitted through her as the smile slipped from Leah's face. Marie's small shoulders rounded as she headed back outside.

Minutes later she raced back in, socked feet skidding across the tiles, tears streaming down her freckled cheeks. 'Bruno's got out. The gate was open.'

'For God's sake.' Carly could feel the anger in her chest form a cold, hard ball. It was one of the last times she ever allowed herself to truly feel. 'Who shut the gate?'

Marie bit her lower lip.

'I did,' said Leah, slipping her shoes back on.

'You're supposed to bang it until it latches, you idiot. You know it's broken. Three times. You bang it three times.'

The girls pelted into the garden, calling the dog's name.

Marie hesitated at the gate. 'Perhaps we should wait—' Under her freckles, her skin was pale. She'd been off school yesterday with a stomach ache and although she'd gone back today, she didn't look well. Carly knew she should ask if she was feeling okay but instead she shoved her roughly into the street. 'It's your fault, Marie. You search that way.' She pointed down the avenue lined with beech trees.

Marie grabbed Leah's hand.

'No,' Carly snapped. 'Leah can come with me.' The twins could be silly when they were together and she had enough to worry about without them getting into trouble.

'But I want—' Marie began.

'I don't *care* what you want. Move.' Carly grabbed Leah's arm and led her in the opposite direction, towards the cut-through at the side of their house, which led to the park.

It all happened so quickly that afterwards Carly couldn't remember which order it all came in. The balaclava-clad face looming towards hers. The forearm around her neck, the gloved hand clamped over her mouth. The sight of Leah struggling

7

against arms that restrained her. The scraping sound of her shoe as she was dragged towards the van at the other end of the alley. The sight of Marie, almost a blur, flying towards the second man also clad in black, who held her twin, pummelling him with her small fists.

'Stop! You can't do this! Don't take her. I don't want you to take her!'

The soft flesh compacting against hard bone as Carly bit down hard on the fingers that had covered her mouth.

'Run!' she had screamed at Marie as the man who held Leah grabbled to find something of Marie's he could hold on to, clutching at her collar, her ginger pigtails, as she dodged his grasp.

'Run!'

ONE PLACE. MANY STORIES

Bold, innovative and
empowering publishing.

FOLLOW US ON:

@HQStories